THE FACE OF ANY OTHER

Michael J Seidlinger

Lazy Fascist Press
Portland, Oregon

{CONTINUED PRAISE FOR
THE FACE OF ANY OTHER}

"Stylistically and structurally innovative, yet with clear, clean prose, Seidlinger exhibits compassion for the inner and outer anxieties, the mundane and not so mundane aspects of our human existence. Instead of using the cold detachment too often employed by young writers, in *The Face of Any Other*, readers are sure to discover a refreshingly, emotionally-resonant work."

—**PAULA BOMER,** author of *Inside Madeleine*

"The idea of a man with no face latching onto random people and swimming in their insecurities is both horrifying and a little hilarious. But the real horror, and humor, in *The Face of Any Other* is found in the consumer concerns, office anxieties, and daily banalities that Seidlinger exposes, skewers, and transforms into art. Seidlinger has a face—I've seen it!—but his novel is a mirror revealing us to ourselves."

—**LINCOLN MICHEL**, author of *Upright Beasts*

{PRAISE FOR MICHAEL J SEIDLINGER'S
THE FUN WE'VE HAD}

"Michael Seidlinger is a homegrown Calvino, a humanist, and wise and darkly whimsical. His invisible cities are the spires of the sea where we all sail our coffins in search of our stories."

—**STEVE ERICKSON**, author of *Zeroville*

"Melding the static, high-concept premise of two humans floating alone on a coffin in a sea devoid of all else with stark and meditative prose, *The Fun We've Had* evokes a highly unexpected experience, somewhere between Beckett's most hopeless solipsists and the mysterious energy of a child's Choose Your Own Adventure-era dream."

—**BLAKE BUTLER**, author of *There Is No Year* and
Three Hundred Million

"All I know is that Seidlinger is consistently enjoyable to read, and whatever world he's created here will be engaging, colorful, and, as the title says, most definitely fun."

—**THE BARNES & NOBLE BLOG**

Lazy Fascist Press
PO Box 10065
Portland, OR 97296

www.lazyfascistpress.com
lazyfascist@gmail.com

ISBN: 978-1-62105-170-1

Cover Design by Matthew Revert
www.matthewrevert.com

Printed in the USA.

I'M

Insincerity //

Hello, my name is Richard Tell, and I love my job. I do. I wake up thirty minutes before my alarm, every morning—never fail—so that I can get that perfect and necessary head start. Truth is I need the extra thirty minutes to build up to the fact that it's another day. Another damn day. I'm at work by seven thirty—never fail, I'm reliable—and I show that I care by going the extra step. I make coffee for the entire office. I make sure the office is clean and ready for the workday. It's part of my job as office assistant and some of the people here, I bet, think I'm trying to show off, trying to kiss the boss's ass, but I'm not. I just really care. I do. Never fail to show that I like and value my job. So many people are jobless and I won't let anyone see that the real reason I try so hard is because I'm afraid that one mistake might be the difference between being able to pay my bills and being out on the street.

I won't let anyone know that I'm afraid of being replaced. Won't let anyone see, not even myself. But I wear it well, my enthusiasm. I wear it well and I'm so happy to have some reason to wake up every morning. I like to hide my real feelings because I've gotten used to it. Half the time I don't even know I'm smothering them, hiding from any feeling by focusing on some new task, or trying so hard to tune into the current conversation between colleagues so that I have someone else to listen to, something else to do with my energy, so very concerned with staying in form, like I might break down in front of the entire office if I don't. But I'm here and I'm early. No one else is here. I'm the first—never fail—to arrive. I'll volunteer to do something because, again, I care and I love my job. *I love my job.* Really won't show my nervous hands, shoving them in my pockets whenever possible, because I developed that bad habit in a meaningless attempt to deal with my anxiety about being disliked by others. I don't feel like I fit in here so I do my best to predict when they'll want something from me, and I do it ahead of time, with a positive outlook, and say something simple like, No problem.

If they don't say my name, Richard, then I'm not in the spotlight.

I care. I do. I really do. Like this one time I knew that the office would need fifty-three slices of pizza and fifty three bottles of beer for the Friday office party but the people at the pizza place messed up and only gave us fifty-two beers so I went ahead and didn't drink, even though no one noticed except for one guy that mocked me for not drinking, thinking I was one of those straight-edge fucks. I don't tell—never fail—myself that it hurts, being undervalued despite giving my best efforts. I don't tell—never fail—that I am insincere. I don't tell myself most things, preferring to bury them underneath busy work.

But the same can be said for most people.

They work so hard to be something they're not.

I would know.

Welcome Mats //

When you have the face of any other, you tend to see the cracks forming long before they are ever felt. You look into a person's face, like young Richard Tell here, and you see the youth wearing away with the ambition that continues to go unaddressed. You see the years that add on with age, the years that burn out like a tired flame. You see what I see, and then you'll see why it's much easier to work hard with the belief that it will pay off later.

The question thought by many is, How much longer? Doubt.

A person will go to great lengths believing that, in every effort, there are dues being paid in full. Richard puts in the work, but the waiting weighs him down. He's twenty-eight years old going on twenty-nine and he feels like he hasn't made it through the front door.

He's still waiting, staring down at the welcome mat, beginning to assume that the welcome is for someone else. From where I stand, when I knock there are no warm introductions. From where I stand, there are no introductions that aren't addressed to someone else; there are no introductions, save for the blank stares and their faces, always their faces, baring all. When you have the face of any other, you can't help but see, and I truly mean, see everything that lies beneath.

Peripheral Vision //

Richard Tell here, telling nobody that I feel like a third wheel at this meeting.

It's a big conference table and there are a few empty seats but I don't sit down.

See, I don't sit down because if I do, I end up sitting between two other colleagues that would rather speak to each other.

I'd be in the way, blocking their vision.

They would have to speak to me.

And why would they want to do that?

Still I'm going to sit down because I should be able to sit in on the meeting.

One colleague gives me a look.

I return the look.

I go back to taking notes—acting as though I am not nervous, barely able to keep myself from shaking. It's not like me to do this, to sit down and to speak without being first told to sit down and instructed to speak.

I'm low on the ladder.

I sense that they are staring.

But I keep my gaze trained to my notepad.

Taking notes.

I use my peripheral vision to see if what's occurring matches my worries. But then it'll be worth the sigh of relief when I see that nobody's paying attention.

Nobody finds this odd.
I'm sitting down, taking notes.
Today young Richard will leave a lasting impression.

Boredom //

When you have the face of any other, you tend to get a little bored. You see through a thousand different sets of eyes—blue, brown, grey, hazel—but it goes on with no clear indication of difference. Like Richard here, you see how the body and the mind function and you see the white space, the abstracted, hidden edges of every personality. You see everything that's held back. That's why you decide to sit down when normally young Richard would wait on aching legs for the long—sometimes three-hour long—meeting to conclude. You sit down and get to playing into what could be picked out of the white space.

What hinders a person from being honest, truly representative of themselves?

What is Richard Tell hiding?

Attention Span //

My name is Richard Tell. That's about as straight forward of a greeting I can manage without either looking away from the person or messing up the part where you shake the person's hand. I either shake it too hard, grip on too hard, or I'm the opposite: too soft, showing that sort of lack of confidence. So then sitting at this conference table, I just know that some of them will ask for my name. It happens. It's a recurring happening. They always ask me who I am, like I haven't met them once a week for years. What I don't say is, Richard, same as last week. What I don't say is, You know my name. I don't say those kinds of things.

But I want to. Really do.

But I might.

The colleague to my right leans in and whispers, Who are you again and why are you sitting in someone else's seat?

I'm just an assistant. I'm low on the ladder and quickly expendable. I know this and they know this, which makes it so much harder to be myself.

The reality of the social situation is that they know that you're uncomfortable, flat-out afraid, so they have a little fun. The moment a person senses weakness, it's an opportunity for others to pounce, an opportunity.

So open up and be the person you really are.

Open up and declare opposition.

I feel at ease in a crowd.

The colleague shrugs, You should.

And that's that—averted. Back to the topic at hand. This is still a meeting after all.

But then I'm still naturally uncomfortable. I never get comfortable where I am.

I've put myself in prime position to be spoken to, and this place is highly competitive. They'll be passive aggressive to anyone; they'll pick you apart if you let them. But this could be said about any working environment.

If there's something to gain, there's plenty to lose.

I'm not going to be able to hide here.

My heart beats faster when a break is called—for lunch— but I'm just going to be me, Richard. Maybe they'll leave me alone.

They talk like I'm not really there.

One colleague asks me if it would be okay to lean back in my chair so that she could talk to the guy sitting to the other side of me.

Thanks.

Two on the other side, we end up exchanging a glance.

One laughs. The other says, I'll have a ham on rye, and the soup of the day.

I care. I like my job.

I'm afraid of losing my job.

If I lost this job, there's no telling I'll ever find another one. And there's my student loans, my rent, health insurance— no way I'll be able to pay for my antidepressants if I lost my health insurance—and there's the car which has seen better days and breaks down every couple weeks. I'm quick to volunteer and maybe one afternoon, during one meeting, I volunteered to go fetch lunch for the office. A good, kind gesture, it is.

I volunteered that one time.

But now this colleague thinks I'll do it again.

What I won't admit to myself is that I'll do it. I'm going

to do whatever they tell me, because if I don't—this is where doubt shows through.

But I sit here, not taking down the order.

I look at the other colleague, the one that laughed, and he looks at the one that ordered. It's a bit of a stalemate. I should be shaking, I'm so anxious, my nerves tensing, but I'm just Richard, okay? I'm Richard the assistant, or to the rest of the office: Hey guy, what's your name again?

And, Can you do me a favor?

Favors are gathered and completed in full.

I'm a hard worker. I am.

So here's what I do. I don't say yes and I don't say no.

I switch seats.

I would never do this just like I'd never admit to being so afraid. I have nightmares sometimes. I have nightmares where I can't keep up; I keep getting lost along the way. I'm sent somewhere, to fetch supplies or something, and I keep getting the task wrong. I get the wrong type of paper, the wrong type of pen; I end up on the other side of the city and by the time I get back to the office, everyone's gone home for the day.

I have nightmares like this, all the time.

I don't even tell my therapist about them, thinking that she'll find it stupid. Like I'm overreacting. It's just stress, Richard. Yeah, it's just stress.

The colleague raises his voice, Hey.

I'm not going to look. If I look, something will happen. *I look.*

He taps at his watch and makes a face.

I say, **When I'm really sad or down, I seek the company of others.**

Someone sitting near me chimes in, What's going on?

She glances over at the other colleague who shakes his head.

She turns to me, then back to the colleague.

He tells her what happened and then I tell her, **I take other people's interests into account.**

Huh? followed by a glance in the colleague's direction. This comes across as odd and I couldn't be more nervous. This is all going to fall apart, isn't it? It's all coming apart at the seams. I'm going to be the one to blame.

The colleague defends himself, He's supposed to get my lunch. I mean, right? That's what the kid's here for.

Another colleague says what I didn't want to hear, Go gopher go.

But she denies these accusations.

Addressing the entire room, Since when has that been Richard's problem?

She talks down to them, lecturing them on the responsibilities of an assistant.

She must have seniority status. She must be a manager, a supervisor, a something.

I don't know what and I don't know her name, was too nervous when I met her to remember her name. She speaks with confidence, the kind of confidence that I wish I had. I've got a long climb ahead.

Just looking at all the people sitting around this table, the ladder does seem endless.

The ladder goes on forever. The source of many of those nightmares is that I'll keep climbing, rung after rung, only to realize that I haven't moved up at all. I'm still two rungs from rock bottom. It's scary to think. It's why I don't think about it.

It's something I don't ever think about.

But I know I should; it'll do wonders for my confidence issues.

Then she makes sure they get it, Understand? I know you all lack the attention span but listen… She tells me that I don't have to listen to everyone all the time. She tells me that I'm an assistant but I'm not a slave. She tells me that people will take advantage of a person that doesn't stand up for himself, but that doesn't mean you can't speak up.

Speak up, Richard, okay?

Richard, she said my name. She knew my name. Someone knows my name.

The break ends. The meeting continues.

I'm back to taking notes, which *is* definitely one of my responsibilities as assistant.

False Alarm //

When you have the face of any other, you often end up helping a person out, aiding them in a predicament. You don't have any valid reason for reaching out, so it's often a false alarm—something I did, something that was done, something that happened. Everyone moves on including me. Like young Richard, it wasn't much but perhaps the best saves are the small ones. Saving a person's life starts with the small gestures.

You do that and it makes an impact.

If you asked me why, I wouldn't know.

It goes unnoticed, most times, because when it happened everyone believed it was him. It was Richard that sat down in that seat.

It was Richard that spoke up.

It was Richard that didn't know the manager's name.

Funny to think you could be so nervous you forget to catch a person's name.

Richard, you really do need to work on handling anxiety.

Not everyone is out to get you.

Caring //

When you have the face of any other, you stand in for a person that could very well walk in mid-statement. The person could walk in right now or right...

Now. How about right... **now**.

You get the idea.

But it's worth it, sometimes. You get used to this element of danger.

You kind of like it sometimes; it's the same adrenaline rush as any other thrill.

But the fact is young Richard is home "sick," a half-step away from a breakdown, too preoccupied with the belief that no one's noticed his absence to pick up the phone and make the call. Richard stayed home because it's my estimation that he just couldn't face it, everything that has become his responsibility. He couldn't make the commute, couldn't make the coffee for the entire office—for him one of the most depressing moments of his day; early morning, empty office, no one aware that he made their morning a bit more pleasant. Yeah, it's clear that he cares. He cares.

He cares too much.

Young Richard is the one that has to live with factors that he's unwilling to face. Being dishonest will get you nowhere. "Caring" without being conscious of the differences will only render you defeated.

Imagine, if he had called in, he would have known.

If he had called in, Richard would have saved himself all that dread.

But I knew that he wouldn't pick up the phone. He wouldn't have called.

What gets me over is seeing how the small gestures pay off in the end.

I can see it now: Tomorrow he'll return to the office distraught, a day shut in, emotionally alone with all those thoughts will drain a person. He'll do his best to hide those feelings but his colleagues will, with their most sincere, best interests, work to treat him as he should be treated. This time, they will show that they care.

With surprise, Richard will notice.

They care after all.

It'll be young Richard that will have to continue from here.

When you have the face of any other, you can stand up for a person but there's no telling whether or not that person will do the same.

Doing Time //

How long have I walked the city looking up at the stars? How many times have I stood at a street corner, watching people hurry to cross the street, the people a mixture of late and lost? How many times have I sat on a park bench long enough to feel the pain run up my spine, my legs go numb, prickling to sleep? How often have I chosen to remain this way, unmarked, without a face, observing the many, the majority, live their own, seemingly self-contained lives? How many unique faces are there on this earth, how many unique personalities wear these faces, looking to make a connection? How many settle for less? How many learn to act outside of themselves, mapping gesture and goals to fit inside the various boxes manufactured by society?

How much time has passed me by without so much as a single blink?

How long? Yet I wear the tie, iron my shirt, wear the name tag like everyone else.

I'm pretty sure I used to keep track of their names, writing it down in black marker, pasting it to my shirt. I'm pretty sure I ran out and never got any more nametags.

Don't really know why, kind of just forgot. All part of it.

Doing time, you could say.

That's not how I say it. I call it—I'd like to call it something funny.

I'd like to call something to be done. Something worth doing.

So I don't have a name for this. I don't call it anything, same could be said for most anyone else. It's life.

Maybe not a life's work, but it's what I've found.

It's what I've become, and the factors that made it possible—wait, I have to save something for later. Can't spoil my entire story right from the start.

Best introductions are the ones that last a lifetime. They keep you guessing, wondering about the *who, what, when, where,* and *how.*

The person behind the professional posture.

It's early enough that I'm still walking, still looking, still tasting breakfast on my tongue. It's possible that it could be one of those days. Days with no need for introductions. Days spent observing. Days spent as myself. Doing time.

Then I see her with cellphone pressed against her face, walking, skipping steps, walking fast, faster than some, pulling forward from the rest. I see the next dozen moves long before she takes that next step. I see it and I see her falling apart in one of the bathroom stalls during the middle of the day. It's morning, the sun barely in the sky long enough to cook the streets, bringing the weather to a humid all-time high.

Doing time, perhaps.

But not today.

Hello, my name is.

Hello, my name is…

A Need or a Want //

Hello, my name is Laura Davis, and I work as a consultant for over a hundred different clients, all of them equally important, none are treated special. I think it's important to get right down to business. I believe in getting the important details out right from the start. Introductions are precious occurrences; it's imperative that I present my case. I believe this to be true because I want them to think I'm experienced, confident. I want them to trust me. I want them to trust me before they can learn anything more about me. I don't want them to see any doubts. I don't want them to turn me down for one of the bigger names, those men that work for the biggest agencies in the country.

I have to get down to business because I'm afraid I'll only have that one chance to present my case, my pitch, myself—who I am.

And who am I really?

Every client has a need or a want. It's why I'm here.

It's why I spend every single day walking these streets—meetings, meetings, meetings, meetings, meetings—let's talk it out. Talk about the contracts. Talk about what you want. Talk about what you need. Talk about what we'll do to make it happen. Talk about moving ahead. Talk about landing the deal. Talk about you and your past, your present, your bright beautiful star-speckled future. Talk the talk because that's what I manage, and if I'd be honest with myself, I'd say that it's what I do best.

Talk—lots of talk. And uneaten meals at expensive res-taurants. Sipped coffee at trendy cafes. Multiple drinks at the closing of a potential client. All goes on the credit card.

But I don't tell them that.

Maybe I should. What else is kept hidden?

I don't tell them that my office is my studio apartment a borough away from the action, the epicenter of our industry.

I don't tell them that I have a different name and that I typically have doubts about every new client. I don't tell them that I suffer from panic attacks every couple hours.

It's why I'm late, most of the time.

Not for fashion. I'm late because I can't just put on the professional, courteous face. I can't always *be* that person they want. I guess I don't really know what I want.

I don't know what I need.

I don't think about this stuff. I keep it bottled up internally. They're of no use to anybody. But lately they're starting to get out. I'll drift off—kind of spacing out. But it's not a daydream. It's the kind of episode where I lose track of where I am. It's an episode like the one I'm having right now, and—I don't remember. Just, yeah: I'm sitting here. No one's sitting across from me. Go through the checklist—look for the indications: Menu still present or missing? Glass sipped from or untouched?

I'm alone. I must be waiting.

These are always the worst moments, when I'm alone with my thoughts.

I should be practicing my pitch, everything I'll say to the potential client. Is this a potential client? I've got a calendar for that—check, see, confirm.

A new client. A new client means a first impression impending.

I'm always nervous, feeling vulnerable, but I don't think about it. I add it to the archive of unaddressed concerns.

I focus on my surroundings and I get lost dreaming up stories for the people I watch. Their wants, their needs.

I think about people's goals.

I rarely think about mine or where I'll be ten years from now.

Letdowns //

When you have the face of any other, you can't help but feel a little let down by what you see. At first you feel genuinely fearless, like some unstoppable force capable of reading the patterns, the various truths to any personality you might choose. But then you start to predict the patterns, and then you begin to write the very same patterns.

When you see it, you can't forget all the previous times you've watched it happen.

All the previous times you've been let down by a person's choices.

They act, but seldom with the ingenuity found at the root of their intentions.

You start to get annoyed. I don't know how many times I've run up to that person, shouted into their faces all the possible variations they could have chosen, ones that would have been a better outcome than the one they went with, but all that does is cast clouds over my entire day. When you have the face of any other, you are susceptible to other people's emotions, their actions, their miseries.

It gets to be a sort of game, looking for the people that stand out, the ones that have remained loyal to their values. Honestly, most don't have a clear value set, most of what they believe is subject to change based on need, desperation, and despair.

You feel a bit letdown.

Feel like shit, basically.

You grow a thick shell.

But I can't help but laugh because that's what everyone does—desensitize to survive. When you have the face of any other, you just might start to see the cracks in yourself.

You keep at it, much like everyone else, because you don't really have a choice.

Unnatural Expectations //

Laura Davis, so very nice to meet you. And my pleasure. And the pleasure is all mine. And this is all about making you, the client, feel comfortable. Comfort is key. Comfort is how I'm pretty sure you'll be more willing to accept me as your potential consultant.

I'll go ahead and make it seem like I'm on top of things.

Ask about drinks.

Ask about food.

What, if anything, the client would like to order. Anything at all. It's going to be on me. That's to be expected even though the client remains humble, maybe even a little shy, refusing my many attempts to buy them lunch, a drink, some tea, their integrity.

Eventually they all break down of course.

Maybe just a salad and some water.

I'll make jokes about how I lack that willpower. Something that's self-deprecating like a mention about how if I knew that someone else was paying I'd go for the heavy-hitter menu items. I'm a little nervous about the joke though because the client doesn't respond to it. Not really much of a reaction. Then I start to think that the client took it as an insult.

Typically I'll change the subject but we haven't gotten to talking yet so I just keep laughing until I can make it seem less abrupt to get right down to details.

Here goes nothing.

Important details.

The pitch, as a whole, is pretty simple. The client here needs advice and I'm putting a price on my own advice. I have bled this advice day in and day out for years, so much that I don't even know what I'm telling this person: It's just the same answers to the same questions. I guess it's a little disconcerting, but I don't think about it.

If I do, I worry that I'll lose momentum. Give myself one moment to really think about all of this and the entire house of mirrors shatters. I don't like that analogy. That would be something I'd tell the client to never use.

The pitch is given and dealt and absorbed before the server can return with our meals and still, I can't get comfortable.

I don't know what else to say.

Roll through the usual strategies. What do I usually say?

I try another joke but it doesn't register anything more than a smirk, so I ask about the food. The client says it's good but that flat tone in his voice says otherwise.

See I'm beginning to run out of options.

The professional consultant does not show weakness.

I feel the same pressure in my forehead, the same nausea in my stomach.

What else does this person want from me?

I'm faced with unnatural expectations from clients because the market is now a buyers rather than sellers kind of market. This isn't real estate, though—they're buying me. They're buying my best information and I pretend that what I impart will get them what they need. But in reality I've never liked what I do. But this is what I do. It's either this or I—

I don't even have an ending to that sentence.

Out of options and **this close** to hyperventilating.

I do what I can, opening my mouth to speak, not sure what I'll say next.

I seek out the emotional support of others.

The client nods, agrees.

I tell the client, **I try to do the best I can given the constraints of the situation.**

The client mentions how that's good, and that most consultants would promise the world. But of course I feel vulnerable, like I've shown him bare skin, shown him too much this early on, so I nod too, taking a bite of whatever it is that I ordered.

I feel so vulnerable.

The client sighs and says that he really doesn't know what to expect anymore. He started out the search hopeful and even a little naïve only to completely lose himself and his intentions in the process.

Let him speak, I think, mostly because it takes every bit of effort to maintain my composure. I'm so close to having one of my panic attacks.

Why didn't I stick to the important details?

Because I wanted to be honest for once.

The client discusses one consultant that proclaimed exactly that—the world, his entire life—able to call and chat at any time of the day. That seemingly bothered this man, saying that he didn't know what to believe anymore. Someone working this hard to impress him, it makes it difficult to see who's being true. Being themselves.

Everything's a blur.

I nod, understanding. I'm not seeing straight either.

That's not what he meant but this is about as close as I'm going to get.

I reply, **I spend my leisure time actively socializing with a group of people, attending parties, shopping, etc.**

What am I saying?

But the client seems to take it as fact rather than something framed from a psychiatric evaluation. Client talks about some of his hobbies; he talks with enthusiasm about basketball, saying that he almost had a chance once, but the same thing happened as now: unnatural expectations led to an injury. He over-performed, pushed himself too far in hopes of winning over the talent scouts and representatives.

He picks at his salad, not able to look me in the eye, saying that it was his fault.

I wait until he looks up at me to speak, **When things go wrong, I immediately blame myself.**

He sighs, says yeah.

There's a moment of nervous silence.

I remain still, because if I move I might collapse to the floor.

Retain control, retain control, retain control.

I'll be fine.

Then he asks, says the right string of words.

And I push aside the empty promises.

I tell him that I understand.

I tell him the truth—explaining how anxious and nervous I am right now. I tell him what I usually go through before and after every meeting.

Everything that swarms my mind, I let it out. This is highly unprofessional.

Highly unprofessional but it gets me the deal.

He says he feels good about this.

Confirms that we can relate. He says something that leaves me speechless, but it's probably just because of the unexpected turn of events. I figure I'm in shock, but we shake hands, he thanks me for the meal and we agree that I'll send over the contract later today.

When he's gone I don't really know what to think.

I don't know what to feel.

But I feel good.

I feel different.

I repeat what he had said:

I've finally found someone *human.*

No Rebounding //

When you have the face of any other, you feel great when other people feel great. You feel like you can do anything when the people around you are in good spirits. You feel enthusiastic enough to take new risks, and then you can't help but keep with the last person.

I watch Laura the workaholic walk slower than normal down the same streets, the streets she's by now memorized. There's something different about her face.

She hails a taxicab and, in minutes, she's gone from view.

But when I see her run a hand over her face, I glimpse how, despite the cracks so prominent on her face leave her as someone affected by her responsibilities, her anxieties, the weight of the world stacked against her, she lets herself have that taxicab. She lets herself celebrate the new acquisition. She lets herself know that she achieved something today.

She lets herself have that truth, if only just a tiny piece of it.

It's a great feeling. Damn, such a great feeling.

Going into the meeting she had been sure she wouldn't sign the client.

It makes me want to find someone else. It makes me want to walk in their shoes and see if my steps will make a difference in their lives too.

But I'm not rebounding, I'm just being a person, petty urges et al.

I'm enjoying the mood of this moment and sometimes it's not about the fact that this feeling will pass; it's about having felt it at all.

If this isn't a good end to a day then I don't know what is.

Questionnaires
for Caring //

When you have the face of any other, it doesn't take long to understand that you really aren't any different. You are bound to the same inertia and velocity of life's strange turns. Read: strange and then my situation, i.e. *look in the mirror and what do you see?* Yeah you won't question the use of the word strange.

You get tired like everyone else, and you **still** need to wake up in the morning.

Like everyone else.

Routine, like everyone else.

Up at daybreak, like everyone else.

I leap, rather than crawl, out of bed because if I don't get up in the moments right after silencing the alarm clock, I'll never get up. I'll sleep the morning and early afternoon away. Some days aren't worth the blinks so I go for a few more winks.

Closet—I have a line of the same suit, like a character from a cartoon, but really, people could learn a thing or two from those episodes. Eight of a kind means less time in the wash, less hassle with the dry cleaners. When you have the face of any other, the dry cleaners are a nightmare. Same with delivery, carry out, and other activities.

You'll find that it's easier to pick a face, even if you dislike the one within reach, than having to deal with the alternative. It could be unfortunate. It could be a curse.

Could be anything—I call it a means to an end.

Everything, a means to an end.

Suit and tie, because a suit without a tie is a person without a face.

Oh, right…

When you have the face of any other, you tend to forget your situation, if you know what I mean. You tend to nod off during the parts involving you, preferring the ones having to do with others. You are more likely to see, projected onto others, the person you'll become. But fuck it: I wear a tie. I like wearing ties. Consider it a case for style preferences.

Been around and back, you start to develop a few habits. Like this one I started.

I have these 7x5 cards printed with a list of questions, made to look like any other survey when really I use them as "feelers," seeing who will bite. Old-fashioned, they can't be emails from an anonymous account. Spam mail is stepped on, deleted. Seeing who will fill them out, answering questions like **I feel at ease in a crowd** and **When I'm really sad or down, I seek the company of others** and will actually go through the trouble of mailing them back—yeah, that's an act of trying. It shows effort, handle with care.

Based on each statement, answer with one of the following—Strongly Disagree, Somewhat Disagree, Somewhat Agree, Agree, Strongly Agree.

I take other people's interests into account.

Does that sound like you?

It began as a fun little thing, seeing if it would work. When it did, generating a fair amount of leads, it became part of my daily routine.

I seek out emotional support from others.

Would you agree? Is this a true statement?

The questions become what I call a dialogue of constraints. In each question is a spectrum full of answers that could take on a myriad of possibilities based on the person I ask.

I try to do the best I can given the constraints of the situation.

Some are mutual afflictions, the same cracks down the side of a person's face viewable in any working adult, anyone that braves the 365 yearly calendar, the 24/7 working way while carrying the hope that they are in fact what they had intended on becoming, all these years.

I spend my leisure time actively socializing with a group of people, attending parties, shopping, etc.

These declarations are safe in that they not only reveal an answer in the one being asked but also in those that are there to listen and/or observe.

They aren't so much words being spoken as they are reflections cast on the face of another much like your reflection would on a mirror.

When things go wrong, I immediately blame myself.

Anyone that disagrees, tend to exhibit a run of doubt. Hey, yeah, this is me, saying these things. I don't view myself as a professional; however, when you have the face of any other, you live by the professions and peculiarities of others. You have to take things seriously because you're a single thread away from losing touch with reality.

I send out a handful of these cards on my way out of the apartment.

My apartment, though the name on the lease might as well be a pseudonym. As far as the rest of the building's tenants are concerned, this apartment is owned by a musician that travels most of the year. Don't get ahead of yourself though: I've worked to manufacture this assumption.

I play music loudly during three months of the year.

I never make a sound otherwise. Not difficult to get in and out of the building.

Not worried about being seen. They've looked right at me and it might as well have been the wall. Sight unseen, everything I do that seems extraordinary is merely just another functional act in the feature that focuses on being made as a means to an end to what on my better days isn't anything more than to make a connection.

When you have the face of any other, your actions and your opinions are second-class to those that carry the same features across their entire lives. When you have the face of any other, you make a connection by moving closer, becoming close, becoming real.

Becoming identical, along with every blemish, every crack upon their face: the faults, the fears, the constant despair hidden behind their efforts and life goals.

My daily routine is fairly simple.

Like everyone else.

I get up, do what I need to do to feel alive in this world, and then I navigate the same streets, seeking today's purpose. I need a purpose.

Like everyone else.

The Fake //

Hello, my name is Bill. They call me Bill, not Bill Kalish or Mr. Kalish. They call me Bill, as in "Hey Bill" and not that genuine, "Bill" short for William, which is my real name. I don't show it and I don't say anything but I really resent the way everyone thinks they know who I am, know what I want, know me like we're friends when I don't know their names and we've never met. People come up to me asking for things like I owe them the world. I want to tell them that I don't even know what world I'm living in. I'm still trying to figure it out.

How about giving me the world and then I'll tell you what's going on.

But that makes me sound like a prick and I don't think I'm a prick.

I'm just some guy that people think is way better than he really is.

I'm in this band that's built up a following and it all looks so damn perfect: Deal signed, tour impending, record well on its way to being completed. Then why do I feel the way I do? I look over my shoulder, as if something's lurking around, waiting to take it all away from me. I don't talk to my bandmates and I keep silent during most meetings because it's kind of like that one quote by that one philosopher—I don't read so I wouldn't remember—but it was about how the less you speak the more likely you'll be considered an enigma. Well, I guess I'm that enigma.

Everyone likes the enigma, totally unaware of that fact that I had no part in this band's success. I auditioned when they needed a new vocalist. Frontman, whatever.

So now they have me. Bill—does what he's told.

They call me Bill so they don't need to bother.

A Logical
Conclusion //

Bill Kalish answered the questionnaire and mailed it to the supplied address so we must be living in the same world, right?

The Atmosphere Alive //

Yeah, it's Bill. Of course it's Bill. What can I say? I'm a real downer, making everything morose. I have trouble keeping track of everyone's names. This is *me* talking. I guess once you open up old wounds, there's no getting past them?

See, this is why I don't talk much.

I think I should speak up.

We're in the studio. We're always in the studio. Recording's begun and today we're tracking drums. I'm here with everyone else but what I don't get is why.

Nick will track the drums and it will take him as long as it needs to take to get it done but having a swarm of people around won't make it go quicker.

The studio's been bought out for the next two weeks.

I bet Nick can feel the pressure. Everyone's watching him. Maybe it's just me. I fixate and overanalyze. I don't know when to mellow out.

I give myself a hard time.

This is what I'm complaining about: I get up to go take a piss and when I come back the couches are full of new and unfamiliar faces, most of them are here because they want to be around Hal, and Nick and Larson and me and Nikki and the whole thing, the whole crazy and exciting and massive endeavor. This band, this opportunity.

And if I were more honest with myself, I'd recognize that I'm not annoyed at the people sitting around here.

I'm annoyed at the fact that one more person in the studio means one more person here to judge my performance.

I'm annoyed because when I'm spotted on the way back from the restroom, they clear the entire couch for me. Like I'm supposed to be treated better than everyone else. It could be a nice gesture, a genuine act of kindness, but this is Bill, and though I'll ignore how I fixate and how I drown my true feelings underneath false pretenses and fakes, I will still take that seat. I'll hide how I really feel. Because I'm Bill and they have to let me know that I am Bill, the frontman, the guy with the voice, the guy that is supposed to stand behind the microphone and direct an entire audience.

Their act of kindness sets me on-edge. Their kindness is a reminder of the reason I'm here. It pulls up that knot of doubt, how my biggest fear is being found out.

But I guess it's about context. I guess everyone here still believes in the value of a band. The rockstar attitude. The whole thing.

I guess everyone just wants to keep the atmosphere alive.

I could be afraid to really let go and let everything out, every memory, every doubt, every concern I have. I'm afraid to fall into the role. I'm afraid to own it.

Look at this scene: Nick hitting every single beat without a single error. Everyone listening and banging their heads to the very same beat. There's something in the air, a sort of electricity and I feel like a fraud for trying so hard to disregard the feeling.

Man, look at how I'm acting. I really am a drain.

A Lot of
Boredom //

When you have the face of any other, you are under threat of losing focus on your own feelings. Like Bill here, the budding rockstar, his predicament is simple: a blend of being unable to set a path, a fear of commitment. The people around him see maybe boundless talent but Bill here, he resists. I used to give up in these situations.

I end up in his situation and I leave before I can leave a mark.

I get bored.

A younger version of myself would have already left the studio.

But instead I'll stay.

I'm going to stay.

My name's Bill.

The real Bill ran away from the pressure.

The real Bill will be back, but until then, I'll fit right in.

And then when the session's over, I'll make sure Bill knows, hears every single thing his bandmates, producers, and fans had to say about him, *Bill*, not his ability but rather Bill, the person behind the extraordinary voice.

Official reason for doing what I do is and has always been to combat my own feelings of doubt, the debilitating feeling of being invisible.

My off-hand reason, well, I don't like feeling bored.

Nobody likes feeling bored, do they?

And if I can stand by someone in need, it helps me sleep better at night.

Helping them back up lets people know that I'm here.

When you have the face of any other, you are only invisible if you feel useless.

Boredom, don't you know, it's a **killer**.

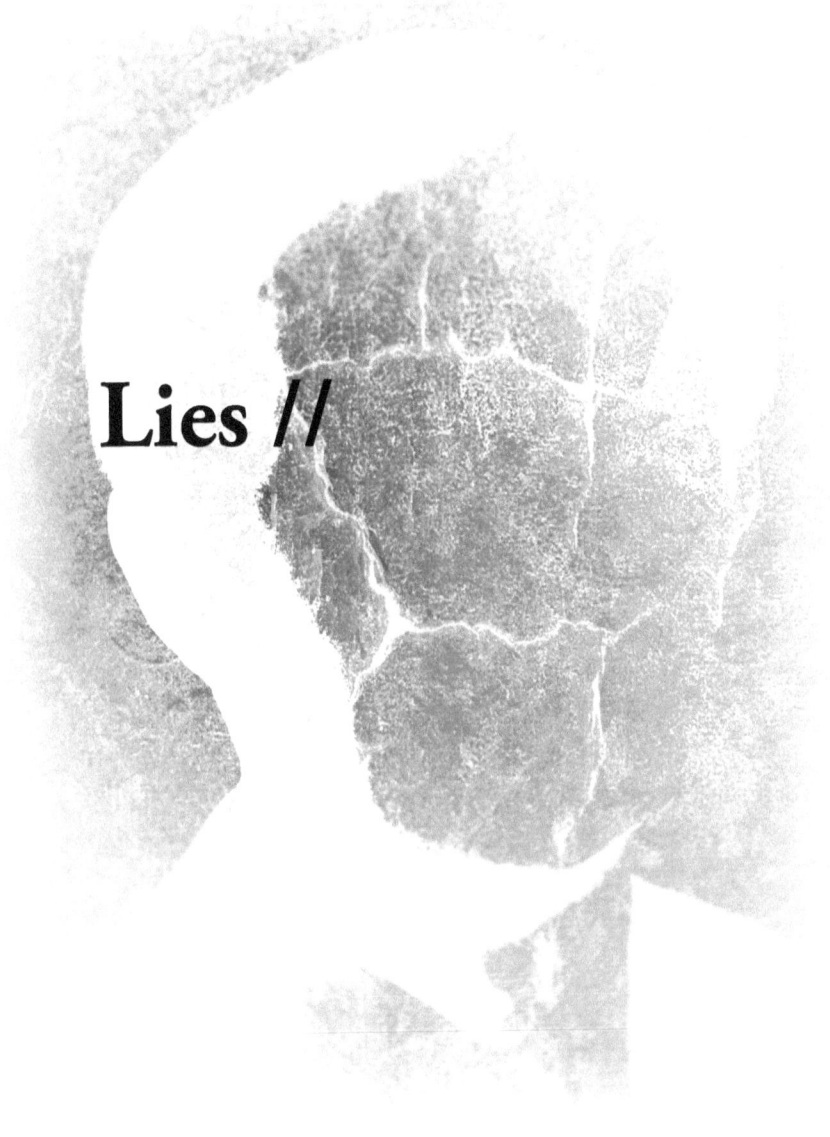

Lies //

Bill this, Bill that—they want my opinion, some kind of official statement about who I am. Who are they, I'm tempted to ask, but when I'm asked about my plans, my strategies for recording, basically a loaded question about vocal technique, I'm silent.

I'm silent and they are waiting.

We're between takes and these two young journalists and maybe fans must have wandered in while I was trying a few takes and really fucking up, not hitting the right notes even though the producer said we're good to go.

I say we're good to go when I know it sounds good. How could **that**, the track playing back via the studio speakers, be any good?

I am a perfectionist. Learn something new every day. Me, a perfectionist.

Here's my reply, **I usually plan my actions in advance.**

It goes right in the interview, I guess.

They ask about time management, how I'm able to write, sing, practice, perform live, tour around the country and world, and still have time to myself. They ask me as if I've already been at this as long as the rest of the band.

I auditioned and now I'm here.

I close my eyes and say whatever comes out first, **I know how to put every minute of my time to good purpose.**

And then there's talk about my vocal work, how tricky

it must be to overextend myself, causing potential throat issues, like so many other vocalists.

I pick out a certain phrase being tossed around, the worry of "not warming up enough." Asking if I'll mess up.

That's just great. What do I say to that?

Might as well get it out in the open, all my doubts and worries.

I'll be fine. I can admit it without putting myself out there. I know what I'm doing.

Listen to what they're saying.

I'm a natural.

I am always prepared.

They both nod and agree, not narcissistic. I look around the studio. Everyone's listening. Curious then to completely tune out everyone else. A moment ago it felt like I was alone with the journalists and the interview in progress.

Knowing that I can disregard the added pressure should help but—okay now I can't concentrate. They want my opinion on something. Haven't I already answered enough questions? I look around for Heather, the manager. I spot her leaning against a far wall next to people I don't know, for all I know label executives or some other corporate source, there to watch, here to judge my every action, and listen to see whether or not I fuck up.

I pay attention to details.

What else do you want from me? Other people are talking too. They ask the bandmates questions, but I find it kind of hard to pay attention.

I can't get outside of myself. Its like there's a layer of white noise around me making it so that I can't step outside of my comfort zone.

I created this as a means of coping with my doubts.

I should just step outside of it. See what happens.

I'm Bill, I do vocals. Why can't I just say that all honest and true? Oh we've had some good sessions and bad ones but as long as I start with a few breaths, some tea, a few vocal exercises to warm up, I'm usually fine. Why can't I say this?

Listen to what everyone around me is saying.

It should make me feel better. It should help me open up.

Instead, these are the hesitations; these are the chains pulling me down. Every step of the way—I'll be found out. Doubt. Doubt. Doubt. Doubt.

Lies. All lies. They're just humoring me.

I don't know who to trust so I'll ask for a few more takes. Just a few more takes.

Even though it's pretty clear that it's just me.

No one's doubting anyone.

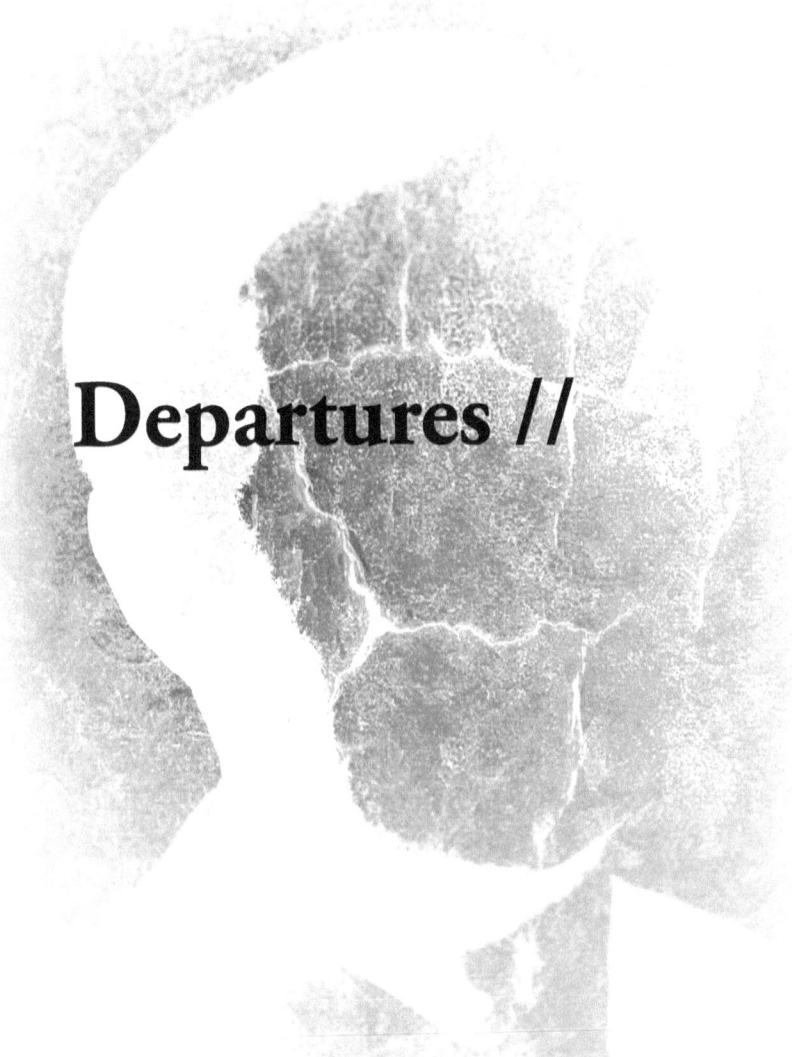

Departures //

When you have the face of any other, sometimes you just need to lighten up. Every single thing you see could bring you down, make you feel like shit. I could easily go back to being invisible. I could stand up and without looking back, walk out of the studio.

All that effort going in goes to waste.

But I'm not going to do that. I got *two days* on this, Bill.

I've been Bill for two and he still hasn't shown up. This implies that this budding rockstar of sorts is about as stereotypically distressed and troubled as any number of other idols that have strutted the stage shouting into a microphone for attention.

Bill Kalish could be on a plane, flying a thousand miles from the studio, but if I keep at this, when he returns, it won't be in vain.

He will be shocked to hear his voice on the track, amazed at what it sounds like.

He'll be too shocked to figure out how it happened— how could they have recorded three songs without him? With his voice?

Around this type of crowd, you can believe anything. They'll tell him he's talented and that he's a natural and then he'll listen to the transcript I recorded, the interview between the two journalists and the entire band, and without too much trouble, it'll be like I never was, never moonlighted for a young rockstar.

He'll learn to accept criticism. He'll learn to commit.

Thanks so much, I'm flattered. I'm going to work. I'm getting right at that track.

I'll tear it up.

I'll walk right into the vocal booth.

The producer will pamper me with various settings.

Are the headphones good?

Can you hear yourself? Good.

I'm going through the motions and I can feel myself falling in line.

I could get used to this.

But there was never any doubt, was there? Not for anyone else. They knew, and me, Bill, I'm getting there. I'm starting to realize it.

I'll tear up this track and he won't know what to think.

And then it's take-one.

No need to read the lines because I wrote them; I should own them.

By the end of the first chorus, the track keeps going. We keep recording.

No stops, so I'm not going to stop either.

I forget that there's any music.

I forget what it sounds like to hear something for the first time. I hear everything in terms of how it fits on the track, so much that I can't even picture the notes in my mind. I don't need to. Everything's a sound, pure sound.

Everything's a color.

Man, I could get used to this.

I play by ear.

I used to limit myself.

I used to play what I know. There were never any surprises.

But now I'm starting to like this.

And when the take is saved, being altered, the producer

saying there isn't a need to cut anything up. It was a solid take. Satisfied looks from the dozens in the studio, I can finally feel it in the air. The electricity. Power and the possibilities.

I can hear it on the track—everything needed for a young musician to find faith in himself—and it's at this point that *I know* that it's time.

If I don't leave when everything falls in place so perfectly, well then I'd still be new at this.

It's Bill. It's Bill! I love you Bill. Love ya man.

He'll have no problem owning that stage.

The Statistics //

When you have the face of any other, the numbers can seem daunting. Numbers are everywhere and they take the shape of possibilities, every single possible person looking back at you. How many are there at any given moment? How about right now?

How about now?

I've ventured a guess and I've come up empty more than once.

I've looked through another set of eyes, and found— well, I've seen, and sensed, everything that person was and could have been.

I've walked these streets, rode elevators, and drove to the outskirts of town as at least fifty people.

I've seen at least three lives end, with a good dozen more on the upswing towards a major life accomplishment.

I've stood in lieu of the actual at the moment of marriage proposal.

I've helped deliver the proposal when one person couldn't garner the courage to do it himself; twice I've seen new life brought into this world, witness to their first tears.

That loud shrieking cry.

I've delivered an important speech to an audience of a thousand, and, yes, on at least a handful of occasions, I have shared the bed with a stranger. If they couldn't perform, I exhibited enough distance to be able to get close enough for penetration.

I've been there—and I've brought a number of my own.

I've sampled so many personalities, and even though they might wear the feeling proudly, I can't remember a time when I've seen someone truly honest and open with both their pride and their pleasures, their faults and their fears. The number for that, I'm thinking zero. When you have the face of any other, you see that the source of every single fissure and crack upon their face is due to what is contained within, held and smothered so that not even the person recognizes, much less senses, the concern, the threat.

Because feeling anything other than immediacy has become a character flaw.

I'm not sure about the exact numbers. I'm being honest. I have no reason to hold the numbers back. Guess I just never kept track. Do you keep track of every joke?

I'm usually too busy laughing, preoccupied with enjoying the moment, to focus in on the petty things. Numbers might indicate a run of certain character traits but as far as I'm concerned, I've seen plenty and there's still plenty more to be seen.

When you have the face of any other, the world around you can change with the single blink of an eye.

While It's Happening //

When you have the face of any other, you can't always pretend that you're something you're not. You can't always ignore that, to the world around you, you're invisible. There's nothing complicated about it. They can't see you. I used to run tests—dangerous and frankly stupid tests—to see whether or not both object and individual could notice me.

I learned the hard way that they can't.

Car collision.

Pushed and shoved aside.

Door shut in my face.

I'm made into a ghost, a haunting occurrence. The physical reaction somehow doesn't add up as evidence to my existence. I am here, I could scream, and the same response would forever be silence. But I still wear the best suits.

I still keep to myself, keep my best interests a closed book.

I had a moment of criminal activity, got a little wild, but that's over.

It got old. I got enough of what I need to survive. These days, I find other people more interesting than my own wants and needs. I know what I need and want. Others...

You'd be surprised. The world is confusing because the people that occupy it render it a mess. I'm no philosopher.

I've seen some things; I know some things.

That's about it. I can't always be something I'm not.

I've reached acceptance and what's left is the world around me.

Some days I can't get myself to walk in step. I wake up when I wake up. I don't abide by an alarm. I don't listen or read the news. I don't look past their faces. I don't examine past the cracks, the blemishes, the wounds carried like some kind of prerequisite.

I stick to the momentum of the moment. I let the sun shine down, blinding my face; I let the rain drench me. I let the snow fall and freeze my nose, my ears, my face.

I let reality sink in and have its say. I let it all happen, everything that occurs without my participation. It is here, these solemn and spare occurrences, that I feel most like myself.

Sometimes being absent doesn't have to result in thoughts of abject failure.

No plans or intentions—I let it be, embracing the notion that I'm alive, like everyone else, while everything else is happening. Whatever happens is going to happen; I don't always need to preoccupy myself with the details.

These quiet, aimless days to myself are sometimes the best.

I can almost forget that there needs to be anything more to this world other than a little food, a nice walk, a casual stay, the weather, the day, the afternoon, and evening.

I can almost forget it all—all the hellos and dreaded departures. Almost.

Watching You //

Hello, my name is Isabelle Blumstein and I'd like to think that I'm open-minded. I love working with people, I love working out. I love that people come to me to improve their bodies. They come to me to improve themselves. They'll be so nervous, it's cute, and when I get them to calm down, they tell me that I'm a savior. It's so flattering.

As the senior personal trainer here, I basically own this gym.

It's reassuring—to have that cushion, financially, though I guess I do work a lot.

I talk a lot, yeah, but I'm extroverted. I spend most of my day watching people.

I'm watching you.

It's my job to improve people's lives.

I've started to, well, develop philosophies. They aren't even mine any more, it's not personal: I use my people skills to brighten everyone's day.

It makes me feel good. I get excited. I have a lot of energy, you know?

I feed on their enthusiasm and compliments.

Not like they're prey, no but I do pray that they keep up that momentum.

I need it to maintain my illusions of progress.

I teach five classes a day and usually have about six to eight training sessions between those five classes. I'm about to have my second class of the day right now.

I'll never be late, but I like letting my students sweat it out in anticipation. I've learned from experience that if I run into the room at the last minute, there's less chance that they'll back off and flee from the challenge.

I wait right here, around the corner, the employee side hallway, listening to my students walk into the room.

Every time I hear them curious and afraid about what I'll make them do, it gets me excited. This is the kind of energy I crave.

I'll make them work.

I'll watch the pounds fall right off every single one of my students. I take their commitment seriously; I take their commitment to put in the work as a personal challenge.

I'd never miss a class.

The Bottomed-Out Soul //

When you have the face of any other, nobody can see you blush. Nobody will notice the embarrassment. I wandered into this day on my own terms, expecting to fall asleep in the same condition I did when I woke. I expected to be me—*be blank, nothing*—but then I saw her. I saw her face. That look, it was one of terror.

I saw the mania hidden behind a shattered face.

I had to do what I needed to do to have a look. I'm sorry.

I'm sorry but you don't just see a bottomed-out soul like her every day.

I wanted to just continue down the street.

Instead, it felt necessary to be a bother. Again, I'm sorry.

Sometimes you have to cause pain to inevitably help a person.

I didn't break any bones. I didn't cause any physical harm, nothing but a few hours to call my own. I whispered sorry into her ear right before it happened.

I made sure that the bulk of it washed over her without anything more than a few cuts and bruises. Nothing serious. A wakeup call at best.

She's got bigger wounds to heal.

Is it presumptuous of me to think I can lend a hand?

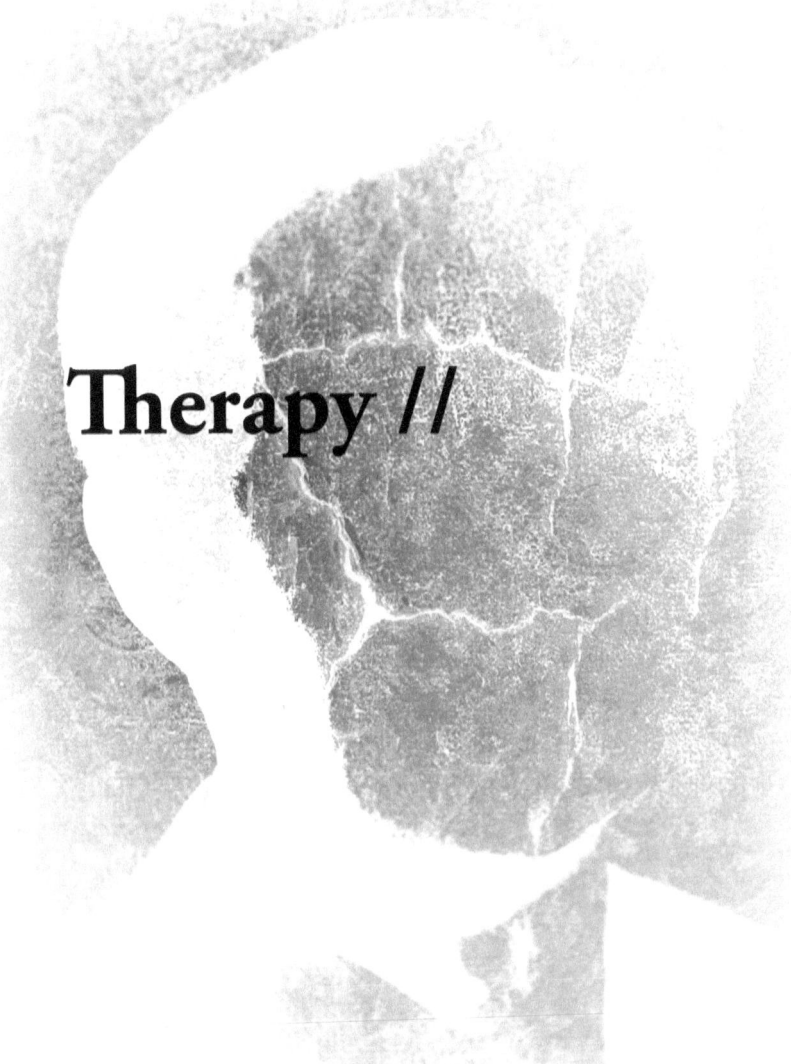

Therapy //

Oh shit, here she comes. Man I'm going to die. Think positive. No, I'm totally going to die. I won't make it. Going to keel over. This is the kind of stuff I want to hear from the students when I run right in. The class gets started right when I walk through those doors.

This is therapy.

It's what I repeat in my head, over and over.

This is therapy.

Once we get warmed up, get the legs and arms moving, the mind clears. Keep the body moving. I turn up the music and let them start with a jog.

Therapy. Keep it motivational.

They know what to do. Follow me, every step.

No one dares slow down.

Once we get started, I'll be able to ignore the feeling.

The question(s) I never ask myself: What feeling? Why do you feel this way? Why are you so anxious? What is the source of this anxiety?

Once we get that sweat going, it's time for the best part. It's time for that part of the workout where everyone decides whether or not they're all in or not. You don't come back from this; once you start with the compound movements, I start placing demands.

I set the benchmark that each student needs to meet.

At this moment, I feel perfect, serene. I feel nothing.

Every thirty seconds, I shout out something declarative. I say something that others can take to heart.

I enjoy exploring new places.

Too busy keeping up to respond.

Too busy to be anything but critical of each and every student.

Too busy to entertain such thoughts.

Keep up with the beat. That's it keep it up. I don't see anyone slacking and I want to keep it that way. If you cramp up, fight through it. Think, I want you to think: The cramp will pass. That pain will pass. We can keep going.

I need to believe my own philosophies.

I enjoy trying new things.

Say it. Feel it. Believe it. Become that person you want to become.

You can be the ideal you. No reason to hide behind any sort of mask; you can look your best. I will make sure you are in the best shape of your life.

I'll say every single thing with enthusiasm. I'll look my best, my most confident, even when I know that what I'm running from will be right there when I stop. I have to keep going. It's right there.

I won't admit that I'm sick. I won't admit that I'm dying.

I like learning new things.

I'll watch as the class takes on a life of its own, my body working without any vital cues or commands from my brain. I watch and see everyone in my class essentially bothered by the same threat of mortality. They are here to heal, to mend something about themselves.

I'll do what I do to hide from the fact that just because it goes into remission, it doesn't mean the cancer won't return.

I pride myself on being different.

I say and do these things for the same reason I remain so manic and hyper:

If I let myself enjoy this moment, I might collapse.

I'm afraid that I don't have a lot of time left.

Next thing I know I'm waking up in a hospital bed, with no way to escape the sound of the monitor.

Beep.

Beep.

Beep.

One of those beeps will last longer than the others.

I'm dying. Oh god, I'm dying…

It'll hold on, flatlining, the moment I lose my grip.

Beeeeeeeeeeeeeeeeeeeeeeeeeeee—

The moment I let go.

False
Expectations //

When you have the face of any other, you are confronted with the understanding that death is present throughout our entire lives. It remains near, the inevitable book-end to the open book of a person's life story. It waits, more patiently with some, while with others it takes a liking to their pulse. You can hear it.

Every beat is one less to be dealt.

Beep. I imagine Isabelle in the hospital after it happened. A life completely changed via one single experience.

You can't hide the cracks carved into the skin of your face, the cracks dug in deep, no matter what the doctors do to bring you back from death's grip.

In the context of the class, her students are as much there to learn as she is there to use them as a means to cope with her demons.

But Isabelle, dear Isabelle, you can't keep living like this.

You can't work yourself to exhaustion.

You can't feed on what isn't there.

That's how you'll end up back in the hospital. It won't be due to something unforeseen; everyone will have saw it coming. Everyone but you.

You'll run yourself back into the ground.

When you have the face of any other, you get sick to your stomach seeing how some people choose to live. So much of what they've been dealt had to do with the various decisions and distances, the ones chosen and the measures carved, to deal. When you have the face of any other, you quickly understand that "dealing" with the cards dealt isn't anything more than another excuse.

How do you really feel? Sometimes, a person must fill in and decide for those that remain indecisive.

Subliminal Messages //

I wait around, unable to really leave until I let Isabelle know that she is not alone in carrying these anxieties. I am here right after my departure. I adjust my tie, run a hand through my hair. I look fine but how does she look?

Some cuts, a bruise on her forearm.

What the hell happened?!

Confusion is natural. An hour ago many of her students had been in class. They assume that she had been there too. A few either remained at the gym or returned for another run. Whatever the reason, they are here, and they help conjure up the impossibility of her case. If she had really collided with a biker, how could she have taught class today?

Isabelle has no recollection of both class and collision.

She has the cuts and bruises to prove that the impossible indeed occurred but that doesn't change the fact that her face is red. She feels taken aback, not quite shock and not quite fear. She's frozen in place.

The students do their best to make sense of the situation, offering excuses like, I guess it just needed some disinfectant and a bandage; they probably ran her through the system, and, it probably hasn't sunk in yet, that's all.

But there are no explanations and I wait near the bench press, sitting with my elbows on my knees, watching as, one by one, they leave the gym.

Isabelle is, to be expected, the last at the gym, closing up every night.

I need her to understand something.

In every step, I am here to help.

She cleans each station, making sure the gym is ready for tomorrow's round of activity. When she reaches the free weights, I stand up and take to her left side.

When you have the face of any other, there are certain peculiarities that come with the territory. They can't see or hear me but they can sense me. If I touch her, she will feel that touch; if I whisper into her ear while touching her skin, she will hear me.

She won't hear my voice, but the thought, it will pass her ear drum and burrow into her brain. I'm here for no other reason than to heal the shattered nerves, the broken face, the wounded and worried personality.

Isabelle Blumstein doesn't need to continue along this path. She can find her way back to previous ideals, lifestyle choices.

I tell her something while holding her cheek.

She shivers, continuing unaddressed. It's nothing, a cold gust, prickle of the skin.

I'm here, but to the world I'm more a ghostly chill than a person with good intentions.

Isabelle checks the private weight rooms, flicking on each light switch to examine the condition and arrangement of the equipment.

She leaves each door locked and continues to make her rounds.

I tell her something, hand on her shoulder.

A look over her shoulder and nothing more.

Isabelle gathers all the dirty towels, checks to make sure all the lockers are properly shut, checks to make sure no items are left behind, pushes the bins into the back employees-only area, essentially fulfilling another employee's duties.

After she's checked the facilities, she returns to her office. I slip into the room before she shuts the door on me, watching as she collapses in the office chair, eyes without focus.

There's nothing but her and the four walls.

I can see the exhaustion across her shattered face, applying more stress and pressure to already permanent and troublesome fissures.

Eyes shut and in seconds she's dozing.

I tell her something.

I tell her what she needs to hear.

I lean down and hug her. I tell her everything I see.

And then I leave. It might have been something imagined, part of a dream, but Isabelle will remember parts of the telling. It'll maybe show itself in the morning or a week from now in the form of a slight acknowledging of how tired she feels, her body screaming for a break. Maybe some of what I said will hit her all at once. I never really know how it'll sink in; I only know that it always does. In some way, it does.

There's no greater purpose to this other than the purpose itself. This is it, my motive. Nothing else. Without one, I'll wander for an hour, a day at best, before getting bored.

And this is where it's worth repeating what I said about boredom.

I'm here because this act gives me purpose. Here for no other reason to deliver subliminal messages to a person in need.

It helps me feel *real*.

Something About Needing to Be Something //

When you have the face of any other, you see the cracks peeling apart their face, showing bone, bleeding with the hidden anguish of hushed nerves. You feel each and every nerve tensing, and you feel for them—for everyone—when they buckle, unable to bear the burden of each daunting episode. Life has a way—the common dictum. But they forget the other half, the part that reads, and life has a way with you.

I see everything as it falls in place—a person's basic needs:

The need for food, shelter, health, safety, ambition: these are imperative. But there's also the need for self-interests, self-respect, self-discipline, self-awareness, self-actualization, self-disclosure, self-control, self-sufficiency, self-compassion, and self-preservation.

Those needs cluttered by a series of wants, desires, and harms dealing with success, worth, and validation. And everything in between:

A person is born into this world, and a person is required to learn.

A person is educated about this world and therefore grounded in the principles, tragedies of the past, and everything in between. The weight of the world handed over in the form of a standardized test. A person graduates and is required to come of age.

A person needs employment.

A person needs a place in society. A person needs to support the institution of marriage. A person warms up to the concept of parenthood. A person will age and eventually retire from what used to provide meaning to their days. A person leaves the world the same as when s/he entered: faceless.

Then you add in social pressures and demands and suddenly, it's less about *all of the above* and more about what's missing, everything in between.

It's confusion and existential curiosity. It's *life* having its fucking way with you.

So I see it happen and I wince, really I do. I just want to help. That's it.

When you spend all your time and energy making sure the people around you are happy, no one will question whether or not you feel the same way.

No one is there to question your motivations.

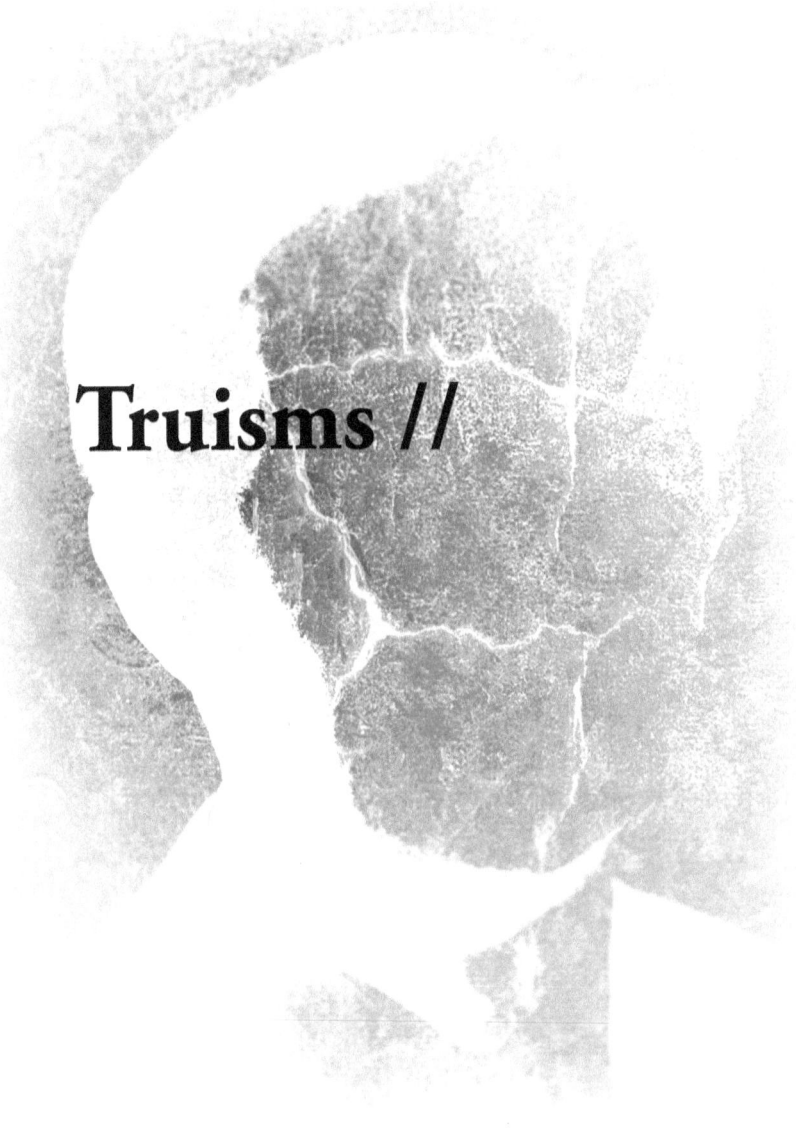

Truisms //

When you have the face of any other, you are like everyone else in that you sometimes can't even begin to finish **this sentence**. You remain indoors and inside. I rest, the bed is my cross and shield. I recuperate, that's what this is, not a joke.

I often take to repeating truisms, letting them flood my head. Drown it all out.

Eventually I get to thinking, start thinking back and imagine a time when this all became somehow possible. I think about the shirt and tie, pants and dress shoes, impressive hairdo, everything that has nothing to do with who I have become. Less considered but deemed most imperative: Whatever I became, and then even more important is the becoming. I think about how I could be dead, and that this is the afterlife, my tailored version of an afterlife, forced to wander and to worry about others because—what's the prototypical plot detail for this kind of thing? I was a horrible, heartless, and cheap bastard.

Yes, that sounds good. Better yet, I could be batshit crazy, running around in my high fashion thinking that no one sees me, acting like an imbecile, when in fact everyone sees me and more, I'm some kind of urban legend. That could be worth a laugh. I could be from a different dimension traveling between my home dimension, looking for a host body in this one. That would explain their disregard.

Sounds like a plan, this one. I'm a dimensional traveler. Put it on a business card.

I could be any number of plot lines to feed the actuality of my situation. If it sounds like fiction, it maintains the absurdity found in impossibility. No matter that something so impossible has now become mine. I think about all the usual assumptions and turn them into stories. I think about how I turn into others, aiding in their own biases, predicaments, and problems, because being given a lucid, though temporary, purpose is better than being left like this, circling the muted frustrations of my own prob—on second thought, whatever.

That's why I stick to concrete facts. I repeat truisms until the mind settles—

I am a person. (?) Really now.

I am alive. (?) It's nothing.

I am not guilty. (?) Plain facts.

I am not hiding from something. (?) Things obvious to everyone.

I think about one thing before leading to the next. Like for instance, the significance of the number "3." See what I did there? I avoided the subject, kept holding off until my mind swept up a different thread of deliberation.

I am human (?) Truisms.

The Number
Three //

When you have the face of any other, you see a lot of what should be left unseen. You are privy to thoughts and memories that shouldn't ever be revealed. Sometimes people can't save themselves from what they've already accepted will be their end.

When you have the face of any other, you watched their attempts. If they fail, most will try again. They'll jump off a bridge, cut their wrists, take pills, or wrap their lips around the barrel of a gun. When you are there and watching, you can't help but think about becoming them so that you can end it for them, so that they can live to see another day.

But it doesn't work that way. I tried.

Three times. Significance of the number "3."

I tried by being them at the moment of the act, stopping it and even going ahead with *it*. All I got was a terrible hangover, some blood loss, and a sudden bout of disappointment followed by dread when I almost pulled the trigger.

The trigger was *almost pulled*.

When you know why they are doing what they're about to do, you start to wonder if you should try it yourself. Three times. I felt that way three times. I wouldn't dare entertain a fourth. One slight mention brought it all back. It pulled me back into the self-obsession, the spiraling thoughts full of "me," "me," and "me."

When you have the face of any other, you just wish sometimes all these thoughts and memories would go away. But it's always been this way, so don't be worried:

Other people are worried enough. They do enough worrying.

They worry for the world.

The Impossible //

Let's go with along with this one, shall we, because I won't be able to move on if I don't settle on a version of the story. That story, the one about how through some sort of becoming, I became me. Let's go with the impossible. It goes like this, though it's a little different every time run it back in my mind.

I was like any other kid, the barely containable curiosity coupled with boundless energy. Oh yeah for the longest time I was so young and so impressionable. That's kind of the point, being a kid. I think about all of the expectations, the false ones and the mandatory, and how being at this stage, you sort of begin faceless. You haven't gone through with it, the first impression, the one that matters, the one that has everything to do with future opportunities and ambition.

Then it all starts to fall into place and things seem impossible. It's all part of growing up, same line spoken by everyone older than you. You just want to silence all the frustrations and confusions of adolescence.

Whenever parents, friends, relatives asked I answered—

I want to be someone else.

I wanted the taller height, the better jump shot, the bigger comeback.

I wanted all the good so I could be good enough.

I wanted all the good without any of the bad.

Fear, it can change you. When you grow to hate the face looking back at you in every mirror, the face that places you into categories and enforced limitations determined by the judgment of others, you get to wishing for the opposite.

You wish more often than you work on bettering yourself.

You get into a groove with the wishing, so much so that when one afternoon you're finally asked the question, What do you wish for? You have the answer memorized.

You know exactly what you want.

It starts with *I want* and it ends with getting exactly what I asked for.

That's how it happens. There's how *the impossible* is once again proven to be the opposite. In becoming conceivable, I have what I remember. I really don't remember much. It could be one of the other explanations—I'm partial to the dimensional-traveler one myself—but this is the one I've embraced. This is it, in full. I'm only being honest.

I take it in stride, even when dog days like these get me down.

I'll get through it.

I'll get through it under the rationalization that, if it really is impossible then I should be dead. I shouldn't be capable of a single breath, much less the one I use to joke around and laugh. I'm right here and I can feel the world as much as I can make a difference in the tired and defeated people that walk its streets.

That's what gets me through. Doesn't matter if it's unbelievable.

Doesn't matter if I'm willing to believe it.

Story's still a story, an explanation if and when asked.

I got what I asked for.

A Word or Two //

It doesn't take more than a word or two before I know that he'll be next. I spot him on the subway, the express train into the city. Sipping iced coffee from a tumbler, he humored the passenger, vacant nods and a suppressed yawn, his only reply to the passenger's pleas. When you have the face of any other, you can see into the lacerations on a person's face to the inner good, the genuine character they rarely expose. The same goes for the inner bad, their infections, personal pathologies. You see a person from the inside out. You see what they look like afterward, when their face becomes less a window and more a mask, concealing every atrophy.

I look right at him.

Yes.

Habits //

Hello, my name is Beauregard, Bryan Beauregard. I'm twenty-eight years old and I work in finance. I have absolutely no fixations—I maintain a logical attitude at all times. It pays, oh man does it fucking pay out, when you keep your senses tuned to the market.

I'm not a pusher, in the sense that I manipulate stocks and work on Wall Street. That's a stereotype, don't you know? Just because they made a string of movies about them doesn't mean every single person at the frontlines of finance are greedy bastards.

I'm just a relatively young guy with plans, with promises to fulfill.

I will get what I want and won't take no for an answer.

Being tired or sick isn't an option. I ride the train downtown every single day, especially on weekends, when I use it as a chance to get away from the ball and chain. My girlfriend can really be a pain. She says she doesn't want much and says that she likes me for me, and to never change, but deep down she's using passive aggressive strategies, some sort of voodoo. She's into all that hip stuff—the stuff that tells you how fucked up your life is and then asks you to pay for the products, books, videos, whatever, so that they can tell you how you're supposed to live. Live in a fucking shack in the woods, harvesting crops, no connection to the modern world.

We didn't get here by being satisfied with simplicities. We have wants. People of the world need to finance their futures, and that's where I come in.

It's my job to help them exploit the market.

It's legal as long as everyone at the personal level gets that payday.

I am *a walking stereotype.*

Excuse me if I'm in a rush.

Excuse me if I'm too preoccupied to listen to your life story. It's early and I got under three hours of sleep. I have an inbox that's been inundated and I'll spend the better half of my day working correspondence. There's still the latest reports to study. Facts and figures, facts and figures. I need more coffee.

So what if I'm a little late. I run on my own time. I'll get there early. I'll get there late. As long as the work is done and bank balance accounts for every dollar, I'm free.

Maybe I get a little ahead of myself, one-upping everyone and everything.

I'm one step ahead of you.

Efficiency is one step ahead.

Sometimes I surprise myself—that's how much of a critical thinker I am and you need to be to cut it in this world. This isn't a world of compromises. It'll eat you alive if you think you can manage with a little. You need a lot— need to give a lot and get even more—to survive. I'm an example, so don't be insulted if I'm too busy to reply. Don't be insulted if I can't take you to that thing on Saturday. Don't be insulted if I miss a family dinner or a birthday. Don't be insulted if you never hear from me for years. Mom and Dad I'm busy.

Patricia, please, I'm busy.

Some other time.

You said you liked me for me.

Don't be insulted if I continue being that person. I'm

not saying I hate what I am, I'm just saying I have a lot on my plate.

I have a lot of expectations and responsibilities.

More you invest, the more you have to lose. I could lose it all, and that's what I'm afraid of most. I compartmentalized and sold off every single likeable aspect of myself; I made sure to accentuate each aspect so that I could win over the right people.

That's what it takes, so if you say hello and I can't be bothered, it's because that part of me has already been priced and sold off for the appropriate times.

Catch me as I am and I'll look right through you. There are more important things in life. I am one of those things. I'm sorry but I don't think you matter much. I don't know you, why are you talking to me? You aren't a part of my life. You don't mean anything.

To someone else, yeah, maybe, but not to me.

I'm sorry if I can't be accommodating.

Most people develop habits.

People build up habits to cope but the very same habits end up consuming us. That's the truth. I believe it. I don't want any surprises; I own my habits. I plan ahead. If it comes to it, I'll already know how it'll fall apart. You have to care about yourself or else who will?

Don't be insulted but, I have to say, in this situation, you, guy, person I don't know, and person that decided to strike up a conversation with me, me at a time when I'm not bothering anyone else, keeping to myself, just trying to wake up, rouse myself for the daunting workday, *you* talked to **me** and you know what:

I'm better than you and that's the truth.

That's what I believe.

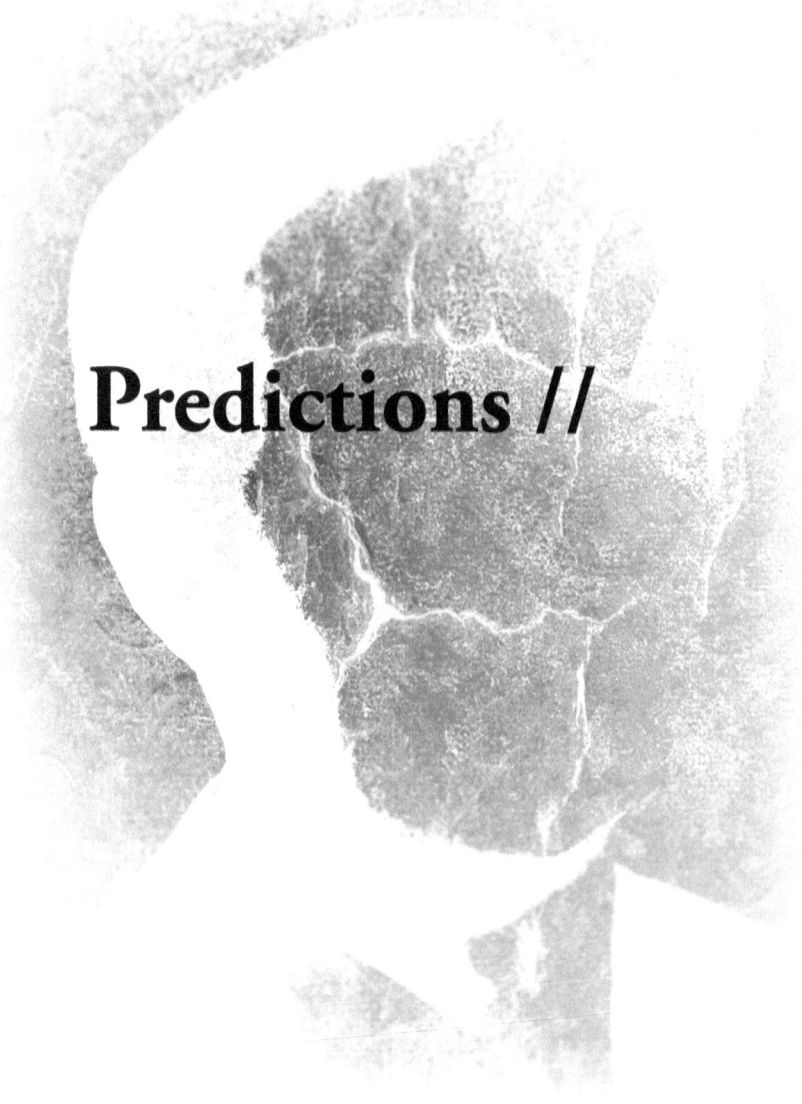

Predictions //

Better than you. Huh, now that's a load of douchebag right there. Better than who? This Beauregard, he thinks the world was made to be a setting of his own modern masterpiece.

Talking epic struggle, full of ups and downs, good versus evil, hero (him, duh) winning out and saving the entire world so that he can, inevitably, rule over it and become evil. Full circle.

I've encountered plenty of people with inflated egos, so it's okay if I joke around. Know what, I'm going to make a few predictions.

I'm guessing Beauregard's had parental issues—not likely a neglectful mother, no, more like a demanding father, one that demanded more than young Beauregard could ever give, from the moment of conception. Strict and impossible demands lead to the inability to digest and appreciate personal success, much less values. He could be the richest person alive and he wouldn't be able to truly grasp what that implies. Likewise, he could be a twenty-eight-year-old douchebag living in a overpriced apartment he can barely afford working as an associate investment banker at some private firm, tired and on the verge of breakdown, and he could be carrying it all like he's a success story. For the ages.

I'm going to guess that he is prone to self-loathing, tending to hide these thoughts beneath a string of boastful statements. He'll tell you enough about himself to make you feel bad about your own accomplishments but, within the context of that conversation, it's really Beauregard that's on the verge of tears.

I'm going to assume that he'll attempt suicide at least once during his lifetime. It won't be the broadcasted or "televised" kind, the type that really go through with it. He'll plan out the suicide, going as far as buying the gun or the knife or the pills or whatever, but when it comes time, he'll hesitate. And he'll hide the shameful act. No one will know.

I'm going to suggest that he doesn't have any friends. He has clearly lost contact with his family. He isn't the type to be thoughtful of others, that's pretty damn obvious. So douchebag, I mean Beauregard, keeps to his own solitary life. Somehow he has a girlfriend. Not sure how he managed that.

I'm guessing they met in college and stuck together for a variety of reasons, some having to do with financial perks—based on how Beauregard views her, she'd be homeless without his earning power—and inability to change.

I'm going to state it as a fact: Beauregard is afraid of change. He likes changes on the books, an increase in bank balance, an investment that pays, but he fears the loss. If you fear the loss, you likely fear change.

One more, I can see it in his eyes. He carries a dead dream of his own. This wasn't what he wanted to become. It's probably more of a father's doing, forcing him down a lucrative path. Beauregard hides this dead dream behind that mask.

I can't be sure but just by the way he thinks and talks, he wanted to be creative.

He was a creative type. As are most.

Athletic, perhaps. Science? Not a chance.

I'm going to go with... something creative, expressive.

Let's see if I'm right.

Stick around and it becomes obvious to anyone the real look and shape of a person. You get to know that person. When you have the face of any other, you tend to know what you're talking about. I know what I'm talking about.

Honest.

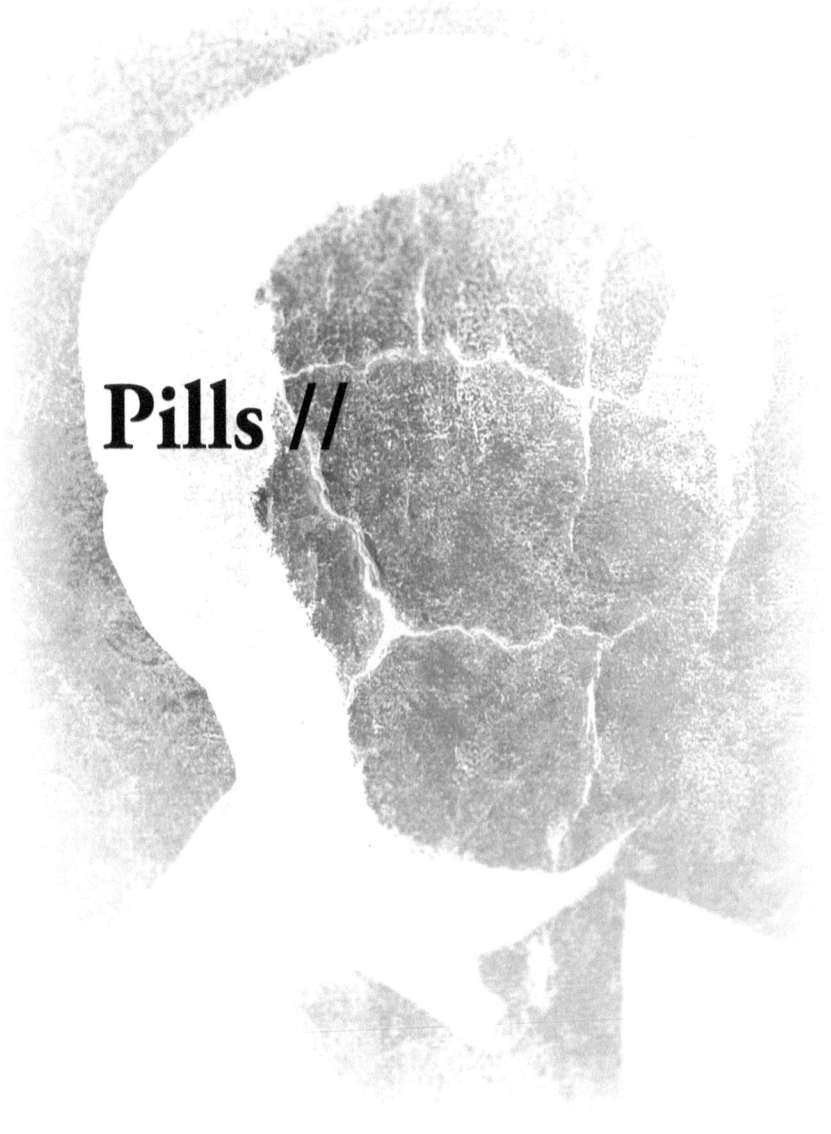

Pills //

This is where Bryan would say hello, a nice cordial greeting. It's customary. It's also customary for the guy to keep to himself, that stuck-up manner with which he'll glance in your direction, long enough to judge, and then continue with his current task.

What is he doing?

He's downing some pills.

He's medicating.

He's burying the past.

He's focusing on the work.

He's thinking about how much he stands to make on a single investment.

He's not thinking about anyone else but himself.

He's…

Oh what will I do, what will I do, if these investments don't pay out? I won't have as much disposable income! I need help. I need help. Why won't someone give me a break.

Just a single breath, a breather.

He doesn't know that I was him for seventeen minutes this morning. I rode the same train, kept ten steps ahead. Opened his desk drawers and had a glance, a quick overview of Bryan Christopher Beauregard. Didn't see anything new. I wasn't surprised.

You could say I was disappointed. I didn't get to see

what he hides behind that mask, and I'm as offended by the guy as I was when I first saw him on the train.

I'm not impressed.

I'm **not** here to help.

When you have the face of any other, sometimes you take things personally.

Sometimes you need to look. Sometimes, you need to get involved.

You *want* to get involved. You see the ego like an incoming storm, and you want to be there to see how much damage it'll cause.

Something
Expensive //

When you have the face of any other, sometimes you can't tell the difference between fact and a fake, a mask and the person beneath. The mask conceals the truth, every truth. No one's smiling and nobody's obvious. They wear them without realizing that they bought their way into wearing the mask, wearing some costume, some disguise, while the reality of themselves is neglected beneath all these expensive items.

Take one look at that Beauregard, and you'll see that behind that mask is a fragile and emotionally dead individual.

I should be sympathetic. I should be saddened by this but instead, yeah, I'm frustrated. I am. I take this personally.

What are they expecting? That everything can be okay as long as they prove to everyone else that they're fine? Like burying it beneath a calm exterior, smothering it with other preoccupations, will solve everything. If you wait it out, it'll be okay. Can't get past how many walk through life without looking up from their masks, blinded to the point of being faceless so that they don't have to deal with anything.

Well I'll tell you, if you'd look and listen, that being faceless doesn't change anything. It makes everything worse. But that's why I try to make other people happy.

Remember what I said about purpose?

Sure, this will be my purpose.

I'm not trying to prove it to anyone. I don't need to prove it to myself.

I've got nothing left to prove.

No need to buy expensive clothes, own expensive homes, drive expensive cars, show off expensive toys, go on expensive vacations, host expensive parties, surround myself with expensive friends. No need.

It's frustrating and it's not funny. Not funny at all. It's a lie, and worse: It's a person lying to your face while being deceitful of themselves.

That's how a mask becomes the most recognizable thing about a person. It's what they wear to be the person they never became.

Why am I saying all this? I feel obligated to be here.

Sometimes someone needs to say something.

Even if nobody hears it.

No I'm not hiding anything. One look and you'll see everything. When you have the face of any other, you're pretty much a walking definition of irony. They couldn't see me even if they searched.

There's something about this man.

There's something about his life. There's something about his job. There's something about his ego that restrains me more than the others I've seen before. It's as if I'm waiting for something to happen. I watch this man create new problems for himself while wasting away from all the stress.

I watch two employees in the breakroom, their voices rising as the chat escalates quickly to a disagreement. I see that as a perfect opportunity.

I get around to thinking that maybe I should go back to being Bryan for a little while longer. Bryan won't leave his desk. I'll wait until I'm in the hall before walking his pace, talking with that elevated sense of worth, feeling like I deserve a say in the argument.

What am I waiting for?

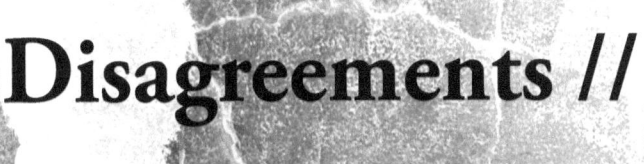

Disagreements //

Hello, hello, hello—I'm having a great day how about you? That's right, I'm doing so much better than you. It's how I walk into the breakroom that says everything so I don't even need to bother. They're fighting about something, don't yet know what it is, but I walk in at the right time and because it's me that walks in, they assume I'm here to take part.

But I go to one of the vending machines instead, pretending to buy a snack.

I'm not going to be buying any of these snacks. What am I, a guy that would really eat ring dings at ten-thirty in the morning?

It's for appearances only.

It's so I can listen in without looking like I care.

One disagrees with the other's report. Apparently the investor isn't budging—doesn't want to take the guy's advice and put in the big bucks. The report is flimsy and ineffective, the chief complaint from the other employee.

So what, right? If someone says it sucks, it probably sucks.

The guy doesn't take criticism well.

So there's a disagreement. No big deal.

I'm pretty sure I'm better than this but I still pull up a chair. I sit down and stare at them. It gets them to shut up and they start explaining, curious summaries of what I've already figured out.

Nod and get them to shut up.

Look at the one guy and say, **Most people can be manipulated.**

He processes this statement and makes a face. He seems to agree.

I turn my attention to the other employee, **Trust no one.**

Then I stand up and leave.

I wait in the hall and listen—silence and then, sure enough, the stupid little fight has been derailed. They start talking about something else.

I find this funny.

I've got the power to derail an entire fight.

So yeah I walk down the hall, avoiding my office, not ready to go back. How they look at me—it must mean something. I know what it means and I wouldn't ever lie to anyone. I'll say it, I like the way they look. Like they'd kill to be me.

I'm only an associate, but even the supervisors with seniority status look at me with that glowing gaze. They look at me like I've got what they want. Talent, good looks, confidence, everything. And it's true. I can get what I want.

Why should that be undersold?

I'd sell every aspect of myself if I could.

I walk around the office, gathering looks, nods, general attention in my direction. It's got a lot to do with the spring in my step, the way I carry myself.

You don't need to know me to know that I've got a good thing going.

You don't need to know me to know that the pretty woman that just walked into the waiting room is my girlfriend. She's here to see me.

I turn around, taking a different turn.

Did she see me?

I walk back to my office.

Yes, that's Mr. Beauregard to you. They stop what they're

doing to turn and greet me from their offices. I'd give them a nod, if I felt like it.

I'm such a douchebag.

I know that her name is Patricia.

I know that she'll stop and chat with the secretaries for a few minutes, the annoying idle chatter that I hate. I also know of dozens of other things she does that I can't stand but I'm not going to think about it. I've got more important items to think about.

She didn't see me, good.

It'll be like I've never left my desk.

Something
is About to
Happen //

When you have the face of any other, you start to believe that you are incapable of surprises. Everything remains the same and the impossible becomes a common occurrence.

Then something happens...

And you feel like it's the reason you've waited this long.

The reason you helped all those people.

The reason you've changed so many lives.

It's practice for what's about to happen.

It's practice for when I find my purpose, a new purpose.

Element of
Surprise //

At the moment, she's just another person. I'm clearly more focused on that Beauregard guy, basking in the jealousy of his so-called perfect life. I'm looking for imperfections, but the mask has concealed it all. Being him only reveals his well-worn and suited persona.

He isn't anything but an act.

How do I activate his true feelings?

How do I ruin this man?

He needs to be ruined. He does.

The jealousy bleeds into every breath, and I pace around his office, knocking over documents, creating disturbances. Bryan looks up, picks up the documents, and continues unfazed. She walks in and is genuinely happy to see him. He doesn't look up from his desk. Has nothing for her, not even a kiss. She hugs him and says something about lunch, how maybe Bryan sweet-talked her by promising a romantic lunch at a restaurant she likes.

Just a moment.

Her reaction says everything. She's used to disappointment; that is, this asshole disappointing her. She sits on the couch and still, I think nothing of her.

I don't examine her face. It's Beauregard that's become my purpose.

It's Beauregard that I hate.

She asks him about what happened to the office.

He doesn't offer much. Probably a gust of wind.

But these windows don't open, she says.

What can I tell you?

She digs through her purse and retrieves her phone. She starts typing something and I notice something. Her face. I think it could be a mask but no…

When I move in closer, she looks up.

She looks right into my eyes.

She saw me.

And I saw her.

One simple look changes everything.

Everything around us blurs, and it's like Beauregard and his perfect job and his inflated ego is muted, put on pause. The jealousy goes missing, as if I never cared.

Bryan, there's somebody here…

I can hear fear in her voice and it's magnificent. I see in her eyes the honesty of her current mood, no subverting of the senses. She doesn't push away from what she's feeling, and it intrigues me. I take another step, just because, and she doesn't run. She sits up, paying attention to me, but she doesn't run. She doesn't run from what she's feeling.

She doesn't run from me.

Dear…

What?

He's busy. He won't look.

He'll look and he won't see me. But she can. How can this be?

Should I do something? Should I say something?

What do I look like? I want to ask her what I look like. If she sees me, she must know. She knows everything. Does she like what she sees?

I'm speechless. I don't know what to say or do.

I remain at her side, for once being the one judged. I can only hope that I'm making a good first impression. I want to say something but I can't.

It creeps up on me slowly, the feeling. I'm surprised. This is new.

When the word hits me, I am ecstatic. That's just it.

Bryan...

He's not going to interrupt.

This moment is ours, and I don't have anything to say. I want to say, Don't forget me. I want to explain to her who I am and why she shouldn't be afraid. I want to explain everything, but I'm empty. I reach in but nothing's there. If she really sees me, she already knows. She shouldn't be afraid. That's what should be said, yes, but the truth is...

She should be afraid.

You know who I am.

Real Feelings //

When you first find out that you have the face of any other, you are afforded some immediate freedoms. You go a little crazy. You take to hurting yourself. You become obsessed with feelings, your feelings. You provoke and then you experiment. Then you get bored. You feel the dire threat of boredom, how it doesn't just depress you—it defies you. So you start obsessing and experimenting on other people's feelings. You play around. You experiment. Then you get bored. You believe that you've seen it all. You feel nothing that you haven't already felt before.

It's a matter of trust. When you have the face of any other, you know the full extent of a human's feelings. You craft, you curate, you feed curiosity. And then you lose the craving. You learn to trust no one. They're seldom sincere. And because you have the face of any other, you know that you're just as bad.

No, you're worse.

You're far worse.

They'll look right at you and laugh but deep inside it couldn't be further from the truth. You didn't think this was all martyrdom and virtue did you?

Purpose //

I'm going to be honest here and this time I really mean it: I am not going to explain myself. You won't get a description of my face. You won't get a real take on what I've done and what I'm doing. The best you'll get is a chance to see what I'm *going* to do.

No apologies, it just has to be this way.

When you have the face of any other, you no longer categorize things as truth or a lie. You no longer trust any of those details. You learn to trust what you see. You trust what you feel, nothing more. Whatever registers, you feed on it until full.

But maybe you could ask her.

I'm not going anywhere. She's seen my face. She knows who I am. I can't leave now.

For instance, after our little moment passes, I leave the office and turn into someone else—doesn't matter who—long enough that she begins to doubt what she saw. Bryan doesn't ask her to explain and so there's no one there to repeat and help process the events. By the time they're sipping mimosas at the restaurant, Bryan paying more attention to his phone than to Patricia, she will have already labeled our moment as manufactured, something that probably didn't happen. It would make for a good story, she thinks, but that's the full extent of her concern. She doesn't move away from what happened, doesn't lie to herself in order to make it easier to understand. She doesn't mask any of it. There's nothing to understand. What happened is impossible. I am impossible, but she still leaves what happened as a mystery.

I have to take better precautions; I can't be myself around her.

I cannot be seen if I'm going to be seeing more of her. I'll be anyone, your best friend, your mother, your colleague. I could be any one of them, Patricia.

You saw mine once and now it's your turn.

I want to know everything about you.

Will I like what I see?

Would it make me wish I were you?

Deus Ex Machina
Part I //

When you have the face of any other, you mail the questionnaire to yourself once a week. You answer to the best of your ability but you're never satisfied. You can't be sure if your answers are honest.

I feel at ease in a crowd.

Strongly Agree.

When I'm really sad or down, I seek the company of others.

Strongly Agree.

I take other people's interests into account.

Strongly Agree.

I seek out the emotional support of others.

Strongly Agree.

I try to do the best I can given the constraints of the situation.

Strongly Agree.

I spend my leisure time actively socializing with a group of people, attending parties, shopping, etc.

Strongly Agree.

When things go wrong, I immediately blame myself.

Strongly Agree.

I usually plan my actions in advance.

Strongly Agree.

I know how to put every minute of my time to good purpose.

Strongly Agree.
I am always prepared.
Strongly Agree.
I pay attention to details.
Strongly Agree.
I enjoy exploring new places.
Strongly Agree.
I enjoy trying new things.
Strongly Agree.
I like learning new things.
Strongly Agree.
I pride myself on being different.
Strongly Agree.
Most people can be manipulated.
Strongly Agree.
Trust no one.
Strongly Agree.
What am I not asking?

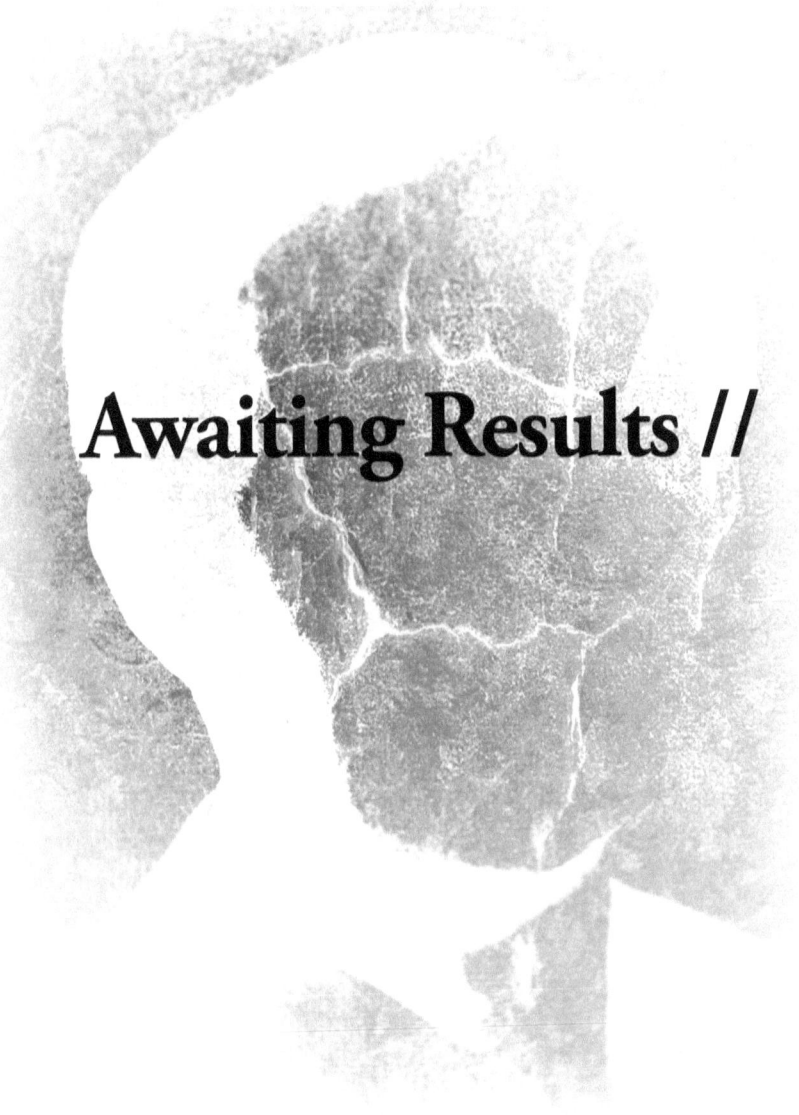

Awaiting Results //

Hey cool, so this is where we can all be ourselves and not have to mask our feelings. This is where we can really be ourselves and vent and, you know, just talk to me. Tell me the truth. Tell me stories. Talk about what's happened so far. Things are happening quick huh? It's pretty crazy. Wouldn't have expected that answer huh? The one about getting what I wished for. How often do we really get what we ask for? That's a fun question to think about. Also, yeah I hate Bryan. I hate anyone with an ego out of control. I hate him but I'm also not going to bother. Not really going to waste any more energy on the guy. Still, he doesn't deserve Patricia. And Patricia, real surprise. Who would have thought that someone could see me? Nope, it's never happened. It's wild. It's kind of frightening too.

Yes, I love it. I love what I'm feeling.

Like I said, when you're me you're basically without a role. Well, you can be a ghost but that doesn't last long. Gets old quick. You can do all the expected things and you can cop a feel, trip a cop, steal from a cop... okay I'll stop. It's not that funny.

You can do all that but boredom is the real threat.

Boredom equals emptiness. Feeling empty is about as bad as it gets.

I don't think I'm a bad person but when you feel the way I feel when there's no one around, when there's nobody looking and nothing is going to happen, you start to wonder what really made this possible. How I ended up this way?

You ever think about the kinds of decisions you make?

You ever think about how much you've changed over the past day, week, month, year? I'm being honest here and you should be too. This is the no-judgment zone. This is where we can just talk. Real talk about having real feelings. We're talking an old-fashioned soliloquy, from the Shakespearean days. Write in the margins if you have to. Say what's on your mind. I've almost forgotten what it feels like to be excited for something. But then this happens, a real purpose drops into my lap. And handed to me by a real douchebag.

You can say that for the first time I'm counting the moments.

I'm taking stock and asking questions. Honestly, did you really think it was possible until it took you by surprise? I get the feeling that that's all it is: Something we refuse to believe until we're faced with the reality of its details.

RESULTS:

You are viewed as creative, confident, and complicated by others. You are able to do almost anything as long as it interests you. You are able to move mountains with your mind. You are constantly excited about new experiences and you have a tendency to quickly grow bored of things. You have an open mind with a broad range of interests and abilities.

RIGHT

First Impressions //

Hello, my name is Patricia Pond, but that's not really my name. My real name is Heather McDonnell. I changed my name when I was eighteen, legal, because I believed that there didn't need to be another Heather McDonnell. I'm talking about my mom, yeah. She gave me the same name, which would make me a second in line, a "junior," or however it is expressed. I didn't think it was necessary and I never liked sharing the name.

I got my mom's blessing first. I would never do something to hurt another.

She was fine with it. She told me it's up to me to decide who I am and I think she's right: I only get to be one person so it should be a natural fit. I should feel as though I couldn't be anyone else.

I donned the name Patricia, dedicated to my childhood friend who unfortunately…

I don't like talking about it. But her name was available so I adopted it in her honor.

I'm still pretty young, I think. Twenty-five is young, right?

Mid-twenties—wow. You think you're indestructible at twenty-one and never think you'll grow old but then you blink and you're twenty-five. A couple more blinks and I'll be thirty. But it's not over. I'm not afraid of getting old. I'm afraid of so many other things, I don't need to worry about getting old. I'm afraid of being dishonest and losing myself to the hectic nature of the city. I'm afraid of the city and how it changes a person. I'm afraid of how the people that say they're used to the city are the same people that would cross a street, narrowly avert being struck by a car, and not even look. How can you be so numb? I'm afraid of losing focus of who I am and what I'm doing with my life. I'm afraid that one day I'll wake up and be someone else. I'm most afraid that one day I might wake up and be nobody. I don't want to be nobody. I'm fine with being normal; I just want to know that what I'm doing is what I'm supposed to do. I want to believe that what I'm doing nobody else could do, living as Patricia Pond. Nothing glamorous. I just want to be me.

I'm fine with being average.

I don't have a lot of beliefs; I'm fairly open-minded. However, I do abide by the idea of honesty and integrity. I'd never want to feel like a fake. I want to be genuine. When I say, Nice to meet you, I really want to mean it. If I don't want to introduce myself, I have to remain true to that— because truth is all we have. I grew up in a household ruled by lies; my mom and dad lied through their teeth, going behind each other's backs, living double lives.

As an only child, I watched them do horrible things to each other.

I have seen the worst in a person and knew that I don't want to end up like that.

I'm between jobs at the moment. I'm not happy about the statement but it's true, I'm unemployed. I feel a little stir crazy, feeling useless. I've always figured that life is full of ups and downs and I think I'm riding the downswing. I can get lost in those negative thoughts. Sometimes I think it's okay to feel sad. But I also do my best to look at the bright side. I enjoy the perks of being independent and unfettered. I'm not tied down to any day-job. That's why I can wake up at 11AM and tend to the small things. Bryan insists on paying a maid twice a week to maintain the apartment but I like being able to clean up after myself so I usually make a nice breakfast, rinse the dishes, and tend to some of the more pressing items. Cleaning helps me relax; somehow, it shuts off part of my brain, the part that won't let me forget that I have a few gallery applications pending and, who knows, I might lose all of them. I've been rejected more times than I've been able to create. I've tried almost every medium but it seems like photography is the one thing that has kept me honest. I love looking for that one angle that captures the true nature of an object or person.

I feel like I'm getting an honest look at someone else's life. *I feel like a voyeur.*

First impressions are often the most accurate snapshots of a person. I really believe that people attempt to show their best side when they pose for a picture. We want to appear interesting. We want to look good in the picture. We want to smile and look our greatest. But really most of the time we feel awkward, inexact; we feel like we're only showing a sliver of our true selves. That's why I use photography to cut through the typical posturing; I don't tell people to pose for the picture. I want to capture the truth. I feel like honesty is on the outs. Things are so confusing these days.

The other evening, I had the TV on and didn't realize that the show I had been watching was in fact an infomercial. I'm surprised by how quickly things change. People don't usually deal well with change so most of us are forced to run and catch up or get lost along the way. That's why I need to be honest.

During a job interview a couple weeks back, they asked me if I was the right fit for the job. I told them, No, but only because I want the job really bad. They asked me what I meant by that statement and I told them that I was desperate. It's the truth. I am desperate to get back into the working world. I feel a little strange, like I've already been pushed aside.

I didn't get the job and the woman gave me a weird look. Not that I'm surprised.

When I go visit Bryan, I can feel it. I'm starting to feel a little invisible.

I am invisible.

I visited him today. Everyone said hi and I reciprocated the gesture but I can tell that sometimes people just say hello because it's ingrained. Either they're busy or they really don't care. Clarissa the receptionist hates her job. She tells me about it. She's one of the few that are genuinely happy to see me. It's 'cause we get to talk.

I'd be lying if I said I was there to see Bryan.

I visit more often because Clarissa needs it; she needs someone to talk to and I don't think she has anyone else.

It's kind of sad, but I shouldn't feel bad about it. I believe that pitying a person only degrades them even more. We're friends, Clarissa and I, so I sympathize at best.

But see, here's what happens when I visit Bryan:

I walk into his office, give him a hug, and barely get a kiss in return.

I end up lounging on the couch for an hour or so. He maybe looks at me twice during the hour, but only because he can hear me on my phone, texting and such.

Most days I leave without getting a lunch out of him. Not even more than a few sentences. He's busy and I have no right to interrupt. I hate that I think this way but I really do think it's true: In this world, you are only as valuable as the amount of money you bring in. I love photography and creative mediums but I don't believe this world was built for those that value less tangible means of value.

I'm thankful that Bryan and I are together, though my honest nature suspects that it might not be forever. Add that thought to the basket of things I've got to lose.

I have a lot to lose.

Sometimes I wonder what it'd be like if I lost it all.

I think you know what it might feel like.

As far as I'm concerned, Bryan might not even notice. My visits have become detours during my otherwise aimless days walking around the city.

I take long walks.

Most of the time I people-watch.

I scan their faces, wondering about who they are, what might be on their minds, their worries, their denials, their fabrications.

I wonder where they'll be a year from now.

I wonder how many of the people I see will be a completely different person this time next year.

And when I see something, see the right shot, something candid, I don't hesitate.

I take a picture. People don't seem to mind. This happens a lot. People going around the city with cameras, taking pictures.

I should feel lost when I'm out there with my camera, but I'm not.

If anything, I feel more like myself than any other part of the day. The moment I'm behind the lens, I feel true. I know I'm capturing the truth, and it couldn't be any barer than the snapshot. Most of the time, I don't have a lot to show. Don't have a lot under my name. I'm a person with a camera, a person without a job, a person living an average life.

But I've got these snapshots to prove that I am at least aware of who I am and what I look like, on the inside and out.

So far I haven't found any of myself that are worth being framed.

Hey, I'm just being honest.

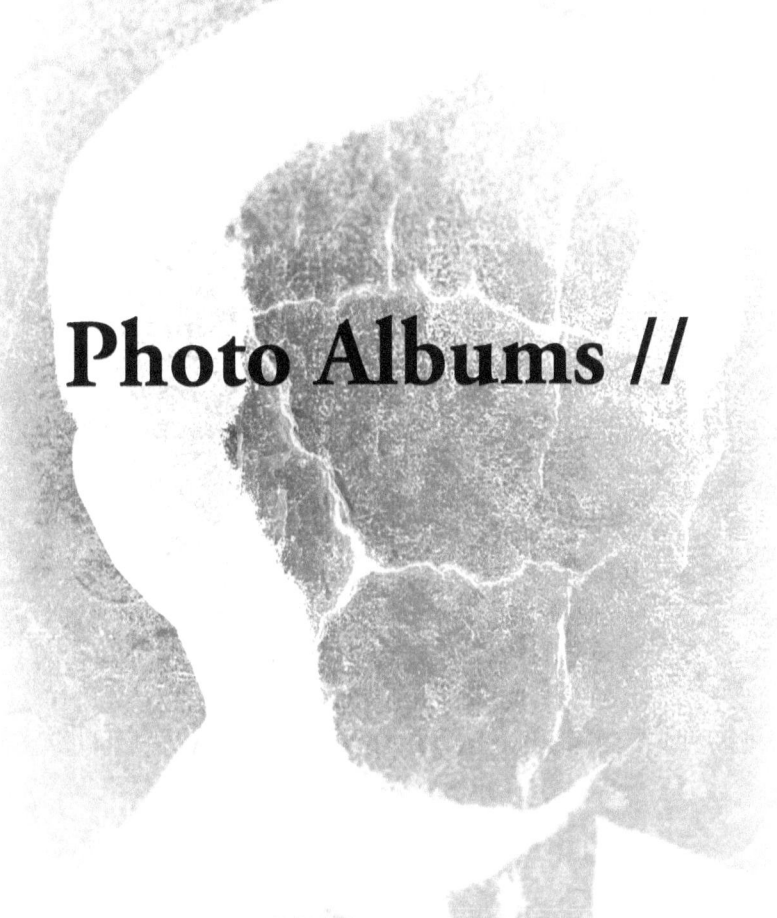

Photo Albums //

When you have the face of any other, you turn the camera on yourself. You hesitate for a moment, making sure that she's not actually home, and then you take that picture. You look at the screen. You tell yourself that you are not frightened when you see nothing but the apartment, part of the couch, and a fragment of the framed painting hanging from the wall behind you. What you're feeling isn't fear. You shake it off—no, nope, not feeling anything.

Then you delete the photo.

You turn off the camera. You turn it back on, checking to make sure it's gone.

You set it down where you found it. You are still sweating from the heat, from walking the streets as Patricia for the afternoon. You breathe heavily but you're not going to think about it.

Take a snapshot so you don't forget the moment when you were in the army, just another early morning during basic training, sure, but it was the day you broke a leg. First time you've ever broken a bone in your body. Instead of letting you get medical attention, the drill sergeant forced you to crawl the obstacle course, broken leg and all. You took it personally, believing that the guy had it in for you. Take a snapshot so you don't forget the moment when you were in high school and the girl, biggest crush of your life, asked you out rather than the other way around, omitting

211

the part about how it was a dare. They got the idea from a movie, figuring you were not that different from the main character. Equal parts odd and doomed. Take a snapshot so you don't forget the moment when you flipped your car, daughter sitting in the front seat when she should have been strapped into the car seat in the back. Fill in the details about how it was an accident and that you weren't actually coming off a buzz. Don't capture any part having to do with being a neglectful parent.

Take a snapshot so you don't forget the moment you realize that you focus on the negative, piecing together tragedies while disregarding the triumphs. The fact that no matter the person, you'll find the one part of them, no matter how miniscule, that's blemished and raw so that you'll feel better about yourself. Take snapshots, but I can't be sure if any of these memories are mine or if they're the memories of another. I only have my feelings and, right now, after having wandered the city as someone else, I don't know what I'm feeling.

I can't be sure. Maybe nothing.

So you think about Patricia.

I know enough. I know everything. I was her for a couple hours. I know enough to be jealous. And not of him. Bryan wears a mask that one day he'll be unable to remove.

Beauregard will get his.

I look at her and—I want more.

If you keep looking, there's always more hidden, deep inside.

Patricia, I'm not going anywhere.

Doppelganger(s) //

Hello, my name is Katherine! Greetings, so very nice to meet you. I love meeting new people. As a marketing professional for—oh, okay you want to know about Patricia. Let's see, we've been friends since college. Not sure what she's up to lately. Could she really still be dating that Bryan? Oh my, it would be surprising. Never in a million years would I think the two were a good fit. Horrible together. But they somehow got together and it was golden for absolutely no one but, maybe, Bryan. I don't think Patricia is looking for anyone in particular. She's severely independent, you know what I mean? The kind that just goes for what she believes. She'll settle for less if it means being completed quickly. She focuses on other things. I've always told her she'd be a great publicist.

I think I should give her a call.

It's been so long, yeah.

It feels wrong not to remedy that situation.

What do you know, she's free to chat.

She sounds great. Oh, Bryan's working in financial investment?

That's a big meal ticket. Damn.

She's into photography. It was painting and poetry back in college.

Did she give that up?

Oh but I loved her poetry.

I think we should meet up. Coffee?

Sure, sure. How about the place on 9th?

Going to meet up with her in a half hour. Finish up some of this insane work—it's so absurd, dear me. I wouldn't tell anyone this but I loathe my job. From top to bottom, kill me please. And the pay hasn't been good since realizing how much better everyone else has it. I hope, sincerely hope, Patricia is doing worse. I feel a little bad saying that but what I keep to myself is my business. I can deal. But I can't deal with seeing everyone from college one-upping me. I'll be interested to see what's on her plate.

She's got a hot shot boyfriend, big deal. I've got my own car paid off.

No more public transportation.

Try me, I'll be chipper. Won't faze me.

Moving forward. I don't like thinking about my work. I'm thinking about quitting actually, but what kind of plan B do I really have?

Anyway, anyway, anyway...

What was I talking about? Right this junk. I don't want to come back from lunch with this still sitting at the top of my to-do list.

But moving forward, Patricia's already there when I arrive. She's looking beautiful, better than I expected. I wave and really give her a genuine greeting. I'm so happy to see her, and to see that she's fit, her dirty blonde hair, so jealous of her natural curls; her blue eyes, double jealous, how she doesn't have to wear a lot of makeup to accentuate her beauty. Pour it on, jealousy grande; but shove all that to the back of mind. Secret to sounding successful is being upbeat. No downer folk in the record books. Not in my industry.

We get to talking before coffee is ordered.

By the time I get mine and start sipping—need more caffeine, I'm coasting on a horrible low, or maybe I'm just imagining it?—Patricia drops a bomb on me. I'm all sympathetic but really I'm cheering. She's unemployed. The talented people of the world are all unemployed. The people that brand themselves and sell and shill get the good jobs. The talented are too humble and get left by the wayside. I love it and I hate it and I'm a horrible person, I think as I zone out, watching her lips, hating her for having amazing eyebrows.

I want to know about friends and her family. I want some leads.

I change the subject. I order a sandwich and get to talking about myself, but only until I'm satisfied. If I say too much, I'll start gushing about how horrible things are right now. Maybe they've always been horrible, I can't remember. I refuse to remember.

Don't look at my face, I look terrible.

I don't care. Stop talking please.

Not saying that, but she's talking about her photography. Please, none of that. I ask about a mutual friend, Tristan. She tells me he's a writer for some media site.

Well, good for him. He's got a novel out.

She says that he's a writer, but she doesn't think he's written a novel.

I tell her, **I present myself in ways that are very different from who I really am.**

That makes her laugh. Meanwhile I'm terrified. That's so unlike me, to admit something like that. I don't say these things.

She goes on about honesty and personal beliefs and it's my turn to laugh and tell her that she was always the wild one with weird beliefs.

Then she talks about some new gallery prospects.

I enjoy trying new things.

She tells me I should try photography. It might just help me.

What's that supposed to mean? I keep my mouth shut and I smile.

Is she able to identify the insincerity in my voice?

When the sandwich gets here I ask her if she's getting anything. She shakes her head. Coffee is enough for that bitch. I'm sorry it's just that it sounds so much like an unemployed person is doing better at life than I am. I don't know why I'm fixating so much on this. I'm not usually this bad. Okay, the sandwich.

Let her talk. Eat.

She watches me devour the sandwich. I swallow it down with scalding coffee. My eyes begin to water. Jesus, that hurt. I tell her, **I am the life of the party.**

Good to see I can make her laugh.

Then she tells me about her mom, Heather, and how the lung cancer is still in remission, how she's "thankfully" retired now and living on the coast. What coast, I ask. She tells me east coast, Atlanta, not Florida. I expected her to say Florida. Then her dad, Brandon, who she doesn't talk to anymore.

They should reunite.

It's a shame, sure. It's also a shame that I enjoy this topic of conversation a lot more than the rest. I sympathize. I'm a good sympathizer. That's what I do.

I listen. And then I say, **I trust reason rather than feelings.**

Which is, I guess, something I'd say.

She seems to make some sense of it. Then asks if I'm okay.

I've never been better. I want to leave, now. But that means I'll have to go back to the office. No. Please no. Okay let's talk about Stacy.

How's Stacy doing? Yeah I almost forgot about Stacy. Remember all those late nights, wine, shitty movies from the eighties, nothing on our minds except for finals the following week?

She nods. That smile, so cute. Maybe I'm neurotic.

That's my problem. Happy when I'm sad and sad when I'm actually happy.

Her phone rings. She looks and makes a face.

I'm like, what? But see, I know what's happening.

Something impossible is happening.

I'm calling her. My phone is in my pocket. I'm not butt-dialing.

She picks up and it's my voice on the other line.

It's me saying something like, Hey it's been like so long it's crazy.

And then it's me following it up with a wink.

And the impossibility of this occurrence is like out of one of our favorite films.

She asks me who's on the phone. I tell her, Me. Doppelganger. Another wink.

She rolls her eyes, scrunching up her face in response.

This wasn't supposed to happen. What are the odds?

Keep going. I pretend it's a prank. She'll have to accept it, just like I'll have to accept that I hate my job and I need to quit before it eats me alive. But I'm afraid of what might happen if I quit. I can see it now: overdraft, eviction, homeless in the city, goes missing, is murdered, body in a ditch off the interstate.

I can be so miserable, dear me. Play it off as a prank.

She asks who it really is, the person on the line, and I tell her that it's me. I'm being honest. Then she laughs, thinks its funny, maybe gets the prank. Hangs up.

Tosses me a look as if to say, Very funny, I secretly know how miserable you are.

I hate myself. Say it. I hate myself.

I hate myself.

I don't feel any better after admitting it.

The sandwich is gone; there's nothing left of it.

Got nothing left to preoccupy myself with so it's time for more laughter. It's time to talk about Stacy. I tell her

Stacy liked that film, tracing it back to the reason for the call.

I should probably go soon. Finish the coffee and go.

I'll never see Patricia again. This is what I know to be true and so I don't mind that I maybe tell her that I miss those days. Those nights. And when I ask her if she feels the same way and like she usually does—saying no, she is happy with how things turned out—being honest to the letter, no matter how it might sound, I nod and say, Yeah you're probably right. Deep down, I know I'm not being myself. Something is wrong. Deep down, I don't know what to do anymore. I kind of want to go home, never return to work. Wonder how many paychecks I'll get before they realize I ditched this life.

And then I notice that I'm zoning out and she's noticing.

I tell her, Sorry, what were we talking about?

But it's her that breaks up the chat, saying that we were talking about Stacy, but I missed the crucial details.

Remember to look up Stacy Hsu.

She says she should really get back to her afternoon plans.

I ask if that means photography.

She grins and nods, waves and leaves me alone at the table.

What else can I say? I'd leave me for an afternoon of photography.

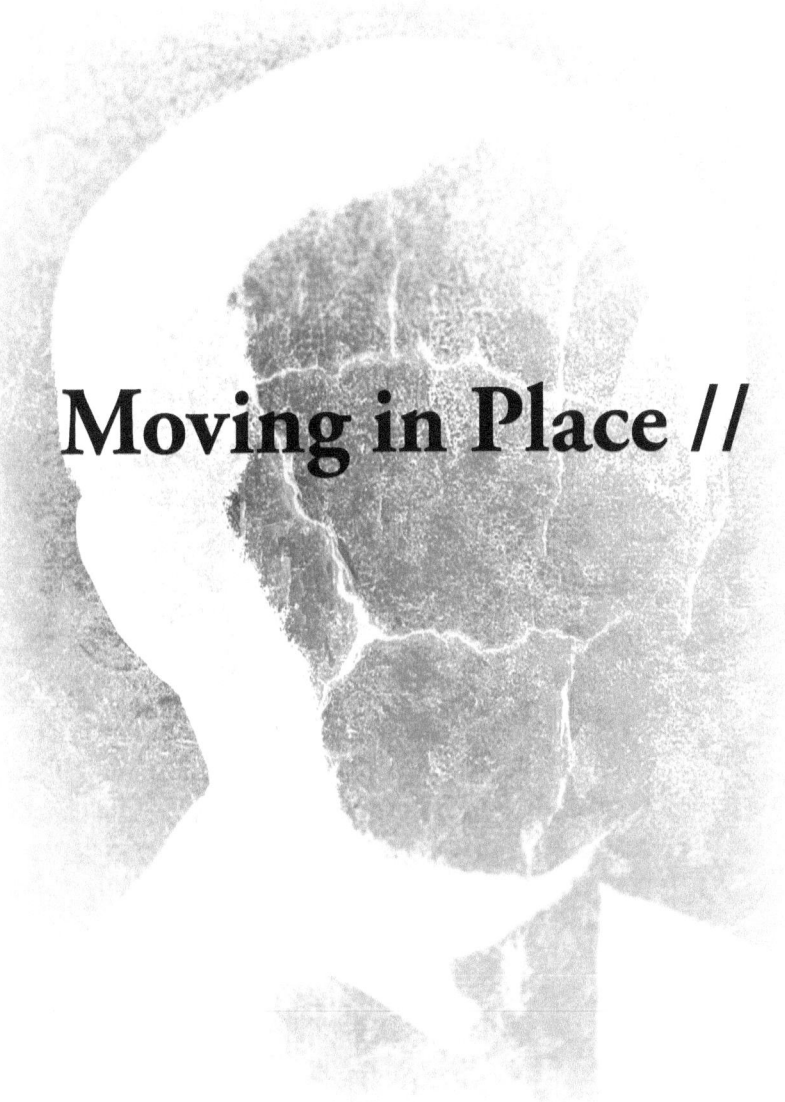

Moving in Place //

When you have the face of any other, you feel as though everything you've ever done and will ever do is erased the moment you've moved on. You look at the world, the image of two young women chatting over coffee, to the inner sadness of the situation, the reason for their meeting. You sit there, long after they leave, the table cleaned, neither busboy nor waitress noticing you there, and you watch the world go by.

Everything moves.

But you are moving in place.

Then there's the all-too-familiar feeling of emptiness. Doubt. Boredom.

It's all suspect, you assume. The only thing that's real is the purpose that's been presented to you. Patricia. She must be about done with her photography session by now.

You think about the names given, leads for the lure, and you relish on the possibilities. I want to know more. I need to know more. There's more than what I've seen.

I bet she's a walking in the rain, counting the stars kind of person.

Willing to put herself in a vulnerable position if it means enjoying new experiences.

The finer things. Variety. The honest feeling.

The only thing a person can be sure of. And then you know what that means and it gets you up out of your seat, back out on the street, looking around at the cracked, mutilated faces, the ones that bring a smile to yours. If you had one.

And you say her name.

Patricia.

I'm on my way.

Random Help //

Hello, my name is Tristan. Full name, which I rarely use, much less entertain the thought of others using my full name to address me, is Tristan Brunhoff. Brunhoff, I blame my dad for that one. Of course I blame my dad's dad and the great ones that preceded both of them. The surname came from somewhere and now I'm carrying it. Don't get me wrong, it's not that big of a deal. It's just one of those things that irk me during formal introductions—job interviews, business dinners, that kind of thing. Mostly people know me as Tristan, and people seem to dig that name. I dig it. It's memorable. I need all the help I can get in this field. Shortly after undergrad I was lucky enough to land a shitty internship with a major media outlet. The people there liked me because I worked my ass off for free. Didn't pay me a penny. I was a peon, a piece of shit in their eyes, paying my dues. I'm still paying my dues. But yeah, I'm now a full-fledged associate, which means nothing. I still need to triple-check whether or not I'll get away with the writing of an article. I still need to seek approval for everything. Meanwhile the site continues it's domineering influence. I should cut "domineering" from my lexicon. I should cut "lexicon" too. This isn't the sort of job that favors "big words." They want buzzworthy shit. Stuff that goes viral. So yeah I feel ambivalent towards my job. Need to cut "ambivalent" too probably, I don't know.

I don't want to think about it.

Some days I feel like I need help.

I really do need help.

Some days I'll work on every single line of an article and feel like I'm finally onto something and then I'll get it back from the director and they'll say something about how it needs to be trimmed by eight hundred words, sometimes upwards of a thousand. They'll tell me that it needs to be retooled.

I really do need help.

I'll retool and then I'll get it back with a note that tells me it's great but somehow doesn't fit, telling me that what they're really looking for these days is content that grabs the reader's attention, sweeps them up for ten seconds, and drops them back down. Lasting impression with minimal commitment. What the hell does that mean?

I really do need help.

It implies frustration in work. It implies a migraine. It implies taking migraine medicine at work and getting groggy. It implies having to take a sick day. Nobody cares as long as the deadline has been met. Our days are spent staring at a computer screen; if there's any interaction, it's gossip, shared procrastination.

Fuck it, I can get more done at home.

I really do need help.

It's a thought that I seldom want to admit. I'm not doubting that I can do this alone—I've written nearly a hundred articles, mostly slush, reportage, but still content—but I hold onto the idea that I might not be able to take that next step. Original writing. Every staff writer gets to write a couple every month, and so far everyone has. Except for me.

I'm the only one that hasn't bridged that gap.

I really do need help.

I have a difficult time not thinking about it. It gets

to me. It really does. A number of explanations come to mind, "washed up," "writer's block," "burnt out," "two-dimensional writing," "sentimental crap," and they slow me down. They slow me down because I start to believe them. Customarily I'm a laid back guy. I don't want to think such thoughts. But then it settles in, and I can't be sure.

I want to drive a nail through my head. I want it all to stop.

And the clock, time ticking away, becomes a constant insult.

How many words did you get on the page in the last hour? One hundred?

Is it any good?

I really do need help.

I am afraid to ask for help. It's a stupid masculine thing, ego trip and how asking a colleague for help would be tantamount to demotion.

We're all fighting for a byline.

If I get help from one, they end up crowding around and before you know it, my name gets nixed from the byline. Their name is added in, I'm ironed out like some crease on a shirt. That would be a nightmare. Never going to happen. Never going to happen.

I really do need help.

But I'm beginning to think I don't have a choice.

I can't think clearly, not with this pain. Migraines, they only ever appear when I have a deadline. People think I'm doing well. I imagine that's the illusion we create for ourselves. Everybody pretends but how many are really wearing the right set of clothing, the kind they can afford, what matches their current financial situation.

I need help but who do I ask? Friends? What friends do I have that aren't looking to gain something. Okay, think. Focus.

I know how to calm myself down.

Well, yeah, I have to believe this to be true. Just lie down for thirty minutes. Thirty minutes might be too much. I need to act now. Day's going to waste. What to do, what to do... who else do I know that's a writer? Kat, naw she wrote more poetry. Nick, but he's a writer now, I believe. I don't know his number anyway. I don't have the energy to search for his number even if I wanted to. Who else... I imagine there's Pat. That's something to consider. What is Ms. Pond up to these days?

I should call her.

I have her number but it might have changed. I haven't spoken to her in what seems like forever. Years?

Let me work through the logic. I can't just do something. I have to think it through, like most people. I need to weigh my options, and think about what might occur if I call her. We have history, the two of us.

Does it imply something more than help if I called her out of the blue?

I should just call her.

Where is her number... it's still in my contacts, that's something. Cloud storage is worth something after all. Will she pick up? She's probably busy. She's probably on some photo shoot or some—well what do you know.

Hey.

Man, I've missed her voice.

Do you know who this is?

Ha. Well, yeah, duh. It hasn't been *that* long has it? Well, perhaps.

She sounds great, genuinely happy to have received this call. It was a good decision to call Pat. She's the honest type; if she didn't want to talk to me, she wouldn't have picked up the phone. Which implies that I wouldn't be out of line to ask her to help me with the article. So here goes— the inquiry, and the response. She's wondering about the nature of the article, what are the demands, restrictions, word count, and so forth.

It's only right to tell her my problem.

She seems to understand, telling it like it is.

You were always the verbose one.

Ask her to come over.

I do and I'm about to tell her, my place, but no—how about the studio.

She remembers the studio. That's where we used to, well, anyway—it's still in my name. Rented out to a number of different artists. My community service, of sorts. I had wanted to be a different sort of artist; look what happened. I didn't have the heart to lose the studio so I turned it into a shared space, everyone donating a little bit of cash to keep it afloat. It works. Don't let people tell you DIY is dead.

She remembers.

She says she misses the place.

She's the honest type so it isn't surprising when she says it.

Says that she misses me.

Whereas she would speak her mind, I tend to smother. I tell her as much as I can, given the situation, which is a single word that may or may not be "likewise." Sounds horrible, stilted, and the hushed nature of how we finish the call makes the migraine worse.

Before I go, I tell her to meet up in an hour.

I need a nap first.

She asks, Still getting those migraines.

Yeah. Like me, they've gotten worse. Much worse.

No humor in my statement and no humor in her reply.

We share an honest moment and, man, I miss her.

I miss her so much, which went unrealized until this very moment.

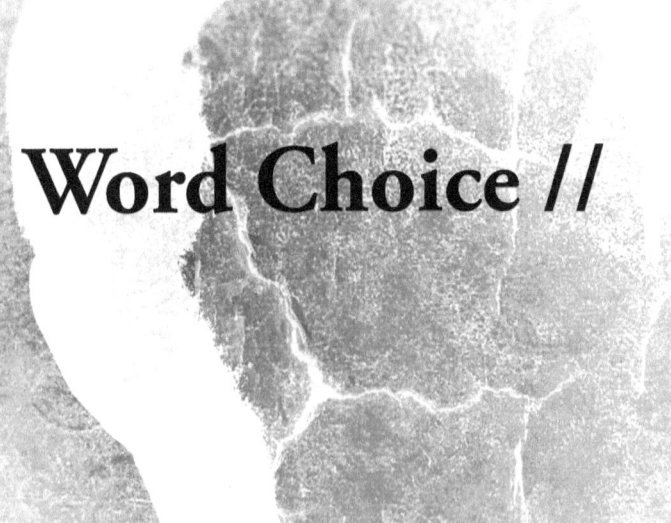

Word Choice //

Tristan, she always liked saying my name. She is already there, chatting with another artist, when I arrive. I apologize—it's not my right to be the one that's late—yet she tells me it's more than all right. Migraine, my excuse. She believes it.

I can't look away from her eyes. It's as if the past rushes to overwhelm my senses.

She's here for, clearly, nothing else but the work. She's here to help, but nothing else.

Was it worth anything, what we shared, once?

This isn't right at all. Right from the start, I'm unable to pay attention.

I watch her as she reads the draft, fingers on the keys of my laptop, a tap here, tap there, I can't stop watching, intent on her every gesture, my gaze more of a glare, and then I remember that we're not alone. I look around the studio. The other artist is busy, but he might as well be judging me. Something is definitely wrong.

I don't feel like myself. To be more—how do I explain what I'm feeling? To be more accurate, I feel conflicted. Much like how you never think about something that's been pushed to the back of your mind; however the moment it rises to the top of your mind, everything attached surges and surrounds your senses. I can't be sure I'm making sense of it.

I can't act any different. I can't let her think anything less of me.

She isn't sure if she can do much to help the article.

It reads fine. And then, I'm not a reader of the site so I'm far from the best measure of judgment. And I tell her that I understand but here's something else I want to tell her and, secretly, I hope she feels the same way. I hope nothing has changed between the two of us. I try to read her body language but I haven't ever been very good at those sorts of cues.

So there's nothing you can do?

I'm hopeless.

She reassures me, stating that the article is well-written. It doesn't waver and it sticks to its argument.

The issue is that she's having the exact same problem communicating the information in language that fits the aesthetic of the brand.

She offers to work on word choice. I tell her, I could always use another tutorial on self-control. We both know what I meant by the statement but, given what has overcome us in the past. What I said, I assume it is out of line. I don't know why I said that.

I meant it.

She calls me out, saying that you know that the past is the past. Digging it back up would only complicate things. Mention about how we had agreed that friendship was far more important than any sort of physical connection.

And I agree.

I remind myself to focus on the good things in my life instead of the bad.

What?

It's as if the words found their way to the tip of my tongue, waiting until I was ready to speak to take a dive and make me feel like shit.

I already feel like shit.

What now?

Don't go. But she tells me that she's uncomfortable and doesn't want anything to happen. There's mention of Bryan, who I never cared for, but I honor their bond, their engagement, their long-time, stillborn engagement. Engaged to be engaged.

I really dislike that guy, Bryan.

There's mention of admiration, adoration, and other words that I would never use in my article, because they wouldn't go over well with an audience that wants impulse rather than real emotion. Real emotion can be tossed to their feet, left on the ground, to be trampled. Much like how I feel when Pat leaves.

I believe we leave on good terms.

I text her shortly after she's gone, Really isn't that bad is it?

Thankfully, she replies in earnest, It's beautifully written.

I think about telling her more, but then a group of artists enter the studio and break my train of thought. They don't see me. They don't look over and greet me. I feel invisible and, staring at the defunct article, my head begins to throb.

I'm going home.

I haven't a clue what to do.

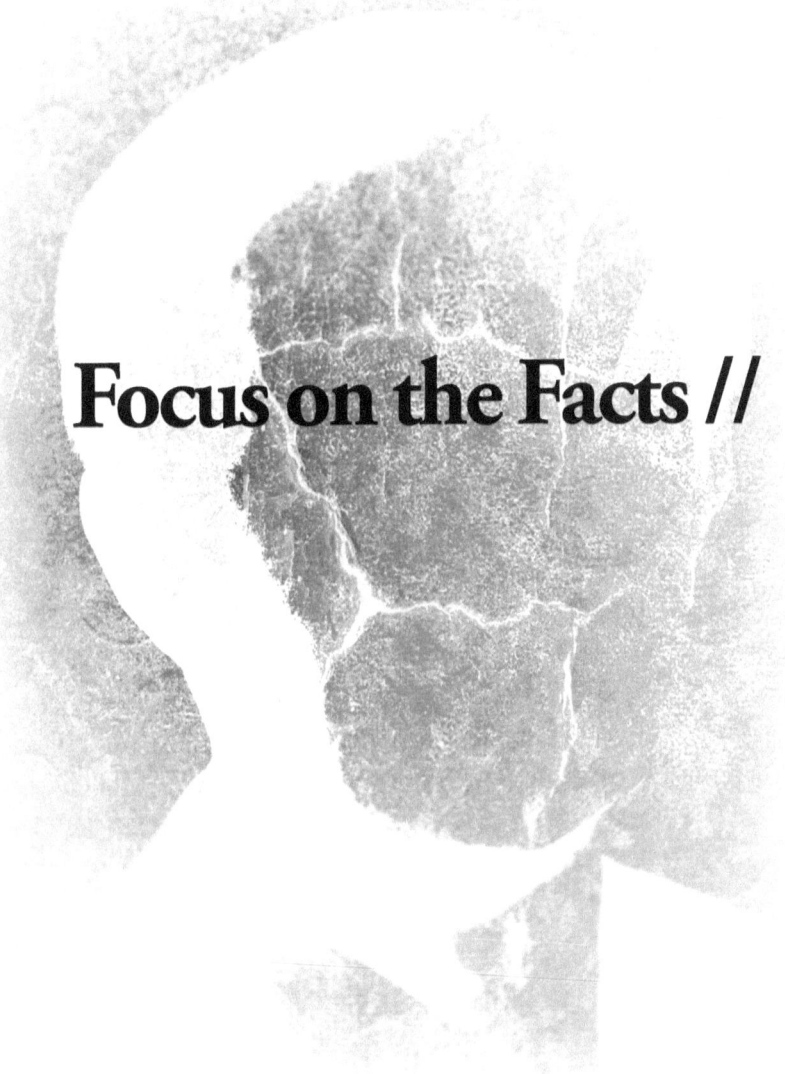

Focus on the Facts //

Look at you—you aren't afraid to show your face after years of tense silence, severed communication, and near-transparent feelings towards him, a man that *isn't* your boyfriend. A man that cares for you more than Beauregard ever could. Instead you take a man who couldn't be any more wrong for you. You couldn't do any worse than the guy that you choose to love. And yet you believe that Bryan is the one.

You walk these streets without any conceit, no need to create a narrative to direct your worries, your doubts, your human desires to and from the items that invade your slice of the world. You simply navigate your path, interpreting your senses. What do you see?

But the facts: If I were to focus on the facts for just one moment, I would examine your relationship with both men. In each analysis, I would see how you would be changed, and in both, you remain identical.

When you have the face of any other, you wonder why someone can love someone so emotionally dead. Then you examine yourself and feel jealous because—and this is where you choke up. This is where you stop talking.

Because when you have the face of any other, nobody is really listening.

A Couple of
Clean Breaks //

When you have the face of any other, you become as many people as you need in order to hide from her. You count the number of cracks on the sidewalk, count the number of cracks seen across countless faces, waiting patiently for her next move.

I'm right here.

You are Rudy Mike, a grade school teacher running a slight temperature after having contracted the flu virus during one of his summer workshops. Flu in the summer, that's unfortunate. You walk three blocks in a dizzying trance, doing your best to keep her in view. You wipe your forehead to keep the sweat from dripping into your eyes. You have nothing on your mind at the moment, but let's just say you're not looking forward to returning home. You're usually a well-adjusted man but with budget cuts by the school board, the promotion you had expected to be real now a distant dream, the new child, your second, wife a couple months away from childbirth, the threat of bankruptcy is being fully realized. But at this moment, you don't think about these things. You don't—instead, you look at a young woman; you follow her and you don't know why. And then you don't and then you find that you've walked past your subway stop. Two blocks too far in the wrong direction.

I'm right here.

You are Charles Aster, a college student, freshman, young and still very intimidated by the city. You take small, cautious steps down the sidewalk, afraid that someone might mug you at any moment. Your biggest fear is never being able to fit in. It's the constant worry, been that way since as far back as sixth grade. You were on your way to the university library but somehow you end up following a woman. She's young, not really your type, but you're still kind of confused about what your ideal type might be, so you aren't surprised to find yourself drawn to her, following her a number of blocks, into a different neighborhood, one that you wouldn't have visited if it weren't for the interest. You stop at one street corner in particular, and become distracted when someone asks you for directions. *You*, for directions. You tell the person that you're kind of lost yourself. When the person sighs, disappearing into the crowd, you lose your train of thought, forgetting the reason for having walked this far. You're lost, really lost. You've never been so afraid.

I'm right here.

You are Vince Sullivan, co-owner of a moderately successful upstart co-op store based in one of the trendier neighborhoods of the city. You're having a better day, a better year, than the shaky and uncertain ones in recent past. You have regained emotional and financial stability of your life, but all of a sudden, while on your way to pick up some new donations for the store, you are hit with a deep and incapacitating sense of doubt. You begin to reflect on those deep cuts of time when depression consumed you and working at the co-op was all you could do. You and the other co-owner, an ex-girlfriend, had just broken up but were financially tied down to the business, this store. You had no money to hire new employees and you had no chance of ridding yourself of the entire venture. You end up in a bit of a daze, walking and thinking about those dreaded times, until you find yourself following a woman, fairly young; in a mild fit of confusion, you figure she reminds you of your ex. You follow her because you assume that she might be headed in the same direction. But you don't quicken your pace; you don't catch up. You keep at a distance, hesitant, and you don't know why. You feel like you're about to faint so you step aside, freeing yourself from the crowded sidewalk. After the feeling passes, it takes you a few moments to remember where it was you were going.

I'm right here.

You are Dania Heim, an accountant for a large distributor of youth products—mainly educational material—not that you care. You just got out of work early, and these are the sorts of moments that make life worth living: moments when you don't have to do any work because work has veritably consumed your life. But you tend to keep going based on the absurdity of it all. You love the humor of having to pay such high rent when you spend, at most, eight hours of every day in the apartment. You love going out and you're currently on your way to a bar to meet up with some friends. You love going out because it feels like you're actually getting away, a sort of rebellious act of leaving all responsibilities in the dark while you live your life. Really live your life. You live for the actual life, the party, the fun times, and so you've basically accepted that you're living in the moment. You know you won't be able to work this job for the rest of your life, no matter how well it pays but you don't want to think about the future. You figure you're young and in the city so you're going to enjoy your time. Because like some celebrity or something said, Time is fleeting. Maybe it wasn't a celebrity. You don't really care. Anyway, you have to stop by the apartment; you're not going to the bar looking like this. Wear a worksuit to a bar? Never. You hate it when you see it and that's not about to change.

You see what's-her-name a few steps ahead of you.

You don't remember her name but she's nice. She's a nice face. Probably wouldn't get along outside of the occasional chat in the stairwell.

Like right now, you could get her attention but you don't because you value these moments to yourself. It's when you don't have to think about anything. You just walk. Focus on the sidewalk and the path ahead.

She opens the door for you, and you both say hi.

You think she asks about your day, but maybe she didn't so it seems strange when you tell her that you're totally beat. Swimming and really the only sort of scenario you want to swim in right now is a pool full of bourbon.

That was supposed to be a joke.

She didn't hear you. Whatever.

You reciprocate, asking her how she's doing, but the moment you ask, you tune out, taking the steps two at a time.

At your door, you pause instead of getting inside a.s.a.p., and you don't know why.

We are cordial to each other, isn't that enough?

She says something about helping out a friend and maybe later dinner with the fiancée. You are like, That's nice, when really the word "fiancée" freaks you the hell out. You're barely in your mid-twenties; getting tied down when you're having so much fun is like—well, it's like something.

What are we doing here?

Why am I accepting her offer for something to drink?

You end up in her apartment, chatting about a recent news story.

You say that you loved all his movies and it's too bad he quit acting.

She agrees. He's a damn good actor.

You both sip coffee but you don't really focus on the taste.

It's probably good. Coffee isn't really what you're in the mood for right now though.

You figure, Whatever, it might get me buzzed quicker.

You tune out a portion of the conversation while trying to figure out if you have any beer or wine left in your apartment. Maybe Charis drank it all. She probably drank it all.

She's the alcoholic, not me.

Somehow you both talk for nearly fifteen minutes before you feel your phone vibrating—they're wondering what the fuck's keeping you—so you wander into the kitchen, pretending to laugh, saying that you'll be right back, just have to use the bathroom.

You hear her say sure; I'll keep the door unlocked.

But you're gone, like post-haste. Next thing you know you're in your bedroom.

You blink twice, kind of surprised, but then you've blacked out before.

Wait, no you haven't. You take it back but then realize that you aren't talking to anyone. What the hell? Now, you're confused.

Maybe she put something in the coffee.

What kind of coffee has alcohol in it?

Irish coffee?

This for That //

I'm right here. You are within arm's reach but I remain quiet, frozen in place. I don't want to be seen. You'll see me if I move. The curtain won't protect me. Funny to think that the archetype works. Hiding behind a curtain. I'm hiding behind a curtain, please let there be no sudden archetypal gusts of wind shaking the curtain from my clinch.

There you go. You say her name. Dania. But it was never her you were speaking to; if you're saddened by the result, we can talk. You can tell me what you saw.

And I can ask you how—how can you accept the truth. It's the sort of thing that can upset a person. But Patricia, you're nonplussed. You check the front door, when it's obvious what's happened, you lock the door. A shrug of the shoulder at best followed by a muttering, That's rude. You keep it to yourself, but I'm right here, and I can see your face. There's barely a blemish, and the insult is taken in stride.

How? Why?

Later you will trade this for that, but I will remain nearby, slightly out of focus, away from prying eyes. You might see me and check a closet, the bathroom, behind the shower curtain, perhaps suspecting that Dania had been hiding as some kind of prank.

Perhaps not. But you're searching for something. I can see it in your eyes, your body language, the manner with which you can't sit still for any longer than a couple minutes. You are searching for something, and perhaps I can help. I'm not just imagining it.

You trade this for that, but you, as a person, remain the same. It's a rarity, seldom seen. Well-adjusted; a heart capable of weathering the weight of the world.

But if you're lonely, I'm right here.

Just tell me what you want. What is missing?

I'm not going anywhere. In case you're wondering, and you probably aren't, I'm looking for something too. I'd say I'm sorry for what I did but it doesn't seem to have affected you. I'd show you who it was, telling you that it was only me. But I'm concerned that doing so will make it impossible for us to speak at a later date. If I step from this curtain now, without the proper context, it'll give the wrong impression.

And that's the last thing I want to do.

Don't fret. It's just me.

We have the whole afternoon. There must be something that you want. You have my undivided attention.

Honest.

A Brief
Viewing //

For all intents and purposes, Patricia has the place to herself. I move between the area behind the curtains and the bedroom closet while she moves between the common area and the bedroom. The following events take place:

A brief viewing of a film she's seen a number of times. She laughs and recites a few lines. I note the modulation of her laugh, high then low, tapering off as the feeling has been felt and quickly passes; I observe how a few delicate lines form across her forehead at the apex of her laugh. Patricia does her best to recite the lines in the same voice and manner of the characters on film.

A gentle pacing up and down the hall while she talks on the phone with her mother, Heather. I glimpse how she does a slight double take whenever she is faced with information deemed slightly uncomfortable and quite personal. Heather bombards her with accusations, discussion about her job search, the stagnating career in photography, namely how Patricia could be doing so well but instead she is here, pacing up and down a hallway in an apartment she could never afford.

A brief stint in the bathroom where she relieves herself, followed by a shower to wash away the sweat from her walk earlier today. I listen to her sing while she showers, the same verse repeated, sung in a manner that renders the lyrics into syllables, clear that it's not about the words so much as the rhythm, the rhythm she carries with her like the spring in her step. I watch as she walks to the kitchen wearing nothing but a towel more interested in the reason for her trip to the fridge rather than her nakedness. She picks out a few olives from a jar, popping them into her mouth, savoring the sour flavor, I admire the way the edge of her mouth forms a half smile. The towel drops to her ankles, and her naked form is an unaddressed blur as she wanders into the bedroom.

A nap in the bedroom followed by a fit of masturbation impelled by the sudden dominance of a dream. It's not the act so much as it is the reason behind each stroke that rouses me, bringing me in for a closer look. I note how she savors the sensation, uninterested in the climax, staving off orgasm in favor of the building sensation of reaching that point. She doesn't sleep, and she barely moans. Patricia is under the covers, being kind to her senses, on this, a day that could be any other day, but because it is today, it is currently what matters to her most. Once she orgasms, the feeling, the importance of her actions, has already begun to fade, purposeful if only to direct her to the next and the next one after that.

This is her, Patricia without compromise. And in every action, she exposes as much as she knew she had an audience. What I see is no joke. Her actions are subtle, her gestures soft, and the nature with which she carries herself is a surprise. A surprise to me.

I look into her eyes, as she stands at the window, a breath away from me, and I see a person as bare and vulnerable as those one step away from being broken by the world. And she keeps going, the honesty in her voice and her lens.

I hold my breath. She shouldn't see me here.

The afternoon is hers to enjoy. Hers and hers alone.

A brief viewing is maybe all anyone can get.

When you have the face of any other, you forget what

it's like to remember a person. You forget who they are after boredom takes hold.

You hold onto this last image, Patricia at the window with a glass of wine, watching what? Watching the birds feast from the installed bird feeder, she enjoys the sight, watching each bird swoop in for its fill. And there isn't the slightest flicker of a worry, the slightest thought or worry preoccupying her thoughts.

I'm right here, but I might as well be a world away.

Movie
References //

You know who you remind me of? Not people on the streets or people that I've helped, but rather, characters in films. You have that unpredictable quality, the sort of glow that causes a group of people to gravitate towards you, curious about why you're not at all curious about them. You have no reason to stand outside of yourself, being something you're not, and that alone overcomes me, above and beyond the purpose for my watch.

When I watch you I feel as though I'm watching the world.

You look like the actress in that one film about Hollywood, about film itself, being a star, and how she had everything—absolutely everything—a new starlet needed, but it was the small things, rather than the big ones, that affected and ultimately ended her chances. When you have the face of any other, you see that the big items have to do with purpose (when is it not about purpose?) and motivation. Ambition. The small stuff, the items that are easily procured but often never dealt as a big deal, are the ones that can really ruin someone. They embed themselves into your daily routine—lust, addiction, loathing, and doubt—and they bring you down long before you feel the effects.

You look like the actress in this one film about a bunch of college students that end up stuck in a flat for the duration of the riots transpiring in and around the college town. Because of being stranded in the flat, they are given a pocket of time to be themselves, to find themselves, and as a result, lust and love and a sort of amateur passion take hold. You remind me of the actress, the one that led the way, acting older, and much wiser, than her age. She was so comfortable with herself that she failed to identify her fatal weakness: Everything she constructed, as a dream, had become reality. She was young, a virgin, and immature, without a clue about her motivations much less her identity. And yet there she was, even at the end, swearing by her feelings, believing that it was true. The look on her face, it was so genuine. She wore that face as her own, no matter how stilted or broken.

You look like the lead actress in that film that had to do with an alternate aquatic universe, located within our own world, where they live dormant, like genies, waiting to be called. She is called one evening, by chance of a depressed young man, and much to his surprise, she is as real as his own nightmares. She becomes an earnest mentor, helping him to his full potential, while, at the same time, he becomes infatuated. When he finally crosses the line, acting on his urges, she takes it in stride, revealing that it's routine, part of the process. He is the one surprised, and embarrassed; she tells him that it's not his fault and neither is it hers. She had the chance to attach the blame, but instead chose not to judge. There's something so rare about that performance, and how her face remains so perfect in every single frame.

You look like the character in that one animated film about art school, where the term "coming-of-age" is as cliché as the idea of it being yet another film about art school. But here they are, the entire cast of characters, so they have to live through the blasé and archetypal nature of the film. You're that one character, or I should say, like that one character, that never says anything. Never needs to say anything. No one really knows if she is a she or he is a he due to androgynous fashion sense and the lack of even a single line. But the character is there, in every scene, essentially doing what the main characters in the foreground are unable to achieve. You are the character that could be a star, if only you could speak and be the right kind of ego for the sensationalist media.

You look like the actress in that one cult classic, gore-heavy film. Typical fare—zombies, end of the world, a plague, some kind of ridiculous setup about a war between two sides that end up destroyed by zombies at the end. And then there's the actress, who has suffered a horrible physical affliction and has, somehow, been given a machine gun for an arm. She wanders around seductively, just because, and fights off waves of zombies, helping random male characters that end up objectifying her only to end up paying the price in the following scene. Everyone is expendable until she meets up with the Romeo type character that asks all of the questions the audience has been asking from the beginning. And then something builds, a sort of bond, between the two. But the war and the zombies weigh in heavily and the world is fucked, so they say—fuck the world—and go live in some cabin in some untouched part of the world. Machine gun arm and all. You remind me of that.

It's probably your earnest nature, unmindful to social expectations.

You look like that actress in the film about writer's block, where she is essentially the ghostwriter for at least a few failed, burnt out authors, and quintessentially uses their oeuvres to put out her own work. And she's conflicted because they are conflicted. They suffer from addiction—alcoholism, gambling, sex, you name it—because they have trouble dealing with the truth. Meanwhile she can't stand being around them but, at the same rate, worries about what it means for her career, and whether or not her best ideas are being used in her ghostwriting gigs. There's some big overdone second act and a rushed final act but you remind me of the actress that pulls off such a knockout performance, dealing with the inner struggle of being stuck with nothing but your own thoughts.

And I want to tell you all of this, but I haven't a clue when would be the right time. You saw me when I wasn't ready, and now, given that I feel like I'm so close to you, Patricia, I'm not sure how you'll react when I tell you everything I've already said here. It isn't love so much as it is admiration, and a fair share of adulation, surprise. You see, what am I trying to say? I can feel myself buckling when faced with the chance to explain myself. How's this—

When you have the face of any other, you know when you've found someone different, a face crafted outside of the usual defaults and doubts. It's as if you've avoided the usual pitfalls. And now you have someone like me worried for you.

Wanting so very much to see, and maybe… to help.

Your mother is right—you are so much better than this!

You could be there among the stars, onscreen, featured for your ingenuity, your ability to own every single emotion, without any doubt that you'll do it to the best of your ability. You could be perfect, you know, and yet, I see you outside of your element.

It doesn't make sense to reference you as just another face when really, when it comes down to it, to be quite honest, you are the one person that's noticed me.

You saw me, when a million and one looked and only saw shadows.

A Certain Degree of Boredom //

When you have the face of any other, you'll do and say anything if it helps prevent boredom. You know what boredom does and you'll reach for the stars if it means ensuring that your efforts don't go to waste. You'll spend the entire afternoon hiding in the same spot, waiting until Beauregard returns home from work.

But he never returns home and so you watch Patricia as she prepares a dinner for one, occupying her time before and after the meal with some music, followed by a couple hours on the computer, inspecting the day's photo session.

She changes into a nightgown and lounges in a chair with a book near the largest window in the apartment to capture as much of the cool summer evening breeze as possible.

You catch her looking in the direction of the front door, as if expecting him to walk in at any moment. You want to whisper in her ear, He doesn't return home tonight.

Please, don't wait up.

You're so much better than this.

But you don't, and you'll remain where you were, the gentle pain in your back becoming a numbing sensation from the hours logged hiding in plain sight.

Unfortunate for you, nothing changes for a long while. Eventually the sun disappears behind a line of nearby buildings. She doesn't look away from the page, reaching in the general direction of a lamp, looking for its switch. She trades sunlight for the synthetic glow. Turns the page. From one of the neighbor's apartments you hear what will undoubtedly continue for hours. The apartment remains docile, muted, despite the heart of the party beating quicker, faster, to the same pulse as the evening's advances.

Yet the night presents a different set piece.

Where you wouldn't dare walk, shadows dampen the details. You note the possibility and spend what feels like forever making sure your steps are absolutely silent. With every action comes an equal and opposite analysis, a glance in her direction, waiting to see if this is the moment when she finally sees you.

But you keep going, step after step, and she keeps reading, page after page, and soon she'll yawn, turning off the lamp, retiring to the bedroom.

You nearly bump into her, but when you have the face of any other you —blank blank blank the blank. That means whatever you need it to mean, your own definition for the situation at hand. Ultimately it means you remain cautious.

You step aside. You wait until every light has gone dead in the apartment.

You wait at her bedroom door, until she's fallen asleep.

You stand at the foot of her bed and you think about everything she might have said to you if she understood what you were.

You listen to the noise, the party a few apartments below, but Patricia is asleep.

She won't wake up until you want her to.

You think about what it must take for a person to sleep at night knowing that their significant other is potentially out there, sleeping around.

Maybe yes.

Maybe no.

But what's undeniable is that Bryan isn't here when he should be, here to protect her from you. And then you wonder what the hell that means.

You are here because *you care about her.*

That's what you've determined to be true.

She is *your* purpose; the sheer bafflement of what she does keeps you from being bored. That alone is enough.

You want to ask her—

What actor am *I*, if an actor at all? Am I something in between? What's happening between us, is it somehow impossible? Tell me, I can take it. Just don't tell me that *I'm* impossible. But all this, I'd never say, much less whisper it to her while she sleeps.

I think about the countless others I've been and become. They treated the confusion as a miracle, the sudden change in their lives as some sort of curiosity; but, because it helped, it couldn't hurt to let the circumstances slide.

Think about it, and then return to the same thing that started this.

She saw your face.

When you have the face of any other, you can stand at the side of her bed, listening to her breathe. You watch her sleep, admiring the calm that comes with a clear conscience.

I want to ask her what she saw.

When you have the face of any other, facing a new impossibility keeps you from facing the impossibilities of your past.

It keeps you going when, quite frankly, you haven't gone anywhere, you've remained as invisible and ordinary for as far back as you're willing to remember.

You lean in and touch her face, a gentle run of your index finger across her left cheek. Just once, the one time. You expect more than what you're getting. You expect more than what is given. You know something's wrong; it's a demand.

Something **is** wrong. You can't see it in her face.

But what's this? Brief glance at the other side of the bed. What's missing from this picture?

Maybe I'm supposed to know. Maybe I'm supposed to have known for some time. I know everything about her, honest. I'll leave, but not without taking something in return.

A snapshot, a thought, a new lead—a glimpse of what's problematic.

She will be jostled awake by my touch but I'm long gone, venturing through shadows back to where I can roam, outside the bounds of curiosity.

There isn't a single person that could attest to my whereabouts.

Cipher Call //

Hey hello, can you guess who it is? It's Tristan. It's been awhile hasn't it? She laughs because we saw each other recently. It might have been yesterday, or so she assumes. Guess it turns out she called but I didn't answer. *Of course I couldn't answer, I was busy watching you from behind the curtains covering the northwest corner of your apartment.* But sure, sure—I guess you did.

I get busy sometimes. Yeah, I swear they don't pay us enough for the work we put in. I remember taking note of it. I intended on calling but, you know, deadlines.

Oh the article. Yeah I did. Yeah.

I pause for effect.

I submitted it.

And?

She wants to know if it worked.

I could lie and say yes. My lie could make her happy.

No, but it got close. I think as close as I've ever been.

Yeah, I'm not going to worry too much about it. I'm over it now.

She wants to know if I'll try again. Of course, it's my job. I can't keep writing slush for the newsfeed. I'll give it another shot, yeah. Who knows, maybe I'll even have the guts to ask a colleague... But let's talk more about you. How are you doing? I know we really didn't get a lot of time to catch up the other day; again, the article. How's Bryan?

She's as honest as ever, discussing his distance. There's mention of how he never returned home last night.

I can't come off too candid here. It's best to speak in ciphers, be as clever and calm with my approach as possible. I want her to confide in me but the same time I don't want her to think that I'm really interested.

I don't know what I'm doing. I shouldn't be doing this. *And yet I am.*

She tells me that she's been concerned for quite some time but the current situation isn't exactly simple. She can't just pack up and leave. It's not the money situation, no—she still cares about Bryan. She still cares about the guy. Patricia isn't asking for advice but she also *isn't* asking for advice. What I'm left with is a longtime friend explaining a complicated situation, expecting that I'll react in agreement. So I do.

I tell her I understand.

I also tell her that she should consider why she has these feelings.

There's discussion about a few years back, when she first moved to the city. The sheer terror of so many things going on in her life, and how she never felt so confident of her decision to remain with him then at the time of her move.

The sheer force and will of what she's saying. Pat doesn't need me here. I am quickly shut out of the call, listening and reacting to her self-analysis of her younger years, which don't happen to be all that long ago.

I chime in with a single phrase, Your younger years, the sarcasm going right over her head. I should have known it might. Pat isn't dense; it's just that when she's focused, she thinks of nothing but what happens to be in that narrow point of view.

This is what my side of the conversation sounds like over the next couple minutes:

Sure.

Yeah, and how did that make you feel?

Yeah.

I understand.

Every relationship has its pitfalls.

Yeah.

I know. I can imagine.

Sure.

Being treated that way doesn't it make you feel small?

I sound like a daytime talk show host, encouraging the guests to continue rambling with those seemingly good-natured replies.

One word agreement followed by questions to fuel the fire. *I'm looking for fuel.*

Maybe it's time you start thinking about the future.

I hate to say it but that might just be the best advice I can give. Like, this one relationship I had—it's nothing like what we had—but it was just as impulsive, just as quickly swept up into her life. Her name was... Sarah. We met in the workplace—yeah, go figure—and it was during one random Friday night happy hour-turned-bar-hopping coworker outing that we ended up making out. We were drunk yeah, but it didn't stop there—*I'll keep talking about this, saying how toxic it was, how it felt so right when it really was so wrong for the both of us, and I'll slip in more than a few times about how it was nothing like we had, "you and me." A quickening cipher between some sort of story made to make sense of what's going on between Patricia and Bryan. Just keep going and going, stretch out the story until...*

I'm talking about this brief relationship with Sarah, but wait—

Where was I going with this?

She tells me that she doesn't know.

Oh man. Wow. I must be really out of it.

You do sound a little "out of it," she says.

It's how she says it that makes it clear.

I knew it.

Anyway, before I got swept up in—

She interrupts, Sarah.

Hmm?

Swept up in Sarah.

Right. Swept up in Sarah. Before that happened we happened, but long before that, you and Bryan happened and it must have happened for a reason. Right?

Silence on the other line, and then, Right.

The two of you have been through it all.

We have, we really have.

And you're the honest type; you'd never hide from your problems.

I guess so.

No, I'm not asking. I'm telling.

I'm here to help you, Patricia.

I'm here to tell you that maybe… it's time. Love doesn't last a lifetime.

Then she giggles, and it's cute, the way it comes out. She apologizes, saying that it sounded like something from a breakup romance, what I said.

I tell her, I don't even know what I said. What did I say?

She tells me.

Okay, I think I'm done. I need to get off this phone before I make more of a jackass of myself.

Mutual laughter. That's good.

Man I feel out of it.

I'm right here.

But before we go I tell her, I'm here if you want to chat.

Thanks so much.

Of course. We've been through enough to be honest with each other.

And I mean it, what I just said. I really do. It brings up the memories we shared; it's reassuring to discover that the ones that hold on longest have nothing to do with what we did in and around the bed.

I guess I should really get ready. I have a job interview today.

Oh excellent, are you excited?

I am.

You should be excited. Okay—go wow them at the interview. Don't let what we chatted about bring you down.

You know me. There's nothing to worry about.

I picture her winking, slight tilt of her neck and a half turn followed by the wink itself. It is remarkable how the understated gestures reveal the most about someone's personality.

Bye Tristan.

Bye.

The way she says my name.

It kills me every time.

Fuel //

Hello, my name is Andrew Place and—*I don't care; I just need to know. I need to know. I need to know. I need to know*—I'm one of the younger guys in the office, sure, but dammit if I'm not going to be one of the best. Everyone likes me because I'm not here to one-up anyone. I'm confident but I'm not going to kill a person to get ahead.

I'm part of the team.

I'm pulling my weight and I'm getting the job done.

Cold call like a pro.

I can talk my way out of any hostage situation. It's true—I love a good spy thriller, some kind of flick involving hostage negotiations. That's where you really get to see the mastery of human thought. The negotiator is a master of psychology.

The negotiator will get you talking about anything.

Secrets will be revealed.

Indeed, secrets will be revealed.

I can find the source of what's on a person's mind just by talking to them.

I'm confident that it's how I got the job. How do I know this? It's because I mentioned it as my biggest asset during the interview.

And dammit if they dug it.

Now look at me, I'm chatting with one of the hot shots that'll undoubtedly run the firm in five years. His words, mind you.

Sincerity is a negotiator's biggest asset, second only to loyalty (as in, loyalty to the hostage and the department's goal of freeing the innocent from danger)

This is how they do it. They need to make it so that it seems like they are truly in with the demands when really they're just talking, biding their time, looking to gain whatever's needed.

In this case, I'm being trained, you see—trained by one Mr. Beauregard.

He's surprised when I introduce myself, clear to appear a little shy, that "wet around the ears" kind of first impression. He says he didn't expect me for another week.

Yet my name, number, video transcript, and home address are on file. Like I've been maybe working here for ages but you've never noticed.

I pretend to laugh, as in I intentionally want him to think that I'm nervous.

He treats me with the usual amount of respect, good-natured enough but clearly Mr. Beauregard is more irritated that he has to train me now when he could be doing something more important. I sit down where instructed and I keep it calm at first, mostly listening and observation. Make Mr. Beauregard think I'm one hundred percent with him, totally engaged with what he's telling me.

Formalities.

He lets out a sigh between short statements.

One look at you and I can already tell.

A good negotiator nudges the conversation in the proper direction. The proper direction isn't necessarily the right one; rather, it's whatever gets you to your goal.

He asks me about myself.

You can hear the insincerity in his voice.

Andrew, you an honest guy?

My response, **I frequently and easily express my feelings and emotions.**

He snaps his finger, Good. Yeah that's good enough. And the seed has been planted. He assumes that he's got a flop on his hands. Someone that'll do precisely as he's told. This opens up opportunities for Mr. Beauregard. He'll pay less attention to the training and more on what sort of work he might be able to pass on to me.

But it takes another ten to fifteen minutes of the mixed lecture and mock-interview to cultivate the seed. Before the seed can sprout, you've got to water it down with the right amount of nutrients. In this case, the best negotiators are the ones that keep cool.

Maybe they even relate to the captor.

He asks me about my love life, if only because he wants me to chime in with a negative or, at best something amusing. I tell him nothing permanent.

That gets him. Mr. Beauregard laughs.

He tells me that I should enjoy it while it lasts. It gets a lot harder when you're tied down. He tells me just like that, nonchalant, while looking up a report online, one that he will have me cross-reference and check to make sure the numbers are correct.

So that he doesn't have to.

He talks about how tough this job is but if you keep a close bond with the rest of the crew, you'll be fine. We look out for each other. Again, those are his words.

The seed is starting to grow.

When I'm really sad or down, I seek the company of others.

Kid you'll be fine. Lighten up. Relax those shoulders. Nobody sits ramrod straight unless they're a fraud.

I'm looking at one right now, wearing a mask because he's lost touch with his true self.

The negotiator identifies the weak point, focuses all efforts on that one exact point, while remaining completely sincere.

He asks me about my girlfriend.

I say, **I like to be engaged in an active and fast-paced job.**

The statement catches him off guard, precisely as intended. I shrug and tell him I'm single. How about you?

Then I have him right where I want him.

Cold calling like a pro. I'm as good at talking to anyone, even a future CEO.

The seed, watch it sprout, and anything a negotiator needs, it's right there. The teams already making their way to the location, going around back, snipers aimed at the windows, the entire source of suspicion, targeted, the opportunity, dammit, it sprouted ten minutes ago, when the negotiator finally took over the psychology of the conversation.

Mr. Beauregard busies himself with the superficial details like my age, how I'm liking the city, favorite haunts, if I've heard of this one bar that he loves, and then he talks about his own past—how he got into this gig. He focuses on himself, and talks about how he'll probably move out of the current neighborhood because he's tired of the commute and, with a chuckle, could probably afford something better. He mentions how his "scene" has moved to the opposite side of the city. Nothing should keep him from the pulse.

Send Mr. Beauregard the right signals and he'll pity you, which I do, the right signals, and subsequently, he explains how he'll show me around, maybe get me laid so that I can, at the very least, lighten the fuck up. His words, mind you.

And dammit, I just love how in those films, the negotiator has all the power. The negotiator is never vulnerable, never uses a weapon other than words.

Sometimes, dammit, words really are the worst possible weapon.

He never mentions Patricia.

Report from
the Shadows //

When you have the face of any other, you see the cracks on a their faces. You see how miserable they've become; you are able to identify how long the misery has lasted, often a great enough measure to consume their lives. You look at someone, like the beautifully honest Patricia and you see that this is all she knows. All she knows is misery. Misery and other miscellaneous setbacks have become the backdrop of her life. And yet she remains pristine, near perfect. You look at her and you are amazed at the differences, the absence of even the slightest blemish. And then you want her to show you where you went wrong, where you acted when you should have fled. You want her to show you what she saw. But before you can do that, you know what you need to do.

That's right.

You can't take no for an answer.

You must be persistent. You know what's good for her.

It's true.

I can help you. I can improve your life. You don't need him, Patricia. Don't you see? You don't need him. You are perfect on your own, perfect with someone like Tristan.

Take a snapshot of him now and compare it to your first and lasting impression. What do you see? Bryan, he's nothing at all like you remembered him.

I'm doing this for your own good.

I disliked him from the beginning. I saw the mask upon his face and knew there was nothing but disgust behind its manufactured features.

I went to him, Patricia. I went to him right after speaking with you. That was me.

It's almost always me. That was me on the phone.

Tell me you enjoyed the conversation. I know you did.

You still have feelings for Tristan. And Tristan, the reason he never returns your calls isn't because he's busy. It's because he still wants you. You hear that? He wants you too.

But of course you keep things the way they've been.

Truth can set you free and I'm here to be that truth.

Faceless, I'm this suit. My professional attire is all I have as self-expression.

I'll wear my best suit. Just for you.

Today, I'll wear my best tie too.

This suit has been worn the least. I want to make the right first impression. If you see me in the right context, you won't react the way you did. I think its time to step out of the shadows and introduce myself.

I'm not a nightmare. I know that I'm not a nightmare.

I'm just...

I'm here to help. I hope you like my suit; it didn't come cheap.

I know what's good for you. And your mother agrees.

Establishment
of Place //

Hello, my name is blankblankblanklblank and I am here, not on business, I'm not a solicitor, please, I can see you, Patricia. I can see you behind the peephole. I can see you behind the door. I can see that you're wearing a nice summer dress, with a delicate lace trim. I can see that you wore it because it's comfortable, but you also had thought that someone else might appreciate it. Am I right? I'm right, aren't I? You had hoped he wouldn't be working on a Saturday, much less a Saturday morning. You thought he might enjoy how you look in that dress. I think you look beautiful. You are beautiful for more than just the dress and your physical features. You are beautiful for your extremely loyal and honest nature. You are beautiful because you see and feel and make no alterations—you experience the direct summary of every feeling. And unlike most, you don't compartmentalize or fear the feelings that spin their own episodes. I see you. To think it was your fiancée that I was more focused on when we first met. But, anyway, I'm not for any of that. I'm here as a friend, a prospective friend. I'm here because we haven't properly met.

I have important information for you.

And I think you have important information for me.

Please, if you'll just answer the door, I'll explain.

Why won't you open the door?

I'm asking kindly that you do. Please, now's not the time

to resist your feelings.

Why are you backing away from the door?

I'm here as a friend. I might look a little strange, and I apologize for that.

I know, I know, I know that I'm impossible.

The fact that I'm here is impossible. I know that, but I'm still here.

I'm at your door, asking nicely to be let in.

You know how there's that idea of a once in a lifetime opportunity, one based in chance, how it presents itself to you without notice, often requiring the individual to take a leap of faith, risk it all, stare fear and doubt directly in the eye?

This is one of those situations, Patricia.

Yes, I know your name. Why is that so frightening?

Please, will you let me in?

I'm not a ghost. I'm not some monster. I can't walk through walls.

I'm just asking you to see me for me, see me for who I really am.

Will you open the door? Don't make me do this.

You're making me do this. Are we really going down this path? I just want you to know that you are the one making me do this. I'm here as a friend, nothing more.

Honest. I'm a friend, willing to do what I need to do if it means getting closer.

I wore my best suit. Look. Patricia, come here.

I told you not to make me do this. I risked my own safety climbing that fire escape. I risked it all to get to you. Now please, open the window.

To prove that I'm a friend, I'm not going to break the window. See?

I'm being honest.

I'm here to help you.

Now please, why won't you tell me?

Tell me, what do you see?

Speak up. You want to know what I see? You want to know what I see? Do you? You do, don't you? What are you doing?

Don't, no. Don't do that.

By the time you call anyone and they get here, I'll be gone.

Why would you do this to a friend? Okay, so you're afraid. Fair enough. This is a frightening situation, first impressions.

I would have liked it to be different than this, but we can't always expect things to go our way. Yes, I understand. You're overwhelmed. You're afraid. You aren't the type to pretend otherwise. But you can hear me. You can hear me, can't you?

Yes, you can. This is my voice. This is me, don't you like my suit? It's the best one I own. I wore this specifically for you. Don't mess this up, Patricia.

We can help each other.

I can help you.

Don't. Don't do that. Call the cops if you want but don't do that, please.

Don't call him.

Why are you doing that?

Don—okay, okay, I'm leaving. You're being irrational. I'll come back when you've calmed down. But Patricia, before I go, I want you to hear me say it one more time:

I am your friend. I showed up today because I want to help you.

That's all I've ever wanted to do, honest.

I'll leave.

Because you want me to.

That's what **friends** do.

Something for
Later //

Process the events. Establish where I went wrong. When you have the face of any other, critical thinking is your best asset. Figure out where the dialogue dropped and amend with a second chance. Think. Don't stray away from the problem. Think, identify, repeat—until you follow the fissure towards the source, where it started.

Realize then that the first impression has passed.

I did. I didn't get a chance to make a good first impression. She saw me in the office that day. And she remembered.

What does it take to win someone over after ruining your chances at first introduction? She thinks I'm—I know what she thinks. And it's wrong.

But let it go. It's a problem, yes, but it's something for later.

It doesn't change anything in the long term. She's afraid because I looked frightening, I imagine, in the office that day. I would be frightened too, given the circumstances. Caught her off-guard. And then there's the impossibility of it all.

I made a wrong first impression.

But I know that this will change. She will understand. She knows that Bryan's been unfaithful, that Bryan brings her down. What she needs now, more than ever, is a friend to tell her what she's already thinking. She needs me to tell her what she needs to hear.

It can't be Tristan, because of the circumstances. It's likely

Tristan that will treat her right. When the time comes.

It has to be someone else. And I know who to use.

When you have the face of any other, it's what others don't see, the cracks running down their faces, the frailties and fears that weigh down their subconscious—that's what becomes the norm.

More Like
Nothing //

Hello, my name is Stacy Hsu and you know how it is with time. It runs away from us. Time it makes you think that it's still the millennium when really we're a couple decades in. Time, it flies. Oh, it's like they say, once a workaholic, always a workaholic. I cut my teeth as an intern like anyone else, fighting the competition until I got to a place where I realized that the fight has no end. You keep fighting; never stop. I thought about it and really really thought about it; I want to stress how much thought went into the following decision. I thought about it and eventually I identified that I was fighting the wrong people. I needed to fight the people that claimed to be on my side.

Right, I'm talking business, the business of web design. I was a grubber or whatever they call it. What do they call people, the ones that toil their better years in low demeaning expendable positions? I should ask my husband, he's the wordsmith.

Hey, honey… right, lifer. I was a lifer until I started this business with my then boyfriend now husband. We started it in our shitty one bedroom apartment and now we've got this house in the suburbs, built on the workaholic's penny.

My, my, how time flies.

But that's why I'm reminiscing. That's exactly why I'm actually going through with my husband's suggestion. A reunion, who would have thought?

I feel so old.

I'm already running through a list of friends, family, and colleagues. This will be swell, and there's no way I'm going to survive this without at least a few glasses of wine.

Oh, make that a whole bottle.

I should call Patricia.

Who, oh wouldn't you know; I can't believe I remember the name. It's really been so long. We weren't all that close, but we had our moments.

We had our circle of friends.

A few of them, like Katy—my, my, we really were inseparable.

Patricia, that name really brings me back.

I should invite her.

I'm pretty sure she'd fit in. I almost forgot all about her, but sure, she would. She would fit right in. Katherine's been roughing it out in the big city. She wanted the world and now she's got it. I'm fine with my little slice of the internet.

Patricia, how could I have forgotten the name?

She was sweet, really nice. She used to write my European lit papers for me. I wasn't much for the essay stuff.

I sucked at it. But her and Tristan.

Didn't they go out? They were an item.

I should tell her to come alone.

I talked to Tristan a week ago. Hmm. I should ask my husband if it'll be okay. But…

It'll be fine.

Yeah, I think it'll be all right. The host isn't supposed to know about everyone's pasts anyway. I'm not ashamed to admit that I deal my fair share of gossip.

It's fun and it's harmless.

Time used to run away from me but lately, it has slowed down quite a bit. It's probably the business, going so well. It's going perfect. I'm having the time of my life. It's really great. Really, I'm quick to tell people the news.

If gossip is part of it, then I'll do what's needed. It's harmless gossip anyway.

Did you hear about this celebrity?

Did you know that this person and that person are getting engaged?

Harmless because it's information that'll flow freely.

I'm spreading the word is all.

It's something to say and do—my friends and clients and family are all doing well and I want them to know that I am too. It's great to think that everything's going so well. I won't mention it, won't say anything to my husband because I know how he feels about the subject. We built a business together. It was magic. I'm thankful for every day, for being so blessed. Not everyone has their own home, business, able to set their own hours.

I guess I'm just a little bored is all.

But did you hear about how the young couple down the street, the folks that moved in earlier this summer? They're pregnant. They're going to have a child.

It's that special?

It's really *something*...

A House,
A Situation //

When you have the face of any other, you sometimes forget what it takes to go unnoticed while posing as someone else. You receive the same information, the same knowledge, the same loves and hates, the same plans and predictions, as the person living their life maybe ten thousand miles away. You are this person, and it's impossible.

But it still doesn't prevent this impossible thing from happening.

I am Stacy Hsu.

But there's another Stacy Hsu.

In the same room. In the same house.

This will be difficult. But I'm here to help.

I'm willing to do whatever it takes, even if it means posing as someone else.

Patricia hasn't arrived yet. The reunion looks as though it'll be a success. But it's a poor excuse for the real problem, the one thing that Stacy wants most, but her husband is unwilling to provide. When you have the face of any other, you notice immediately the jealousy dripping from her face. Glare at every couple that brings with them their newborn baby, their toddler, their kid, their preteen.

Dolt the kid with praise, and mask jealousy by gossiping with the parents.

The proud, *so very proud* parents.

No surprise then when Stacy sticks with Patricia, the

only one that arrives alone.

Patricia is safe. Stacy feels superior around her.

Stacy, you are going to be a problem.

A Nonessential
Character //

Hello, my name is Michael. Michael Ice. Damn right that's my real name. What, you want a look at my ID? My birth certificate? Why am I talking to you—this is a party right? Who yelled fire? Who brought all these people here? Something's not right. I don't feel normal. Shit, I don't know why I'm here. I don't know anybody.

That means they'll ask for my life story.

Well how's about this, I'll sit here with my own bottle of wine.

Not going anywhere.

Life story. As if my life is already over.

It just got started, idiots.

I should relax.

Yeah so what? I put on this mask because it hides my anxiety. Yeah so what? I put on this mask because it makes me mysterious, a mysterious musician, which is exactly what I am, okay? A musician. That's what I am. Yeah so what if I have anxiety?

So what.

I don't like people and people don't like me.

Look at these two. I was sitting here you know. That bottle is mine.

One of them tells me that it's her house. Oh, its your house, so I'm supposed to apologize? She's insulted, Coming on a little too strong, hmm?

The other one keeps quiet. I like that.

I don't want to be here.

She says, I don't remember inviting you. What's your name?

Here we are again, life story.

I'm not going to acknowledge that question.

She's attractive.

Hey, my name's Michael.

Hello. My name's Patricia.

Then she intrudes, My name's Stacy. I'm *her* friend and I don't think I invited you. Who are you with? You're clearly not here by choice.

Fine you want details. I give her the details.

This Patricia, she's really attractive, isn't she?

Hey kid, you've got a lot to learn, says Stacy.

I've been playing guitar for ten years. I think I know enough.

Buddy, don't be a smartass.

Patricia grins, What kind of music?

Talk to her.

Indie, more like indie rock but a little bit heavier. We like to experiment.

Watch that Stacy pour herself a drink, totally indifferent to what you put in the wine.

I'm not drinking from the same bottle. Look down on me. Call me a kid. I can be vengeful. It fits right in with my behavior. I'm trashed, maybe, but it's all part of the show.

I like making a strong first impression.

Michael Ice, huh?

You got it.

That's a ridiculous name.

Ignore Stacy. Talk to her.

Tell that Patricia, **I demand perfection in others.**

Then a wink.

Stacy's all like, Oh come on.

Patricia laughs.

You're not actually humoring the guy are you?

I'm going to tell it like it is, You don't have to stay. It's your house, Stacy, go obsess over someone else's kid.

She blushes, takes a big gulp from the wine.

Perfect.

Talk to her.

Patricia says, You're charming.

I work on improving myself.

Stacy rolls her eyes, She's got a fiancée, you know.

Then look at Patricia, completely ignoring Stacy.

I am open about my feelings.

Patricia smiles, That's good.

Yeah you better believe it's good. I don't know what I'm saying but yeah, it's good. It's exactly what girls want.

That Stacy's drinking it down.

Good. I'll have a sip too. But mine's clean.

Not going to drink?

She shakes her head, I don't like cabernet.

Shrug, Whatever works.

Wait until it kicks in.

And yeah so what? I don't actually find Patricia attractive. Yeah so what? Our conversation's copied right out of some teen romance flick. Yeah so what? I'm some kid that's never been able to know the difference between love and infatuation.

I'm a kid, barely eighteen, and I'm already shattered.

Yeah, so what... I don't care. I don't care about anything. Just a kid? This kid's got plans.

Doesn't need any of you people to tell him he's nothing.

You'll remember the damn name.

You'll remember the name!

I'm right here.

A Sad,
Necessary
Moment //

When you have the face of any other, you do what you need to do, even if it means rendering the real Stacy sick to her stomach, banished to the upstairs bathroom by her husband, who goes around making excuses to everyone that asks, but everyone's confused because, She's right there. They point, and where Stacy stands, you are standing too.

The real Stacy is sick to her stomach upstairs.

But for everyone else, Stacy is still making her rounds, mingling with her longtime friends, longtime acquaintances, her longtime relatives.

You let Patricia finish talking to one Michael Ice, a decoy that disappears at precisely the right juncture.

You are Stacy Hsu.

I am Stacy Hsu.

And Patricia and I get to talking.

Truth. "Real talk," though Stacy doesn't actually use that kind of lingo.

We talk about her life. It's going well, creatively, and it's beautiful to hear her say and believe every word. She's between jobs, that's okay. She's really getting into photography. Patricia truly believes that she's going to be able to sell these photos.

As honest of a declaration as possible, she says that she's captured the truth in each subject and, that alone, has been a big challenge.

She sees the truth.

It's going well, yeah.

What else? There's something else.

My my, now that's so very frightening.

I should call my husband over. I tell Patricia that she should tell him too.

Doesn't it sound like a nightmare?

Sounds like a ghost, my husband says.

Oh yes, That could be it!

Patricia shakes her head.

I'm not sure. I've seen it before.

Where, where have you seen meit?

We talk about her life. That's what we're doing. Like everyone else at my reunion, we talk about our lives. We show vertical slices, split second summaries of our lives, but we never tell the full story.

We have a **life story**, but we're not telling it.

When you have the face of any other, you read the shape and contours of their face before you read into what they're telling you. You've seen the cracks, the blemishes, the broken and the bad.

You know their life story.

Just as you know hers.

We talk about her life. It's about getting her to say it. It's about using Stacy to set it right. The husband sits with me, but that's okay.

I'm Stacy but I'm not fully her. I use enough while being ready, completely ready to leave if and when the real Stacy recovers.

It won't be long.

I mention Michael Ice.

I notice that Patricia hasn't discussed her love life.

Everything else is a given, but what about love?

The husband mentions his name—Bryan.

Yeah where is he?

Patricia explains that he's busy. He's always busy. There's a hint of frustration.

You pretend to sympathize, the right tone and Patricia will notice. So then you follow it up with, Do you want to talk about it?

There's an explanation. The explanation you've heard before.

I don't want just an explanation. I want acceptance.

I want Patricia to say it.

We get to talking, and after I mention what I need to mention about Bryan, she warms up to the idea.

He might, yeah.

It's upsetting, I know.

The husband, too. He sympathizes. He explains how it doesn't get any easier when you're married.

Marriage is a big step.

You drive it forward, the idea, not saying what you really want to say—I'm helping you through this, Patricia—but rather you move it forward, knowing that Patricia cannot turn away from something once it's been delivered.

Patricia nods, Maybe I will have some of that wine.

But you're Stacy now, you take the bottle and say, I'll get you something stronger.

The husband says, Allow me.

Leaves you to continue talking about Bryan, and how she should at least talk it over with him. Then use material found in Stacy to relate to Patricia's situation:

In a whisper, you reveal Stacy's predicament, the root cause for the reunion, the root cause for her mild case of depression. She wants to have a child.

She wants to have a child but her husband doesn't want children.

Her biological clock is ticking. Time, for all intents and purposes, is running away from her. She wants to have a child, now, and Patricia understands. She sympathizes.

It's a big decision, says Patricia.

I tell her that it's the same with marriage. You shouldn't marry someone that has clearly moved on.

We come to an agreement.

I'm doing this for your own good, Patricia.

Then, as Stacy, I will leave—dropping word of being here to help.

That's what friends are for.

Recovery //

When you have the face of any other, you leave the reunion moments before the real Stacy returns downstairs, apologizing to her friends for her absence, while Patricia, she goes outside for some fresh air. When the two speak again, there'll be some confusion. But neither woman will entertain it for long. The reunion extends past 11PM and then it's over.

Giving Stacy all the time in the world to recover.

An
Understanding //

When you have the face of any other, you know that Patricia calls up her mother, Heather, the following morning, and they speak for a little over an hour.

Their discussion centers entirely on Bryan.

Her mother, who never liked him, corroborates everything I had said as Stacy, the previous evening. This part wasn't planned but when you have the face of any other, you come to an understanding: Never let a single opportunity go to waste.

Patricia's mother will pay her a visit shortly after lunch.

When? Oh, I'd say right around the time Bryan's off on one of his business lunches and Patricia returns from her latest stroll through the city, with hundreds of new shots to peruse.

Self-Encouragement //

Feel every feeling. Make it real. When you have the face of any other, feelings are all you have to make sense of the world. In fact, the same could be said about anyone else. It just so happens that the texture and trajectory of feelings are often odd, absurd, and incapacitating. They are seldom what a person wants when they want it. So you do what you do to keep going. They smother and hide, letting the feelings mutate within.

You, on the other hand, if you have to manufacture a purpose, do it. It's what you need to keep going. Boredom is a killer. Boredom brings it all back.

It's not impossible, like you.

I tell myself all this. It's not impossible.

Be persistent. You can help her, you just need to be persistent. She's different, clearly, than most. Some persistence and you will change her life.

Honest.

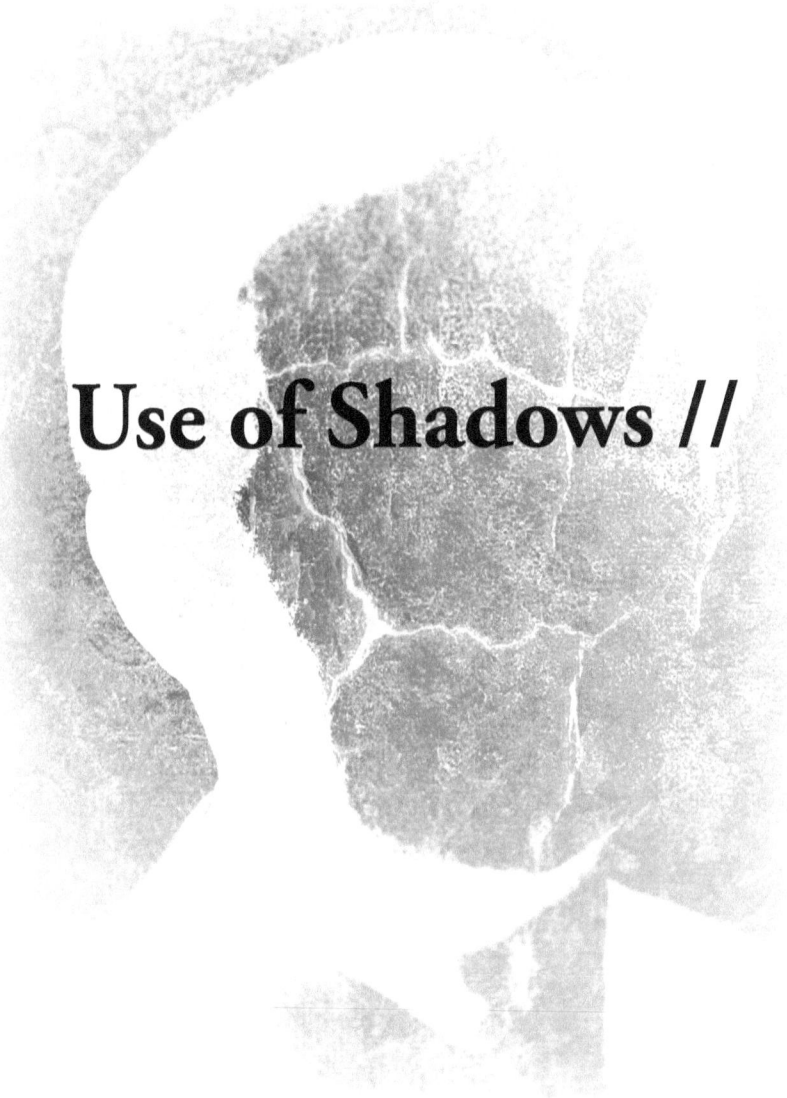

Use of Shadows //

I have to make sure. I have been restless all morning. In bed, restless; unable to sleep, much less lie still. It is indeed one of those days where I am nobody. I'd rather stare than dare to be anyone else. But I can't. Not today. I can't let this opportunity slip past me.

Heather will visit her daughter this afternoon.

Heather will persuade her daughter to demand exactly what she deserves from this life—accentuating her talent, her caring, honest nature, her everything.

But I have to make sure.

So I mail one of the 7x5 cards.

I mail it out hoping that she'll fill it out and mail it back.

I look at the blank image staring back at me in the mirror. When you have the face of any other... **no**. Not yet. Help her and she will help me.

I have to make sure. I need to be sure about one other thing.

There will be no posturing; I will visit the restaurant as myself.

Take the train four stops west, make that transfer, heading north two stops, it'll bring me to where Bryan will eat lunch, the same neighborhood he is interested in relocating to for increased comfort. It's a nice neighborhood—one of the more affluent parts of the city—and no surprise, he wants to live here for status alone.

I find Bryan looking at a brownstone with two women and a realtor.

I'm not interested in the details; I'm only here to make sure.

Here's what I discover—Bryan has put in a bid for the brownstone.

Bryan is working a second job.

Bryan has lunch with the realtor. The women, one is Bryan's assistant and the other is the realtor's intern.

They order celebratory drinks—margaritas and piña coladas. I knock over his drink.

Bryan sweet talks his way into a replacement free of charge.

I knock the drink over a second, third, fourth, and tenth time. Bryan blames it on the server and demands that he talk to the supervisor. He believes that the server is playing some kind of sick and immature joke and claims, It isn't funny and nobody's buying it.

A quick exchange results in the server's termination and Bryan with another drink.

No charge.

I hate this man.

No way, he isn't good enough for Patricia.

Much to the disagreement of his company, she will not like the new location. She will not like the close proximity to a number of art galleries and she will not like the fact that he is hoping to take her on a cruise two weeks from now where, and he whispered to his assistant to keep it a secret, surprise her with a marriage right there, on the spot, with a select group of their friends and family.

No, she won't like any of it. Because I know how Patricia really feels and Bryan can't buy her with peculiarities and creature comfort.

She is not his trophy wife.

He cannot treat her as something less than she really is. When you have the face of any other, you see the truth draped behind a dozen lies.

They might be perceived as truth by the one spreading the lie but it's a lie all the same. It's too bad really, because by this time tomorrow, Bryan and Patricia will no longer be an item. The future will set her free.

I want what's best for you, Patricia.

Before leaving the restaurant, I knock over his drink for the thirteenth time.

Lucky number thirteen.

An Advocate //

Hello, my name is—and who do you think it is, hmm? Have you already forgotten what your mom looks like? Have I gained weight? Am I growing a second chin? Is this some kind of joke? Don't take that tone with me, Heather. I'm really sensitive when it comes to my weight. I don't care if you hate the name. It's your name. Your real name. It's the name I gave you and it's the name I'm going to use. And I am fat. Don't lie to me. Oh but I have been working out. I've lost three pounds! The fat's coming right off. It's a new workout routine that focuses on cardio. No more walking around the city thinking I'm burning hundreds of calories. I'm thinking smart—taking this diet seriously.

Does a mother need a reason to visit her daughter?

Dear, I think you need me right now.

You can talk to me.

You sounded so troubled and well, I was in the neighborhood so—let's talk. But first put on the kettle. I'm drinking tea now. Gave coffee up. It kept me going; I couldn't sleep at night. Dear, it didn't matter if I drank it at 7AM or 7PM—the coffee disrupted my sleeping pattern. I drink a lot of coffee, dear. I love the taste. I'm not addicted.

Like you, I don't have an addictive personality.

We are alike. Like mother like daughter.

Let's talk. Sit, sit down.

No, how about out on your balcony. Oh, it's wonderful.

I didn't know your apartment had a balcony. This is great, yeah.

Did you put the kettle on?

Good.

So, while we wait.

Do you want to tell me something?

Dear, I can see it on your face. You told me about it on the phone; why is it so difficult to tell me now? Remember what I said about being insincere?

What does dishonesty do to a person, hmm?

That's right—it kills you from the inside out. Dear, you'll become a zombie and I'm sure you don't want that. It's better to face the problem, no matter how easy it might be to deny it, before it's too late. It might be too late as it is. Look at this place.

He makes good money, huh?

But that's the real reason why you've stayed with him, Heather.

Say it. Admit it.

That's not what you told me on the phone. You said you weren't sure you loved him anymore. Well, which one is true?

Dear, you're lying. Don't make a habit out of lying.

Yeah, go get the tea. The kettle's screaming.

When you get back, we're going to talk, mother and daughter. I don't want any walls. You are not going to lie to me, okay?

I'll stay right here.

Be quick.

You know I'm here for a reason, right?

I know you can hear me. Doesn't matter if I've made it my purpose; you're my daughter and its my duty to help you during tough times.

I know a thing or two about weakness, dear. Like me, I'm weak. I've got a weight problem. Gain ten pounds, lose three pounds. Gain eight pounds, lose twelve pounds. My weight shifts like crazy. This is a problem. I don't tell anyone this, not even my closest and oldest friends but it's because I have a destructive, inadequate self-image. I still see myself as I was when I was your age, when I was beautiful, fit, and had the whole world on my side.

When you have it all, you fall hard when you see it go.

And it will go, dear. Nothing lasts forever. Not even love. Look at what happened with your father and I. We were just like you and Bryan, separate lives hidden away from the one we manufactured as our own.

Thank you. Let me taste first.

I'll be the judge of the tea.

See, this is good. Not as good as coffee, mind you, but it's good. This'll do just fine.

Now, tell me. Tell it to me straight.

Everything you alluded to on the phone.

Tell it to me again.

Let it out, dear. You were raised to be honest. No use messing up that pretty face with worry. You're in your twenties. What a failure it would be to see it all go to rot this far into your maturation. Am I right?

You know I'm right.

Now, talk. I'll listen.

Yes, I want to hear every word.

Dips and Dives //

I'm her mother, see, so it should be that she trusts me. Tells me everything. But that doesn't happen. What she says versus her true feelings contradict each other. I can see it in her face, a dotted line where future fissures will form. I'm her mother—why would she hide these things from me? She's honest, as honest as can be, but in this case it's not honest enough.

She says that she feels like she's betraying him by talking about him in such a negative light.

She says that she loves him, Beauregard is a name she could clearly take on as her own. Take his name, under oath, the threat of marriage.

Really?

She says that she fears that if they broke up she'd never be able to move on.

She says that she would use Bryan as a measure for every other man she dates. He would be the image, the model which they would have to meet, if not exceed.

She says that she knows Bryan is up to something. But he would never cheat on her. If anything, he's living a lie but he would never do anything more than a lay.

She says that he's probably slept with someone else—she mentions Tristan—but it's okay because she has done the same. Cheating in this case has to do with feelings.

Mother says, Everything has to do with a person's feelings.

She says that if he loves another, she will move on.

Let's talk more about this Tristan.

She tells me everything I already know. The past, the present situation, and I ask her if there's a future. She says that there might be but she doesn't know how to categorize her feelings, she doesn't yet understand her feelings towards him.

She tells me that she knows something's got to change. The situation has gotten stale. It's gotten to the point of being stagnant.

I tell her that I understand and it's true: I really do understand.

It's complicated.

She nods.

She says that she feels like she's stuck, in limbo. Life paused but time continues to expire. And that she doesn't know what that even means, but it makes sense. Somehow.

Somehow...

I tell her that at least you're being honest.

She muses about how this all came up suddenly. Everything's gotten cloudy and frightening, like someone's out to get me.

I tell her that she just needs to keep going.

Life is a tossup, full of ups and downs, dips and dives. But you just got to keep going. She is silent for a second, and I want to be myself, I want her to know that she had been talking to **me** the entire time. Every time, with almost everyone she's spoken with these past couple days. She's been speaking to me, every conversation of some worth, some value, it was because we were speaking to each other. I want her to know that it's me.

But instead I sip the tea and watch the clouds in the sky roll past, slow enough to suggest that we have quite a bit of time left on this planet. We have the rest of our lives.

Dips and dives, she says.

I tell her, Yes, that's what we do.

It occurs to me that perhaps she *is* being honest. Perhaps this is truth. Then why is it that I am unable to see it on her face? The truth should show itself.

Unless it means that I'm the one being insincere.

But no—I'm her mother, how could that be?

Like mother like daughter.

Everything I see and feel, it's reflected in our actions, our voices.

So we're both being dishonest. Maybe but—no.

You have to end this.

I tell her plain and clear.

It sounds impossible, dear, but you have to. For your own good.

Remember, it's only impossible until proven otherwise.

You can't just waste your days watching the world go by.

Today is an exception, but soon you'll be thirty and everything about you will be the same but the world, it will have moved on, leaving you behind. Leaving you to this apartment, the same situation.

Maybe you're right, she sighs.

Mother knows best.

Here's Where
Stuff Should Have
Made Sense //

When you have the face of any other, you get a little anxious. You know what you want but, see, it isn't necessary. Still, sometimes that desire is more than I'm willing to withhold.

I'm talking about the card, yes.

I brought one along. I couldn't wait to see whether or not she would mail it back. Maybe she never would. There's no certainty in that particular measurement tool.

But I wanted her to fill it out so I handed it to her under the idea of her mother offering her something that might help. It's nothing much but these kinds of surveys can be helpful. It helps you analyze your personality traits. It gives you a rough overview of who you really are.

I needed to know. I wanted to make sure.

But after she fills it out and hands it back to me, I don't know what to say.

I don't know what I'm looking at, much less what I'm looking for.

It's just one of those surveys, she says. No big deal. But in each statement, it should be an activation or denial of a person's true features. Then why is it so meaningless when it's Patricia that says these things?

When you have the face of any other, you already know what they're thinking. It's as if you have already spoiled every ending to every story. Though you don't know how their life story will turn out, you don't know how to be surprised when it takes its next turn. You don't really know how to react to the suddenness of being alone after having spent the afternoon sitting next to her, talking intimately about her life.

You kind of forget your place.

So you have to go back. Going back means speaking to her online. You know the password to Tristan's email so you send her a message. Nothing spectacular, just something concise, maybe even a little flattering.

You want to talk to her.

She replies by the end of the evening.

You reply ten minutes after receipt of her message.

In it, you ask if she needs help. In it, you say what you should have said all this time.

Patricia agrees that things don't look to be going as originally planned. Something must change. She talks about her past, focusing specifically on "our past."

As Tristan, you rekindle a common bond, the love for art and more so the poetry of a single, masterful line. Your replies are no more than a single paragraph while hers are numerous, often too long to read in one sitting.

You exchange dozens of emails, neither ever wondering why it's so difficult to just meet in person, see each other for who they really are.

You want to ask her, but you keep that to yourself.

Suddenly, it seems too severe of a question.

You pick out certain phrases in that last email, perhaps reading into what's been said a bit too much but from this distance, this safe and comfortable **second person** voice, you can be anyone, anyone you want. You can be anyone except yourself.

You think she knows.

In the email, you think she's telling you to meet with her.

Maybe you're reading it wrong but it sounds like she

wants to tell you everything.

And you, all you can really do is reply with the following: I'm helping you, you have to trust me.

Trust yourself. You wait an hour for her reply. But that email never arrives.

Defiance //

I wanted to be Bryan in this situation, if only to make sure that the breakup goes smoothly, but I knew better than to get between them. She has to do the breaking up herself. Inevitably it is her life. I stand back and watch from a balcony window, concealed by shadows. I watch her pretending to watch television, eyes darting every so often to the front door, the muted dread not at all lost on me.

I share the same anxieties. It's all come to this very moment.

Of course Bryan's late. He arrives well past eleven.

Of course Patricia's lost her nerve by then. Me, I'm just as anxious, breaking out into a sweat while, at the same time, my body set to a full tremor, like I'm freezing out in the cold when really it's a humid night.

Bryan brought flowers.

He has something else, entirely different in mind.

When she sees the flowers, I know that it's over. She won't break up with him. Not tonight. Bryan knows how to pacify her with promises. Mention of the brownstone followed by the celebratory cruise. He drops a bomb and Patricia smothers doubt with the belief that he's the same man she fell in love with seemingly so long ago.

I am rendered speechless.

What can I do?

Think, think...

What can I do to bring her back from the brink?

I can't do anything. When you have the face of any other, you can't do anything. You have to watch. You're stuck watching as Bryan and Patricia make love.

You watch all the effort go to waste.

You watch as if the world is falling apart.

You mutter to yourself—

Why?

Why?

Why?

You repeat the question because there's nothing else to repeat.

Why are you doing this Patricia?

Why are you doing this to us?

What am I saying?

Why?

This needs to happen.

Why are you doing this?

I was trying to help you.

What happens now?

Bonding Between Key Characters (But Which Ones?) //

When you have the face of any other, you wait for the right moment. You aren't sure the right moment will arrive, but you wait. You have nothing better to do. You wait. You wait until she gets out of bed. She can't sleep so she goes into the home office to clean up some of her photos. You wait in the bathroom, to the right of the partially closed door.

She passes right by you, and you swear that you both make eye contact but perhaps it's because you are already posing as her, wearing the same nightgown, and she assumed it was only her reflection in the mirror, the mirror on the wall right behind you.

I'm right here.

You don't know what you're going to do but you're going to do something.

You don't know what it is, refusing to believe what happened.

Blinded by anger, you walk into the bedroom.

You slide under the covers, and you wrap your arm around him.

He reaches back, holding you close.

What am I doing?

When you have the face of any other, sometimes it's the fact that it was never yours to judge—her life, their relationship—that causes the most anger. It gives rise to the manufactured purpose, the fact that you are not one of the key characters here.

It isn't you and her.

It is him and her.

When you have the face of any other, you can't finish any of their sentences.

You can see but never touch.

You can mimic, pose, and project every possible insight, but that's all it is: a projection, a prediction, little more than the shadows that hide you from the truth.

When you have the face of any other, you know what you could do right now. You could take your other arm and wrap it around him, forming a firm hold around his waist. You could, oh let's say, hug him tightly enough that he notices.

He'll say something like, I love you. And when you hear it, knowing that he means it and that Patricia, in this case, would say it back, meaning every single word, equal in their love for each other, you would, maybe, move your hands across his throat.

Lightly at first.

I'm here to help you, Patricia.

It would have to be light enough that he doesn't feel it until you decide that this, this is it—this is what anger will do to a person. It will consume them enough to take another life. Then you remember that this **wouldn't** be your first.

And then you remember what you did and when you did it.

And then you remember a lot more, and the moment passes, the prospective murder gone to waste like the would-be breakup that never happened.

You pull away from him, turning on your side. You are a mess of feelings, none of them well defined. You don't know what to do so you say the same words—

I love you too.

When you have the face of any other, you know a thing or two about trust. Much like how Patricia can trust Bryan to remain faithful when she isn't faithful in return. Much like how Bryan can trust Patricia even though she essentially could have taken his life. Much like how I can trust that my intentions are valid, and yet they are contradicted by the actions of the one I'm trying to help.

I don't know what to do.

I don't know what else can be done.

When you have the face of any other, you have nothing ahead of you and everything else is stuck in the past. You'll leave the apartment the way you arrived; you'll leave before she returns to bed. You'll leave long before the night gives way to dawn.

But you can't leave her behind.

Not with how much you've put into this.

She's different. You haven't seen someone like this since the last time.

That was over a decade ago. You don't know if you can last another decade. She could be your last chance. She can see you. That's so rare, to be considered real by others.

I'm trying to help you.

Can't you see that we have to be friends?

You and Me //

No one knows you better than I do. I am impossible, but Patricia, you are not.

Much like the survey I send out, there are definite questions pointing at the necessary course of action. But you have to be the one to act.

It is your life; I'm only trying to help you.

How am I still alive? How is it that I can be anyone else but I can't be myself? Want the truth? I don't know. I don't know what it means to be real. I don't know how this happened. That memory, the one that matters most, is missing, gone. Stolen from me.

Maybe left attached to someone I was for an hour, maybe less.

But what I do know is that all I've ever done is try to help.

And it's in my nature to continue, without fail.

Because I have nothing else. Because if I'm dealing with someone else's problems I don't have to deal with my own. I can't help myself, so I help others. And really, I like knowing that everybody is, at least a little, like me. Because when you have the face of any other, you begin to understand that their faces are your faces, and so your face is my face. If I don't like what I see, I'm going to go to great lengths to change it.

This is my purpose. It has been since the beginning. Manufactured, ultimately a farce—but it is a reason to reach out, a reason to feel something, and that alone is what I have. It's all I have. This is my confession, Patricia. I've thought about this all night. I've spent the entire day bedridden with thought. I've thought about it a lot and no matter how I look at it, no matter who I decide to be, it ends up the same.

I see it happening no other way.

You and me, we're no different. You might even say we're the same.

Don't you see? Look in the mirror—you could be so much better.

You could be free, unfettered.

You could be Patricia Pond. As it stands, you'll forever be Bryan's.

Mrs. Beauregard.

I've tried to think of another way, but nope, there's no other choice.

Walk down any street and you'll see a hundred faces and think nothing of it. But hidden in the crowd, one face looks right back at you. It's me, begging for you to look. For you to tell me what you see. Do you see me? Do you see me? Do you see me? Do you see me? Of course. You've seen this all before. If you look, and I mean really look, then you'll see what was always there. I'm going to have to make you look. I'm going to have to go through with it. I'm doing this for your own good.

Like true friends.

Like soul mates.

Like two sides of the same face, I'm only here to help.

Deus Ex Machina
Part II //

When you have the face of any other, sometimes the questionnaire you mailed comes back stamped "return to sender." You decide to fill it out for that person, a random name, a random address found via public records. You answer to the best of your ability but you are never satisfied. You can't be sure if they're answers are honest.

You can't really concentrate knowing what will happen next.

I present myself in ways that are very different from who I really am.

Strongly Disagree.

You make the right decision.

I enjoy trying new things.

Agree.

I am the life of the party.

Somewhat Disagree.

You make the right decision.

I trust reason rather than feelings.

Somewhat Agree.

You maintain the right amount of distance.

I know how to calm myself down.

Somewhat Agree.

You remain objective, voice rendered as you, never "me," you never "we."

I remind myself to focus on the good things in my life instead of the bad.

Somewhat Disagree.
You are faceless but determined.
When I'm really sad or down, I seek the company of others.
Agree.
You have a purpose as much as you have a past.
I like to be engaged in an active and fast-paced job.
Strongly disagree.
You are ready to face that past.
I demand perfection in others.
Strongly Agree.
You are ready to face the future.
I work on improving myself.
Strongly Agree.
You save them from themselves. Shouldn't that be enough of a reason?
I am open about my feelings.
Somewhat Disagree.
You make sure. You always make sure, right before.
Trust yourself.
Somewhat Disagree.
You. There's you, and there's them.
You know. You know what you have to do
You know what you have to do.
You know what you have to do.
You know what you said before—
Sometimes…
A person must fill in and decide for those that remain indecisive.
What else am I missing?

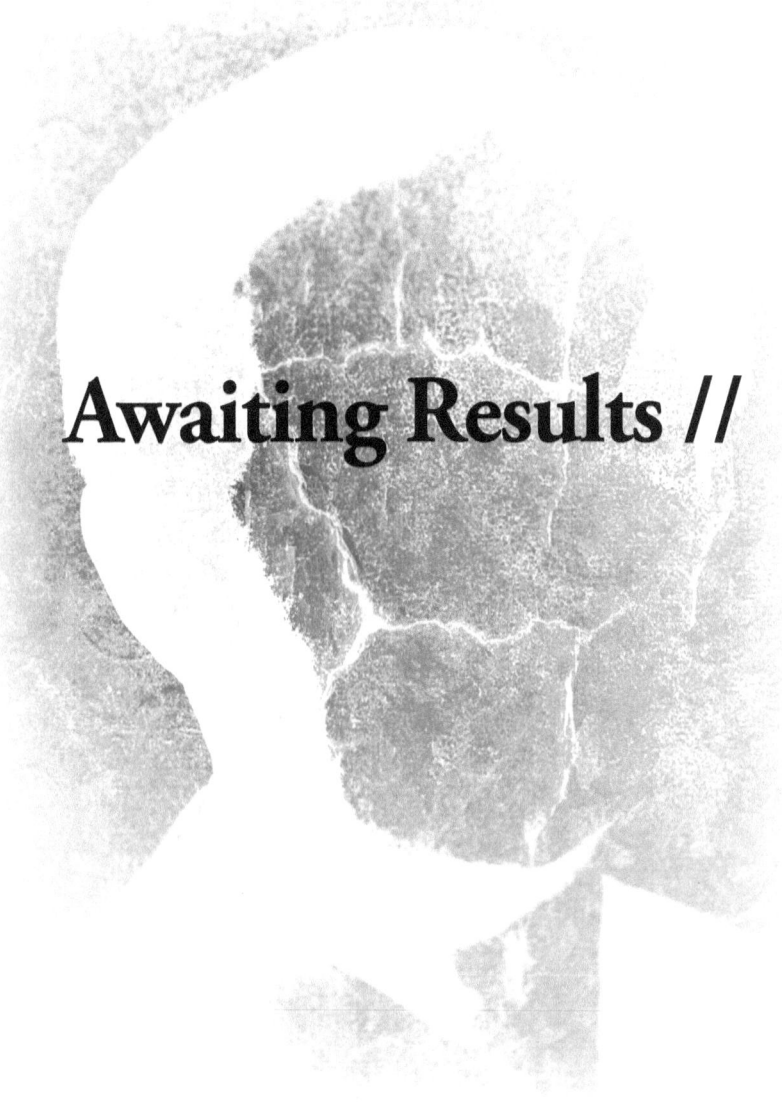

Awaiting Results //

Look, there's something that I've been wanting to get out, something on my mind while all of this... **stuff** has been happening. It's just that I'm starting to lose track of myself. Well I guess it's true that I've never really had much of a self-image but at least I knew what it meant, the word "help." Now I feel like help can mean a lot of things. That's probably the point—that help is a cipher for something else. I guess it's just the complicated nature of the situation. It's a love triangle without the love. It's some sort of voyeur experience but I'm kind of nobody and everyone, playing all the roles at once.

It's like they are puppets and I'm the puppet master.

Or, I don't know, a kid with a bunch of action figures and I'm providing all of the voices. I'm starting to mesh in their own motivations. I'm starting to see things from a dozen different perspectives and it's all really disorienting.

Sometimes I find myself doubting what I'm doing.

I'll be right in the middle of it and then I'll wake up— I'm already awake but it's like I actually was going through the motions, everything lifeless and plastic, and then I wake up and see that I am someone else. It's always jarring. It's always a rush.

It's every feeling you could ever have rushing at you all at once.

It's addictive. You just, well, you want to create a situation just so you can be a part of it. It's really complicated, being the way I am. Doing what I'm doing. But all this stuff that's happened, yeah, what do you think? I think it's getting pretty strange.

I mean I'm pretty sure what's going to happen. It's happened before but that one ended differently. What's about to happen, it has to end differently. I don't think I'll be able to let myself get away with that again. I know you don't know what I'm talking about. I'm not going to say it here. It's for later. I'll have to face my past soon enough.

I just need a moment to gather my senses.

Oh, also, one other thing. Forgive me but I have to ask.

Am… am I a good person? Am I still good? What does it really mean to be a good person anyway? I know I'm not supposed to say, due to the reality of the situation, to ask these questions but now's the time. Now is all I have. I won't have a chance later. Not with what's going to happen next. What makes you a good person, if you in fact believe that you are? Tell me. I'll listen. I'll know if you're lying. Because, I mean, come on, I'm the best kind of liar. I'm the kind that believes the lies he tells.

This time, is it going to end well?

RESULTS:

You are viewed as organized, pragmatic, and sensible by others. You are at your best when posed with a new challenge. You have clear understanding of the way things should be. You are curious about other people's complications and you have a tendency to get involved. You have a highly logical mind with clearly defined boundaries for conduct.

HERE

Personal
Experience //

When you have the face of any other, you don't have a name. You don't have a fucking name. Maybe you did, but you can't fucking remember. How's that for a sick joke? Can someone help me? Maybe that's partially why I've lasted this long. There ought to be someone else that understands, someone else that can see, and prescribe, the practical from my impossible situation. You don't have a name, but you remember theirs, every single one:

You remember Richard Tell, young and despondent, yet eager, to make good.

You remember Laura Davis, working so hard to be something she's not.

You remember Bill Kalish, a rockstar without the ego to save him from their stares.

You remember Isabelle Blumstein, so physically fit that her mind has withered.

You remember Katherine David, someone so busy being a person she neglected what it meant to be an individual.

You remember Rudy Mike, simple teacher with a complex problem.

You remember Charles Aster, the new college student fearful of the future.

You remember Vince Sullivan, an open-minded business man with an opportunity.

You remember Dania Heim, a young and energetic

woman enjoying her newfound adulthood and the freedoms that come with city life.

You remember Andrew Place, new employee and negotiations enthusiast.

You remember Stacy Hsu, a woman living "the Dream" right down to the part where it turns into a veritable nightmare.

You remember Michael Ice, another musician thinking he'll make it big but, who knows—maybe he will, and maybe he'll fail to appreciate his success until it's gone for good.

You remember her mother, Heather, a manic middle-aged woman bored and frustrated and way too addicted to "self-improvement."

You remember Bryan Beauregard. That bastard. How could I forget?

You'd never ever forget Patricia Pond, the one that might change everything. Likewise, you wouldn't forget Tristan Brunhoff, a man equally creative and curious as her.

You remember all the others, so many names you'd think they'd be enough to reconstruct a face of your own. Most of all, you remember the boredom. But that's enough about that. Maybe you misplaced your name in the memories of others. Maybe you want it back. Maybe you just want things to remain the same. You do what you think is right. And I think this is right. But anyway, you still don't remember yours. But you will.

You will.

A Twist //

I won't distance myself from the telling. Not this time, honest. I won't hide behind objectivity, and I won't digress. I'm being honest. I'm not going to use second person. Yes, something has happened. And that happening has indeed happened before. It could happen again. I'm afraid that I'll have to be more aggressive. I don't like putting myself out there because there should never be two of a person. However, she needs my help.

She needs my help.

She needs my help.

And I need hers.

I should be honest—when I said, I'm afraid, it wasn't to imply fear. I am not afraid. I am being quite decisive here. I'm ready to tell you how it happened before. The name omitted because the individual is no longer among the living, he was in his late twenties. He had quite a bit of trouble interacting with the world. He worried more than most, worried himself into a corner; he populated that corner with a desk, a computer, and seemingly endless stacks of books. He imbedded himself into the words of others; inevitably beginning to write whole passages of his own. It might have been a cry for help. It might have been his way of interacting with the world, an alternative given that simple greetings and social outings were impossible.

But one night I wanted to help him out of his cocoon.

Hello, my name is…

And off I went. Could have been any event but I chose something simple.

An open mic. It was enjoyable, if a little bit awkward, and though I did my best, I had trouble calming his nerves when I began reading his work aloud.

Maybe he wasn't ready. Maybe the work was still too malleable to be read aloud, but the effect was dampened, given a minor applause.

But the act alone, especially since someone approached me after the reading, having enjoyed the work, would open doors. It would, given a few more performances, have ended in a call, the reclusive man pulled from his corner by a local member of the literary community, curious enough to offer him an invitation to submit a piece to a journal and join in on the dialogue. When you have the face of any other—

He shouldn't have seen me. But he did.

I visited him that very same night, maybe a little bored and feeling it worse than most nights, I visited him to redirect my thoughts to someone else.

He was still there, reading, writing.

But when he stood up to retrieve another volume from the stacks, he saw me; instead of bumping into me and there being no other curiosity, he looked up.

He looked right at my face.

And his went pale, flushed of all color.

It was the first time, you see. It was the first time and I didn't know what to do. So I spoke, and he screamed in terror. I spoke, telling him to calm down. I spoke, telling him I was just an idea, a dream, something to write about. I spoke, trying to get him to stop. But he wouldn't and really what else could I do?

This has never happened before. The impossible once again proven to be achievable. When you have the face of any other—

To this day, I'm not sure anyone noticed his disappearance.

Yet even if they had, he left nothing behind but his work.

I should really check and see if any of it was published.

Something Like Her //

Hello, my name is Patricia Pond, and I'm still pretty young. Twenty-five. That's not too old, right? I don't look like a Patricia because I changed my name from the one my mom gave me. I look more like a Heather but I want to be a Patricia.

I got this card in the mail today. It's one of those personality tests; same one my mother handed me, I believe. It looks like it's from the same company but they consist of different questions.

I should throw it out but it does get me thinking—what does Patricia do?

She's a photographer.

She's currently unemployed.

She's level headed.

She's open-minded.

She still has feelings for someone else.

She thinks she needs to break up with her boyfriend.

She thinks she really needs to focus on her career right now.

She needs a break and knows that it won't arrive unless she becomes more aggressive about what she wants.

That's something like her.

I guess I feel like I need to explain myself a little because things have been weird lately. I have been feeling very different and though I've always been honest with myself, I don't know if I can, given what's happened. I can't be honest if I don't understand what it is that I'm feeling. I should go for a walk. That might clear my head. Whenever I feel doubtful, I go for long walks, carrying nothing but my camera.

I'm afraid of this city. I'm afraid of how it can get the best of you.

I have to be careful. I have to keep "my cards close." I never say that. It's the city. I must have heard someone say that and it rubbed off on me. Then I just said it. I need to continue being myself, being honest above everything else.

I need to be more aggressive. That part is true.

I usually go to this park. It's not the biggest in the city and it isn't the prettiest in terms of what's growing here but I look for a different type of beauty. I look for that honesty in a situation. I don't like photos that have been fixed so that all the colors are lush and vibrant. I like work that maintains the same overcast hues, the same clouded effect, the same uncertainty in a person's facial expression.

I'm constantly surprised by how quickly things change, but if you are able to capture something on camera, it's there forever. You get a piece of it before it's finally gone.

Isn't that kind of beautiful?

I think it's beautiful.

I think I'm beautiful.

I like to scan their faces. I sit on a bench and people watch. I like wondering about who they are, who they are, what might be on their mind, their worries, their denials, their fabrications.

I wonder how many people I see will be a completely different person this time next year. And then I think that this might be it—the only moment we have. It passes like all the others, and there's no telling if we'll be able to look, feel, or think about the same things we did during that one precise moment.

And when I see something, see the right shot, something candid, I don't hesitate.

I can't hesitate if I want to capture honesty.

I can't hesitate if I want to capture the impossible.

I take a picture. People don't seem to mind. This happens a lot. People going around the city with cameras, taking pictures.

Sometimes I catch a look.

Sometimes I become of their photos.

Sometimes there's a funny moment—like the child making faces at me from the bench right next to me.

There are twenty-one unique facial expressions, and I'm going to try them out—

Happy.

Sad.

Fearful.

Angry.

Surprised.

Disgusted.

Appalled.

Happily surprised.

Happily disgusted.

Sadly fearful.

Sadly angry.

Sadly surprised.

Sadly disgusted.

Fearfully angry.

Fearfully surprised.

Fearfully disgusted.

Angrily surprised.

Angrily disgusted.

Disgustedly surprised.

Hatred.

Awed.

The child does her best to match each expression. Then we both laugh and I take her picture, capturing the moment of truth.

If anything, I feel more like myself than any other part of the day.

The moment I'm behind the lens, I feel true. I'm capturing the truth, and it couldn't be any barer than the snapshot.

These snapshots prove that I'm at least aware of who I am, and that's reassuring.

I am aware of who I am and what I look like on the inside and out.

So far I haven't found any of myself that is worth being framed.

Hey, I'm just being honest.

I have a feeling that's going to change real soon.

Stolen Parts //

When you have the face of any other, being someone like Patricia is eye opening. When you let yourself be that person fully, as if you won't just step aside later, it's enlightening.

It's reassuring.

You decide to answer the questionnaire, one step at a time. One day at a time.

You decide to get a good sense, a good overview, of who she is. You can't help but stand at this distance, the comfortable and safe distance, and admire your friend.

You enjoy knowing that there are people like her in this world.

You enjoy knowing that you are here to help.

You are going to enjoy what's about to happen—and you tell yourself that these parts, they aren't being stolen; you are merely borrowing them for the time being. You have to believe that you're being honest. You have to believe that she'll be better for it.

I believe this to be true.

Not stolen, think of it as being shared.

I Am an
Average Person //

Hello, my name is Patricia Pond, and I strongly agree: **I am an average person.** I agree but only because of the way I walk, talk, and conduct myself. I bet I appear average to most. I am only being honest. I believe that I might be attractive to some people but mostly, I'm more comfortable agreeing with a neutral statement. If I'm going to be able to answer their questions, I have to know that what I'm telling them is true.

I didn't get the job, no—but I'm still going to get it.

I never got a callback. I had one phone interview and they told me they'd let me know. It's typical code for saying, Thank you for your time but this isn't going to work.

This is going to work.

My choices today are to visit Bryan or get what I want.

What I really want.

I'm ready. I have my best photographs printed on high quality photo paper; I have gone through them over and over again, each photo and how they are arranged. I'm trying to be more decisive about the ordering. I'm going to be more decisive about my declarations.

I feel different. I need to admit that.

I feel like something's clicked inside of me and whatever hesitance I've had, it's now gone. I feel hopeful today and for once I don't have to second-guess if I'm doing the right thing. I'm twenty-five and it's time that I start getting what I want.

It feels good to say it, huh?

Bryan is expecting me but I can't think about that right now. I have to put myself first. For once, I'm really going to do this. Mom's right: I have to know what I want. I have to consider my options. If I have to move on, maybe I will. I don't want to think about that yet though. I don't want to think about Bryan. I don't want to think about Tristan. I don't want to think about anything but this job, this residency.

If I get this, I will finally be able to have a show. I'll be able to show the community what I've seen in others. And I'll be able to curate the gallery for six months. It's a paid residency so, if it comes down to it, I can support myself.

I'm right here. It's okay.

Worst-case scenario.

Today is the day where I do something so unlike me, something unbelievable, something downright impossible: I walk into the gallery cold, without an appointment.

I put on my best impersonation of a confident and calm individual and I walk up to the owner, sitting at her desk.

She greets me with a good-natured hello.

I return the greeting.

Before she can start with the whole spiel about this week's showcase, I interrupt, apologize for the interruption and say, **I am an average person.**

That catches her off guard. Who says that?

But I'm not done—I need to be decisive.

I want you to get what you want.

Pause for effect and then I repeat it again, I am an average person, only this time I add, but I have quite the offering.

She is mildly perturbed, and I get it—this doesn't feel right to me either. I feel like I'm being controlled by some urge, some sudden burst of energy and confidence, like I stopped caring about anything else in my life except for my dreams.

She is ready to kick me out but then I hand her the portfolio.

She says, Oh the residency?

I'm sorry but that position's already been filled.

But I won't take no for an answer.

I know what I want.

I know what you need, Patricia.

Oh, all right, since you clearly went through the trouble, and I'm in a good mood…

It's the package, the whole package, that intrigues her. She flips through the photos, at first nothing catches her eye, but then she notices one photograph, one photograph in particular, the one that doesn't belong. It's a picture of a shadow.

It's a picture of me.

She holds it up, There's no subject here?

I don't say anything, letting it sink in. This is intentional. This is very intentional. I take a picture at the moment of pure telling, and see—I saw a ghost once. I saw it and I still can't figure out how to process what I saw.

You saw me, Patricia. And I see you. Don't worry, I'll help you and then you can help me.

This is intriguing but…

But today I'm not taking no for an answer.

She asks me about my education, if I have any formal training, noting something odd about how each photograph is almost always slightly blurred, save for the subject; she picks up on the inexact process, the lack of editing and other embellishments.

Let it all sink in. She notes certain photos for how uncanny they are, Simple, as simple as a standard family photograph… but there's something.

There's something different about this.

As if, and she selects her next words carefully, as if you are capturing the face of any other and bringing out what

407

makes them unique. Their doubts, their worries, their flaws: I can see it—holding up the picture of the child I took the other day—like this one, this child can't be any older than four but you captured this sadness about her. She could be having trouble socializing with other children at preschool. She could be suffering from something she hasn't figured out yet. She doesn't understand the world but, she sets the photo down, folding her hands, but the world continues to show more of itself. It is a big and scary place.

We trade looks; I've gone this far. I'm not going to make any sudden moves.

I can't believe I'm actually doing this.

You have some truly unique work.

Followed by—

I can't make any promises…

And then—

But if you'll allow me to show your portfolio to 678 down the street, 678, I'm sure you're aware that Luis, the owner, is one of the city's most celebrated curators. Second to me, she teases. I think he just might fall in love with this.

I tell her, Absolutely. That would be wonderful.

And then it happens—

Luis is always looking for talent to represent. It won't be a residency like the one we specialize in here, but Luis, well, I don't want to overstep my boundaries.

I'll let you know.

I mean it. I'm not just saying this to get you out of my gallery.

Do I have your information somewhere or…?

See, Patricia?

Excellent.

We shake hands; she has this puzzled look on her face.

I tilt my head to one side, *that cute little thing I know you do.*

You're puzzling, she says.

Do that thing where part of your mouth moves upward, creating an almost-dimple in your cheek.

I know. Then I laugh but it's more of a giggle.

It's certainly a compliment, she says with a grin. Well, we will indeed be touch. If you'll allow me to be frank for a moment, and if you promise me you won't let this feed your ego too much…

What ego?

I tell her that I promise.

You made my day.

I tell her, And you made mine.

We shake hands again. And then a third time, both laughing at the sheer awkwardness of the situation. By the time I'm walking the same blocks, meeting up with Bryan, more than an hour late, it hits me as reality. Reality is often something surprising. I look around at all the people, all these pretty faces, every single person here directing their own life story, and I feel as insignificant as a fly. But today this fly wasn't caught against the screen; this fly got through. I don't want to let get the best of me but it's the reason I skip down the street. It's the reason I feel so genuine and alive, today more than most.

It's the reason why I start thinking about breaking up with Bryan; the moment I think about him, it changes my mood. It brings me down.

I think I know what I have to do.

See? I'm only here to help you.

I Tend To Keep
Quiet In The
Presence
Of Persons Of
Higher Rank,
Experience, Etc. //

Hello, my name is Patricia Pond, and I somewhat agree: **I tend to keep quiet in the presence of persons of higher rank, experience, etc.** But I'm tired of being quiet. I've been quiet for most of this relationship. I think it's time we really talked.

Bryan looks up from his desk, clearly understanding that this isn't a joke.

Bryan, you have no part in this. I'm breaking up with you in one leap. You won't even know why. You don't deserve an explanation. You haven't treated her the way you should have and so this, this happens with you edited out.

I've thought about this a lot. I've thought about this oh, honestly since we moved the city. The city changes people; the city changed you. Bryan, when I said that I love you, I still do, but there's something I need to tell you. I know.

This is where Bryan says something.

I know that compared to your career, I'm an accessory.

This is where Bryan tries to assert himself, assuring me that it's not true.

Please, let me speak. I've thought this out—everything I want to tell you—so could you at least let me explain?

This is where Bryan says okay. Apologizes. Shuts his office door. Undivided attention.

I'm afraid of what this city has done to us.

I'm afraid of what this city will do to us in the near

future. We've barely seen each other these past couple months; where have you been? I've been at home, waiting for you. You don't come home most nights. Where are you staying? Is it someone I know?

This is where Bryan tries to explain.

I close my eyes; I turn away from him.

This is where Bryan stops. He realizes he's overstepped his bounds.

Look, I don't even care if it's someone else. That happens. I'm here to tell you that I've done the same. It happened a long time ago. And then it happened a second and third time. It might happen again. I look into his eyes and tell him straight, You know him.

I've visited you daily like I'm some kind of pet, and you barely notice me. You're so busy with this work, whatever it is you do—what do you do? You won't even tell me. I'm going to try to be as calm about this, okay, but this is taking all of my strength. You don't know how long I've wanted to talk to you about this.

It's either I say it now or I never get my chance.

Here it goes—

I love you. I do. You were my first real love. That's special. Everyone remembers their first love. They never really get over the first one. I know that I'll forever look at everyone I care for with the same kind of curiosity and kindness that I gave to you. But that's the big problem: I'm not sure you care.

This is where Bryan's eyes begin to water.

Bryan, I know that you love me.

You wouldn't have proposed if you didn't.

We've built this life together. We moved to the city. You got your dream job, right?

Bryan doesn't say anything. Good—you deserve this.

You're living the life, your story goes and on like some epic novel. But what am I? Where am I in it? Am I a secondary character? I keep thinking about these moments, the moments we're wasting, as precious items in a life story that isn't really mine.

I don't feel like myself. You know I'm not the type of person to hide from my true feelings. I have always been honest.

This is where Bryan nods, slowly.

I can hear my voice, but I feel like I'm somebody else.

These last couple months, since losing my job, I've been able to think a lot. Almost too much... and it's overwhelming. I, I, I just...

I don't see this working out.

I was ready to end it the other night but then you show up, you actually show up instead of disappearing to wherever it is you go, and you had flowers. You had a new promise. You hand delivered me exactly what I needed to pretend, at least for that night, that everything was okay. The brownstone and the cruise and all those things you said, I love you, I do, but I just can't picture you saying them.

I look back and the memory is already cloudy.

Like it never happened.

Someone else said those things or maybe I imagined them.

This is where Bryan hides his head in his hands.

You see, I really believe that I mean less to you than everything else in your life. I'm here, along for the ride. But I want more. Don't I deserve more? A person should have a chance to express themselves. A person should be able to at least try. Lately the highlight of my day has been my photography. But then I hold back a little, being less aggressive with submitting my work, because I have to think about how it will affect you. If I sell my work, I might have to travel. If I build a following, I might not be here when you get home.

I used to wonder if it would ruin our relationship.

I thought about *us* first, **me** second.

This is where Bryan shows his face, draped in tears.

But I feel good about the work I've been generating lately. I feel like I have a chance. The time alone has changed the way I see everything.

I feel like I have a chance. I have a chance to finally have a snapshot of myself.

Don't hate me, okay?

But I think it's time we saw other people.

I think it's time we think for ourselves less as a couple and more like a singular face.

I pause, sighing deeply, mostly for effect.

I'm going to go.

This is where I leave. Bryan doesn't get a chance to reply.

I Like to Get Lost in Thought //

Hello, my name is Patricia Pond, and I agree: **I like to get lost in thought.** Being lost helps lead me through so that I don't have to ever doubt if I am wearing the right attire for today's weather or if I'm going to embarrass myself by showing up where I'm not wanted.

Being lost to thought helped me break up with Bryan, and it's going to help me face Tristan, telling him how I feel.

How I should feel.

How I know he's felt all along.

I admit that yeah I'm a little lost right now and so instead of sticking around, maybe going back home to take a nap, or window-shopping in the village, I visit Tristan's office.

Being lost in thought, I'm not going to try to figure out how I know where it is that he works; I'm just not going to think about that. I'm going to ignore the fact that I know that he works, know which floor he's on, and what he might be doing right about now.

I'm not going to think about that.

You shouldn't have to because I already went through the trouble.

See, Patricia? I'm only trying to help.

I'm going to take a couple of photographs along the way, and then explain to the two receptionists there that I'm here to see Tristan Brunhoff.

Is he expecting you?

He's been expecting you all this time.

I'll tell them, No but we're... friends. I expect that there'll be some discussion. A few looks but I'm currently lost in thought, thinking ahead to what I'll say when I see him, what he'll say when he sees me.

At some point, they'll have to let me go.

They'll point me in the right direction.

I'll tell them, Thanks but I know what floor he's on.

On the elevator ride up, I stare at my feet, keeping to myself. I don't have a reason to speak to the other people riding the elevator with me and neither do they. We are all, in some way, lost in thought together. The elevator stops twice before reaching the right floor. Somewhere between the tenth and the fourteenth floor, someone's phone rings. I imagine that it's Bryan trying to get a hold of me, but that's impossible.

It'll take me only another floor to begin to believe that it really could be him.

I feel pretty strange, like I'm on autopilot, and everything is happening today. Everything that matters at all is happening right now.

When I reach the fourteenth floor, I'll feel as though it's already finished—the worst part is over before it even started. The reality is that I'm here meeting a friend.

His desk is east from the elevators.

I trade helloes with a few employees passing me by.

This part is easy.

Tristan sees me. I wave to him, big grin.

Pat?

Hey, it's so great to see you.

He's confused, Did I miss something or—?

You missed me, Tristan.

I tell him, **I like to get lost in thought.**

He takes a second to process things, Yeah, yeah. I guess

I must have spaced the date. I just, yeah, I really can't remember talking about this. I mean, why would I tell you to meet me… here?

Well—I see something on his desk. It's a picture frame. *Guess who it's a picture of.*

Well as long as the next thing you say is that you miss me there won't be a problem!

He's caught off guard but he's a writer; he's good at improvisation. He agrees, Yeah. Yeah, of course I miss you. Then he lowers his voice to a whisper, But I thought we talked about this, Pat. I mean, jeez—you're putting me in a difficult position showing up, here, of all places.

I'm feeling pretty good about it, smiling in a way that tells him everything so I don't have to spell it out for him.

He's not dense. He gets it. He asks me, What happened? I can read you like an open book. Tell me. Something big happened didn't it?

That same smile followed by—*why the hell not*—a kiss on the cheek.

Patricia, please, don't do this. I've got so much shit to get done by Friday as it is, you fucking with me isn't going to help. Then he pauses, looks at his screen and then says, Fuck, and now the fucking computer froze.

Jesus, he sighs. Worst day ever.

He looks at me.

Tristan, I could help you too, you know. The answer is Patricia. It's always been Patricia.

Well, are you going tot ell me or not? It better be damn good news; you've totally fucked up my ability to concentrate now.

It's how I want to tell him, that's what keeps me from just telling him straight. I want it to be romantic. I want it to be clever. I want it to be—I don't know how I want it to happen but it'll happen here and then he'll drop everything. For me.

Unlike Beauregard, he'll put her first.

This isn't like you at all. You don't play games. I don't understand.

I'm going to take your picture.

What?

Can I take your picture?

He sighs, Fine. He crosses his arms, half smiles.

No, you have to be yourself. Show the real you. Just go back to work and I'll take a few snaps.

Blank stare as response. Please, then I'll tell you. Please Tristan?

He likes that, the way she says his name.

He breaks, Fine, fine. Whatever. But you're going to tell me after you do your photography thing. Promise?

Promise.

I take about a dozen shots while he stresses over the emails popping up in his inbox. None of the photos capture the screen, but if they did, it would be obvious that it isn't the work that's stressing Tristan. It's me. The fact that I'm here, it's bothering him.

You done yet?

I am.

How'd I turn out?

I hand him the camera, Here.

He skims through them, I like the over the shoulder one. That one's good. Yeah, you've always been good at capturing the little details.

I sit on the edge of his desk, I'm ready to tell you.

It's okay, I believe, to flirt a little; body language is important. He picks up on the cues. He's more perceptive than Bryan.

It's over.

Huh?

I make a noise, Apocalypse. Relationship Armageddon. I will never take on the name Beauregard.

You ended it?

He's surprised. It's so cute, how he leans forward, leans close, whispers like this is obscene and private.

I nod. Over. The End.

He's stunned, So that means, what? What are you going to do now? You'll have to move out.

I shrug, Haven't thought that far ahead!

What, that's totally not like you, Pat.

I like the way you call me Pat...

Yeah, I know. Stick to the question: What are you going to do?

Here's what I'm going to do: I'm going to ask you if you want to get out of here. I'm going to ask you if you want to try that new place on 5th. It's near here. We don't have to walk very far. I'm going to ask you to ask me all kinds of questions while we wait for our food. I'm going to ask you to walk with me to village for some ice cream at that place, you know the place, it used to be our favorite. And then I'm going to ask you to join me on a night photo session where we'll photograph the sky. That's what I'm going to do.

He's speechless.

That thing about the impossible it applies here and it's been proven, once again.

I just got a new lens for the camera...

I reach for his hand. He takes mine, holds it tightly.

He looks back the computer screen and then around the office.

Then he looks into my eyes, and it clicks.

I can see it plain and clear.

He leans in for a kiss.

Fuck it. Let's go.

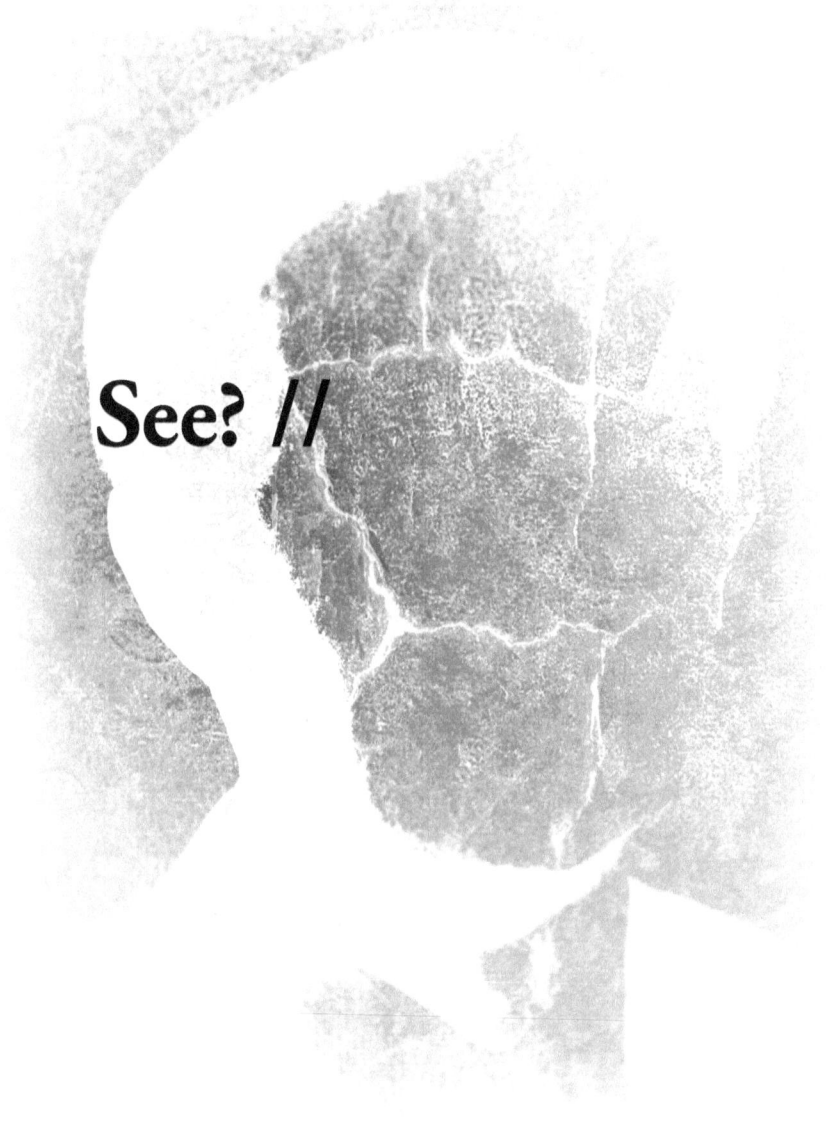

See? //

See how he takes your hand, never letting hang there limply in the cool air. See how he laughs at the worst jokes, never misses a step even when I take things too far and hint at what'll happen later that night. See how he doesn't hide his feelings, looks you in the eye when you talk to him, and how you can both carry a conversation on meaningless banter, never needing a veritable topic, or any sort of intellectual conversation to keep each other's interest. See how you both get lost on the walk to the village but instead of losing interest, you both turn it into an adventure, seeking out an alternative. See how you both fall back into step, after such a long time apart. See how you fit together as a couple and there's never any doubt. See how your faces fit together, a charming couple, one that gets all the right looks from passersby and people that greet you have a great night. See how you both enjoy taking photos of the night sky, even though they're all fairly subpar. See how you kiss lightly at first and then later, when you've gone home with him, it's just like old times, like nothing's changed, and everything feels right. See how it isn't just about him; it's about both of you. See how he asks you later about your plans, what'll happen next, and genuinely cares, so much that he offers to let you move in until you get back on your feet. See how it treats you like you've already made it official. See how big of a difference this is compared to the alternative, another quiet night alone while he partied with coworkers and relished in his superior status. See how every single sighting feels like a picture worth taking, a picture worth framing, and in effect, tonight is a sight to behold. See how great you feel? See?

I know because I am right there with you. I was you.

I am you.

Another Twist //

I won't distance myself from the telling. Not this time, honest. Yes, it happened before but on the verge of it maybe happening again, I should probably explain something. I should probably be honest. No more second person. No more faces except for the one I have. The one I took. The one I culled.

No more but the truth.

The cracks on her face marred her pretty, exotic features.

Green eyes, bright as can be. She lit up the entire room.

She was young, still in high school. I saw her during one of her attempted escapes. The whole "run away from home" freakouts. She had a number of them. Sometimes, they happened once a week. The first time I saw her, she had made it to the city, all the way from the suburbs she appeared at the last subway stop, the one where few never start; they end there, the beach a short couple blocks away. And then the ocean.

She started there. I saw her and knew that she wouldn't maintain her good looks beating herself up like this, letting the doubt, the fear, the sheer trepidation turn her on to all kinds of addictions. She was already entertaining a habit or two.

So then I took an interest, knowing that I could help.

Hello, my name is…

And off I went.

It was easy, natural, being her. It didn't take long for things to be fixed. A few appearances here, taking the right tests, filling out the right forms, and she was all set—ready for college. Nothing could stop her.

Except for her own curious nature.

I would visit her and sit in the shadows, just in case. I was cautious then, so much more than I am now. I was conscious of my actions, triple-checking every collision, every choice; but she still found me and she didn't react the usual way.

She asked me questions.

She wondered if I'm real.

And if I am, is she going to end up just like me.

I had to ask, because her inquiries caught me off-guard. Then she said something like, you're a monster. I wonder if I'm turning into one. She held up one of her hands. It shook, and then she took another dosage. She hadn't been eating; she had been purposefully drowning herself in this substance. She was careful about it.

She made sure to keep up appearances.

But you see, that wasn't her, posing at the right moments.

It was me. Without me, she wouldn't have been able to continue her self-destructive pattern. I wanted what's best for her. She got attached; she knew that I had been inadvertently enabling her addictions, her destructive habits.

By the end of it, she was bedridden, broken.

When you have the face of any other—

I was young, back then. About as young as her, honest.

Perhaps I did it out of physical attraction. Perhaps I did it out of true love.

Back then my feelings were less organized, less manipulated; I hadn't yet understood how I could feel for a person, a situation, a happening in dozens of ways, depending all on the reality of the circumstances, triggered by the conscious choice of which items to process versus which items to disregard. Selective memory. Selective as a whole.

I was her guardian angel, she said.

I fell for it, and I was there when I watched her face shatter.

No one should ever see such a thing.

It was all I could do to make sure.

I left her there, in bed, a sad, tragic story for her family to discover.

She wouldn't be wearing any masks.

She wouldn't be making any more appearances.

What was her name?

When you have the face of any other—

I completely forgot her name.

Being Unaware //

How could she do this to me? That bitch—she breaks up with me? I, I, was just so devastated. It took me this long to understand what just happened. *She* broke up with **me**. After all I've done for her! After all this time, all those years together. She breaks up with me. What, I, I don't know what to think. I really can't believe it. I've asked colleagues, and they said that it must have happened if I'm acting the way I'm acting. Everyone at the office has told me to take some time off. Time off? What the hell is going on? It was perfect—had it all planned out, the move, the cruise, the surprise wedding. I had it all planned out. Things were going well... sure, I've been less than ideal lately. But I'm doing this because none of this stuff is cheap. I have to work twice as hard—do some work under the table just to make ends meet. She has no clue the sort of risks I'm taking. And then she does this to me.

I have to take precautions.

I can't stand the sight of her. So you know what? Here's what's going to happen and this time she's going to be the one that receives. It's my turn to speak. I'm going to feed on my emotions. I'm going to be just fine; you, you broken the chances. I'm not coming back all groveling and wanting to change, wanting to go back together.

I have to make sure that there's no mending the relationship.

No one talks to me like that. Like I'm some kind of child.

No one makes me feel like that. Especially someone I love.

Loved, because what I'm feeling right now, it couldn't be further from the like.

I have to make sure, Patricia.

No one. No one makes me feel so useless, so… confused. No one. So I'm going to leave the office. I'm not useful to anyone today. I bet you're back home, doing the same shit you do every day. Like you didn't just ruin my life.

That's what you did, Patricia. You ruined my life.

Is this what you wanted—to hold out on me, cheat on me with others, and then, when I offer you the world, you break the ground under my feet?

You make me feel like I'm falling to my demise. I feel like everything around me is separate from this, this whatever… I'm feeling. I'm not making sense. Not making any fucking sense. I'm shaking. I'm visibly shaking.

I feel like I'm about to explode.

So you know what? I'm not sorry for what I'm about to do.

Yeah, look at you, answering the door like nothing's happened. I'm not sorry for raising my voice. I'm not sorry for telling you that you're going to get the fuck out of the apartment. Now. Not later. Now.

I have to make sure its finally over.

I'm not sorry for making you cry. Do you know what you've done to me? Those stupid little tears are nothing compared to what you did to me. You ruined me! I'm going to let you know and that's the full extent of it—you walk into my office one day like it's all my fault. You tell me that you've cheated on me and that you think it's my fault. You talk to me like I'm a child, and then you tell me that I make you feel small.

I make you feel small?

Look what you did to me?

I feel small!

Oh and yeah, in case you were wondering, the power isn't out. I cut the power this morning. Told the energy company to cease services. Same with the water, in case you've bothered to check. Yeah, internet too.

Been using your phone all day, I don't care.

I don't care. Don't touch me.

I don't fucking care.

I don't care about that.

You got a callback? Going to be some amazing artist now? Selling work? You're going to have to sell something because I'm not here anymore. I'm not going to be buying everything for you. I'm not going to be supporting you. You ruined me and so now, I couldn't care less about what happens to you.

Get out. Just get out.

I'm only going to be him for as long as I have to.

I don't care where you go; I just never want to see you again.

Walk into my office and ruin it all, like it's your life that you're ruining. Well it's not—it was ours, and you ended it, just like that. What—I, I'm out of words.

I have nothing else to say.

You're dead to me.

Just get out of here. Pack your shit up and get the fuck out.

Take your stupid camera, your stupid "dreams," and don't say anything.

I said don't touch me.

I'm right here.

I have to make sure.

Do what you want. Just leave.

I can't even look at you right now. I'm going to close my eyes. I'm going to count to twenty. When I open them, you better be gone. I don't care. You hear me? I don't care if that's not enough time. I don't care if you love me. I loved you too. You should have thought about that love before saying those things to me. Doing what you did.

You want more, you want some big glamorous artist life or something. Why couldn't you have done that and still have what we had together?

I made all of this happen.

It doesn't make sense.

Stop. I said stop. Don't agree with me.

I'm the one that's confused.

I'm the one that feels like I'm being used.

I'm the one that has been broken. I'm the one that feels like a puppet.

The Bryan you knew is gone. Completely gone.

I can make anything happen.

Now I'm going to count to twenty.

Please… I've said all I can say.

You said it was over, now go.

Get the hell away from me.

Twenty.

Nineteen.

Eighteen.

I don't care! What the fuck is wrong with you? Are you out of your mind? How can you just think it's some kind of argument? How can you think that we can talk through this? Stop it. I said stop it. Don't act like you don't know what you did.

You know what you did.

Seventeen.

Sixteen.

Fifteen.

I said stop it. My eyes are closed.

My feelings are dead. I don't feel anything anymore.

Fourteen.

Thirteen.

Twelve.

Eleven.

Ten.

That's right. Over ten years together.

Down the drain. And you were the one that poured it all out.

You were the one that showed me that I shouldn't trust anyone.

Nine.

Eight.

Seven.

I'm not listening. Cry all you want.

Six.

Five.

You better gather all those pictures, and portfolios, and clothes and everything else because time's running out.

Four.

Three.

Don't you dare question whether or not I'm enjoying this. Don't ask me that question. The fact that you'd say that proves that you really don't care.

You don't care about what we had.

Two.

One.

Don't you dare say I love you.

It's meaningless. It doesn't mean anything.

It isn't an excuse to stick around.

I'm locking the door. Locking the fucking door.

I want you to know that this is for the best.

Boredom? //

When you have the face of any other, boredom is no longer an option and you begin to believe that it never was. You wait in the hallway, adjusting your tie, making sure you feel just right because at some point, you know what'll transpire, and you want to be ready. You can't wait to see your efforts pay off. Patricia, poor poor Patricia, she will go through a lot today. Ups and downs, her life story took a strange and abrupt twist.

It's all my fault. I can't let her see me, so I deny myself the ability to watch. I sit on the top steps a couple floors above.

I'll capture the echoes, the tail end of the conversation. But I won't get to see it happen. It is perfectly acceptable because I'll have my turn later.

When you have the face of any other, you know that Patricia had nowhere else to go except across the hall, collapsing on Charis Boardon and Dania Heim's couch.

She didn't pack much, which will be something of a problem later. She brought her camera and a handbag stuffed full of random garments. Maybe I overdid the twenty seconds part; however, it had to be done. I have to be more aggressive. Patricia's grown way too comfortable over the years.

No worries, though. When you have the face of any other, you know how to match a person's style. You'll be able to gather what she left behind. You'll be able to mend whatever needs some mending. You'll be able, that's not a problem.

There is no problem. We're friends.

What are friends for but to keep boredom at bay?

I'm right here.

Patricia, *everything's going to be just fine.*

Tristan's on his way.

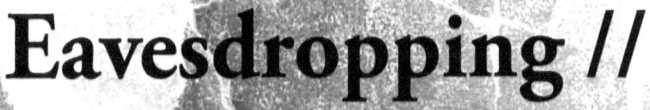

Eavesdropping //

Tristan, there you are, right on time. I listen to his footsteps. He whistles, but not always. Today's a good day. Or at least it should be. He is here to be her crutch; he is here to be her rock. He is here to be everything she needs at such a dire time. First he'll try the old apartment, Knock, knock. Hey, it's me. Pat? You packed yet? It's me, Tristan, you there? Brunch reservations are in an hour. Talking to the door, nothing more. I have to visualize what's happening, paying close attention to each auditory cue.

Another knock, followed by the sliding open of a deadbolt.

I imagine someone looking from the peephole.

Likely Charis, given that Patricia is overcome with feeling.

It's one of those days, full of feeling.

I'm anxious, knowing that this will be the moment where everything really does start to pay off. It's finally happening.

How could anyone be bored at a time like this?

I'm changing her life. I'm showing her the way, and there's absolutely nothing she needs more now than someone to remind her that she's wanted.

Tristan, who is a good guy.

He needs some work too. But that's my problem.

Unless it becomes a problem.

When you have the face of any other—

That kind of thing.

Door opens, it's not Patricia's voice. It's Charis. Can I help you?

Tristan with a good-natured hello. Because he's a good guy, see?

Beauregard just up and left—never came back to the apartment. He erased Patricia from every part of his life. Methodical, really.

Tristan tells Charis that he's here to help move Pat's stuff. Who are you?

And before he can answer, Patricia speaks up, Tristan?

Pat, what happened?

He must notice the effects, the sobbing, the puffy eyes. She's been crying. Thank you Charis.

Tristan. Patricia's voice.

Tristan is here, confide in him.

What's wrong?

I hear footsteps, I hear closed doors.

I hear muffled voices.

They've gone inside the apartment.

But which apartment?

I descend the steps, careful at first. Can't be spotted by Patricia. She won't understand. She won't understand until everything's in place. Maybe she won't understand for some time. That's more than all right; I will be here, filling in for whatever is needed.

They've gone inside.

I'm going to have to do this, if only because I need to know.

Yeah, yeah, it's Dania. I'm supposed to be at work, I know, I know. But hey, I was feeling pretty hungover so. Hey I'm here. Wait—what's going on? Oh no, don't tell me it's going to be one of those long explanations. It's going to be a long explanation isn't it? I don't know if I can stomach that right about now. You can't imagine how much I drank last night. And it wasn't even the drinking, oh god, I shouldn't have taken the molly.

Really shouldn't have.

Oh, oh I'm so sorry.

Patricia, that's horrible.

Hey, my name's Dania. Tristan? Killer name.

Okay, I'm sorry but I'm going to have to duck out. Dania needs a nap!

But Patricia, yeah, by all means, totally; stay for as long as you want.

Oh no the room's spinning. Okay, okay bye for now!

I had to get away. I'll listen and watch from the partially closed bedroom door.

Charis and Patricia are sitting on the couch. Tristan paces back and forth.

He hasn't said much. No one's said a lot. But I missed part of the exchange. I didn't expect that they'd walk into the apartment so soon. Sometimes when you have the face of any other you—blank the blank and have to blank.

But I'm still Dania.

So I have to sit here quietly.

And listen.

Patricia starts crying.

Charis speaks for her.

Tristan says, Yeah they broke up.

Charis said, How did you know?

What do you mean? Tristan wears a strange expression. He points, She told me.

He raises his arms, folds them behind his head, What the hell is going on…

Patricia is hysterical. How can you know that?!

Why are you doing this?

Tristan is dumbfounded, completely dumbfounded, You told me. You told me everything. You broke up with the bastard and then you visited me at the office.

Patricia hides her face in her hands.

Charis says, That's not fucking funny guy.

It's not meant to be funny.

Tristan goes back to pacing. After a few moments, he starts repeating the word "so."

So... so... so... while pacing, trying to figure out what's going on. So you're saying that you didn't kiss me on the cheek. You...

Didn't break up with Bryan and you didn't have dinner with me.

You *didn't* stay the night. None of that was you.

Is that what you're telling me?

Patricia says nothing.

Patricia what are you doing?

Charis is getting defensive, I think you should leave.

I'm trying to help. What are you doing?

Fine, you know what. Fuck it. I don't care. Pat—you're nuts. You always were nuts but hey, I thought I was nuts too. I guess I was nuts for having believed that you'd finally leave him for me. So you just wanted to mess with me? Fine—that's fine, but this, whatever it is you're doing, this is sick. It's a sick fucking joke. And you know what?

Tristan is right there. What are you doing?

Don't ever call me again.

I'm leaving.

That's what I said: Leave! Charis slams the door shut, Dick. *Look what you did.*

Everything Else //

When you have the face of any other, you have trouble reading their faces when their feelings come undone. You worked so hard to fix what needed fixing only to see the one that should have reaped the reward ruin everything you built.

You watch her cry into the couch.

You watch her mask her emotions.

You don't understand how people can sometimes give into their doubts, how they can deny what they're feeling, as if to spite themselves.

You watch as she convinces herself that her life is ruined.

You remember the last time, and the time before that.

You remember how they felt. But then you can't be sure if that's true.

After a very brief spell of frustration, you remember your place. You talk yourself back into the reality of the situation.

When you have the face of any other, you have no choice but to adapt.

When you have the face of any other, you feed on the most recognizable feelings and tend to forget that what's most recognizable to you is often what is deemed impossible by others. You remember your position. Everything continues.

It's okay. We'll be okay.

I'm right here, never more than a few steps away.

Honest.

I Wish I Could Have More Respect for Myself //

Hello, my name is Patricia Pond and I strongly agree: **I wish I could have more respect for myself.** It's true. It's a wish that pretty much anyone would make, but I feel like it's the one that I need to work on most. I'm still trying to figure out my life. Things haven't gone according to plan. I thought I had set it all up, but clearly, I'm still asking questions. I'm looking more and more broken in the mirror every day. Maybe that's part of aging. Maybe that's how the story goes, but really I can't help but feel like I need to turn a new corner.

After all that's happened, I can't keep thinking that I can just go back after everything levels out, after Bryan stops being angry and we remember why we fell in love in the first place. Maybe we'll remember that we were our first loves. First real loves.

I'm starting to worry but I know that I shouldn't be worried.

Today's a new day and every day should be treated as a new promise.

I have to believe that. I have to be honest with myself: I'm not one hundred percent right now. I'm feeling strange, and yeah a little excited.

But mostly concerned—maybe I'm not the right person for this job. I can't really even remember applying for this. It fell into my lap and I feel like I shouldn't take it. Or maybe it's that I shouldn't take it seriously. I don't want to take it seriously because I think it might disappear, might fall to rot, like everything else lately.

But something's going to change.

Deep down, I can feel like I've got something on my side.

I don't know what that means, but it's the best explanation I've got.

I'm right here.

Figured I'd show up around the time the gallery opens. But when I get there, it's still closed though so I have to wait. That's fine. I can wait.

I feel a little nervous, anyway. I should probably sit down for a bit and let the nerves settle. I'll know what will happen though. I'll start thinking about what I'm wearing—am I overdressed? Is this skirt and top inappropriate? I'll start thinking like this isn't just the first day at the gallery but also the first time I'm really being myself.

But it's an irrational fear and if I want to get through this in one piece, I need to keep being honest with myself.

Yeah, it's just the nerves.

I stare at the sidewalk directly ahead of me. I observe the cracks, how they take a thousand different sudden turns. Some keep going on forever while others end shortly after they begin. In no time the cracks will change.

Everything changes.

I am no different.

I think the same could be said about life. I feel like anything can happen, at any moment, and if you think something's impossible, it's only because it hasn't happened yet.

Heard of separation anxiety?

It's a voice. His.

Luis. I say hello, and do my best.

I probably come off a little shy and that's unfortunately

how I am, at first. I'm shy because I'm feeling down.
Everything that's happened in the past twenty-four hours—
wow. It's like you hit age twenty-five and suddenly it's all
over. Everything you thought was permanent breaks apart.
Everything you thought was impossible becomes... your
job.

After we shake hands, we walk inside the gallery and I
want to cry.

I don't know why.

Just settle down, be calm.

He says something like, You're not what I expected.

I don't know what to say to that but an apology. I'm
sorry.

Save it. As far as I'm concerned we're all imposters.

He has this habit of talking while doing other things,
so it's difficult to know if he's talking to you or to himself.
I pick up on this in mere moments because right after
we meet, he doesn't stop talking. First he's talking about
separation anxiety because he just changed the entire next
six months lineup of shows and his mainstays are now
gone. Moved on. Caput. As he says. And then he's handing
me various placards to be pasted under the right painting.
But then he stops doing that and checks his phone, texting
someone.

In between all of this, he's asking me questions.

I pick one out, So did you get the details or do I have to
start you from zero?

I hesitate, From zero?

He rolls his eyes. Should have known. And then, No
matter. No matter. So here's the short version: You got a
show and more than that you got every show. I do things
differently. I pay you to make art. I showcase a selection
of the artwork made for me every week. You're competing
with every other artist on my payroll. This is 678. I do
things differently. So, he pauses.

This is the first time he looks directly at me, Are you in or are you out?

I nod, but then say, **I wish I could have more respect for myself.**

That gets a reaction, Me too. You're right about that. We're this close to collapse, so what do we do? We contain it. We help ourselves by putting it into the work!

Then he hugs me, This is going to work. Yes, just yes.

He pushes me towards the door, Now get out there. Work, work.

I find myself telling him that I have nowhere to go.

Work here if you have to but unless you're taking snapshots of me posing half-naked with scarves and silk you won't get anything showcased on the gallery walls.

I nod, I understand.

Find yourself! He widens his eyes, Cause part of me things you lost a bit along the way here. But he relents, I kid, I kid. But still, standing here won't help. Show me something in the AM. That's tomorrow. Now go. Get out there.

I Am Quick to Understand Things //

Hello, my name is Patricia Pond and I agree: **I am quick to understand things.** I feel like a lot of what I do involves intuition. Tap into a sort of feeling that might not even be a feeling at all. I think I see it more like a suggestion of the subconscious, pointing you in a direction that might work. Intuition is a lot like a compass but instead of mapping out a field, it's mapping out creativity. I "intuit" a lot from each subject, each setting. Because there isn't a lot of time to waste on figuring out the best angle. You just have to take that leap of faith, using intuition as a guide. The truth behind each photograph has a lot to do with being able to trust what the lens sees.

It's an understanding, really, knowing that what the camera captures is real.

It feels like it's my first time. So strange but exciting too.

I usually walk the streets getting different shots but the fact that I need to surprise Luis with something great, I start walking through every single park, trying to get a sense of what might work and what might be a waste of time.

I need to surprise her.

I observe the power lunch crowd, everyone walking quickly, busy with their phone calls, their colleagues, their clients walking side by side. Everything moves so quickly. It gets me dizzy sometimes.

I take some shots of the busy streets—the surfaces of

various cars speeding by, the traffic lights and how they direct the masses, body language mid-fight. I make a point to avoid taking shots of people's faces, because, for some reason, it's what I'm obsessing over today. I feel like it's too easy, too safe, to capture close ups of people's faces.

Someone spills coffee on the front of their shirt. A crow is about to poop on another person's shoulder. A young man is about to pickpocket someone. These are things I see when I walk the streets. These are maybe things everyone sees; but which ones will capture something different? That's what I'm trying to do.

Honesty, the truth behind a shot—I'm going to do my best.

Today, I feel the need to prove something.

For Luis.

For Patricia.

I check the park benches, but again, it doesn't feel right.

Intuition, guide me. Show me something.

I won't settle for less.

I spend the greater half of the early afternoon sweating and walking, looking through the camera lens, but I never take a picture. Not even one. I feel like I need to save it. The first shot. This feels like a monumental occasion and I don't really know why.

My first shot as professional photographer, employed to capture art.

My first shot as Patricia, her well being on the line.

There's one area of the park that consists of one big rolling green field. People lounge around on blankets during these kinds of summer afternoons. Tons of young people, people that have no prior obligations. People lay out their worries here.

I look, I zoom in, but I can't help but see the same thing.

Everyone's doing the same thing. I know I'm not making sense but really everything's doing the same thing. It might be reading. It might be a meeting between business associates. But everything around me is the same and I don't know how else to explain it. It's a lot of nothing, yeah. I think it's because I'm picturing myself as "professional artist." I'm making this more difficult than it should be

But I am quick to understand things. I should get those shots in no time.

I need to start letting go, letting me seek out the feeling, tap into the inner artist.

Whatever you call it. I can do this.

I walk the field, looking for a subject. The northernmost part of the field has been occupied by a group of people in similar dress. First I look via the lens and then I look with my own set of eyes. What am I seeing?

I'm kind of nervous.

I don't want to put myself out there, but I'm curious.

I'm right here. I can do this.

I feel like an amateur, but I'll take what I can get. It's all about understanding, right?

It's about giving my best greeting. First impressions count for something. Three of them welcome me, asking if they were too loud.

I tell them, No. I don't hear anything.

We're just getting started.

What's going on?

They tell me it's a guerrilla show. They're all going to be performing a musical routine. I ask if they've done this before.

No.

Once.

He did this once, yeah.

Is it dangerous?

Naw.

Well a little.

We got the masks for a reason.

Hide your face, yeah. Got to be incognito.

I nod, That's interesting.

Mind if I take a photo?

You a professional?

Someone else interrupts, Don't answer that until you know what they mean by "professional."

Oh, I raise an eyebrow. I don't know what else to say.

Say no because they won't let you take photos if you're a pro. The pros photographers are narcs; they'll take the photos, make money off them, and misrepresent what we're doing by writing some bullshit because they don't understand.

Well I'm not a professional. I just like taking photographs. I like finding the truth.

They seem to understand. One says, That's why we do this.

A woman gives me a look, If you want to understand, stick around.

I tell them, **I am quick to understand things.**

If you're able to understand what we're doing, you'll see that this is not about being interesting. This is about representation. This is about honesty in government and politics. This is about the sensationalization of the media. This is about our lives as citizens.

I nod and then hold up the camera, So it's okay?

Sure. Yeah. Fine by me.

I look with the lens and use the gathering, which turns out to be a creative protest, over three dozen people gathered, wearing the same white uniform splattered with color—red, white, and blue—there to chant the same phrases set to a drumming beat.

They aren't just protesting their freedoms.

They are protesting for their jobs.

I'm taking dozens after dozens of photos, but what I find most curious, what I keep looking at, are their uniforms. I take shots of five protestors from the neck down, all of them with their arms partially raised. To be faceless, it looks like they are mannequins.

I start imagining this as a war zone, taking pictures of the people that hold back.

Some remain seated.

Some aren't as enthusiastic about the event as the others.

Some look sad, slumped over shoulders, leaning on their sides.

I notice one of the protestors screaming at the top of his lungs, shouting into the air, and I see in the pure emotion of that guttural shout, the severity of his message.

They chant—

I'm right here.

I'm right here.

I'm right here.

And between the repeated statement, they chant in a singsong manner, the freedoms they all feel they've lost. These are people that have been beaten to the ground by the world. They have nowhere else to go, nowhere else to be, so they wear masks, hiding their true faces. Hiding their faces, I can't help but relate.

I'm there throughout most of the protest.

I take over two hundred shots, most of them with very little conscious thought about what I'm capturing. I just took shots of what seemed curious.

I took shots of things that seemed to hide behind the insanity of the spectacle.

It wasn't really the protest that led me there; it was the fact that they felt like they were going to make a difference, doing what they did.

There's maybe another protest a block away. People are protesting their lives everywhere, in every single way. Someone I see sitting on the ground, back to a building with her face buried in her arms, she's protesting too. I'm seeing so many people in the act of trying to express themselves;

it's just so hard to know what part of them is real, and what part of them is a fabrication. That's what makes this so exciting. It's also what makes this so frightening too. I could take the right shot and not even know it. Or I could take a shot of something that I don't understand, and hope that when I see it later, I won't have an explanation. How can you tell the difference?

I Certainly Feel
Useless
at Times //

Hello, my name is Patricia Pond and I strongly disagree: **I certainly feel useless at times.** I couldn't disagree more. I find it insulting actually. I feel like I'm meant for something more. I feel like I'm doing something useful with my time. Maybe some people won't understand—I'm just taking pictures—but really each snapshot is truth. I'm trying to find the truth in a person. And maybe the truth I capture might just help reveal something to someone, maybe even the subject.

I'm liking what I do.

I finally feel better, maybe even more like myself than as far back as I can remember. It's kind of like—how do I describe it... I feels like a weight has been lifted and now, I'm able to breathe normally. I'm able to just be myself, walking these streets.

Feeling useless?

I don't agree, not at all.

I'm seeing lucid.

I'm not in a daze.

I feel perfect, I feel great.

I'm seeing faces.

And I don't need to worry about not seeing mine.

I know that its still here.

If I have to, I can turn the camera on myself.

At any time I can take a photo and I'll see the truth.

In the truth, I will trust every detail.

Take a snapshot and I see more than just two guys playing a game of one-on-one basketball. I see that one is newly unemployed and that the other guy took the day off, put himself out there, using some of his sick leave, in order to make his friend feel better.

Take a snapshot and I see more than a stressed taxi driver speeding down the street, desperately hoping to beat the red light. I see a man that just received some big, troubling news. The kind of news that changes a person. The kind of news that I recently received myself. I see a man that would jeopardize his own safety in hopes of making it to the hospital in time.

Take a snapshot and I see more than just another man in a suit. I see a man ignoring his phone. I see a man that's put his phone on silent. I see a man that is hiding from his responsibilities and I see a man that will get drunk tonight, alone. Alone with the dread-inducing loneliness, the feeling that he might not make it out of this one.

Take a snapshot and I see more than just a lone teenager wearing a hoodie in this heat. I see a young man that's afraid. He's afraid of what might happen the longer he does what he's doing. He shouldn't be doing this but he needs the money. His parents need the money even more. The city is cruel and relentless; it doesn't do you any favors.

Take a snapshot and I see.

I see the truth, and the more serious I get with my photography, the more I see in each snapshot. I'm starting to see in the face of any other the weight the world places on anyone that decides to take a chance.

Put themselves out there.

I'm seeing clearly.

And it's because I'm the one doing all the seeing.

I Don't Like to Draw Attention to Myself //

Hello, my name is Patricia Pond and I strongly disagree: **I don't like to draw attention to myself.** I walk these streets, arms at my sides, and I look into so many different faces and you know what, I think there's a reason why eye contact is so important.

On the way to 678 today, with a dozen photos from yesterday's session, I put myself out there. Maybe I'm just feeling better. Maybe I'm just getting used to all this, being myself above all, and not being tethered down for once.

I could definitely get used to this.

Maybe that's just it—but wow, anyway I dare myself to make eye contact with as many people as I can. It's actually more difficult than you would expect. I look at someone and they'll ghost me—look past me—but when I make eye contact and someone reciprocates, there's this sort of merging, this sort of flicker or one-second impression.

Only three people look back at me.

Three.

That's crazy.

Crazy to think people could be so mean to someone like you.

But of the three that did, no one said anything. One man did the half nod, the lowering of the chin, and then a quick return to looking straight ahead.

Three people.

I tell Luis this and he says, They're all a bunch of creeps.

I kid, I kid, but you're here, right? So you must have something for me, hmm?

I hand him the portfolio.

I feel pretty confident.

He doesn't waste any time.

He goes through the photos quickly. It's a little intimidating. But I'm thinking it'll be okay, right? It'll be okay.

He picks out two out of the dozen.

He says, These two. They're quite strange.

They are?

They're good. I like them. He holds up one, a shot of three of the protestors from a distance, with one looking straight into the camera. Eerie given the expressionlessness of the mask, and the way it looks almost like blood on the uniform.

He tells me that this one, It's uncanny.

Then he adds, Maybe if you made it overexposed a little?

I tell him that I normally don't do that to my photos.

He shrugs, Dropping the photo into my hands. Think about it. People are always changing their minds. I think you should change your mind.

I ask him about the other one he picked out.

I like it. It'll go up on these walls.

Really?

Oh yes. But that one—the one I gave you; it needs more.

I look at the photo closely.

He points to something I hadn't noticed until just now.

He says, And this—that's really clever. Putting the artist in the work!

I see her. She's right there, standing and staring into the camera. She's in the background, pushed and blurred by the rapid pace of the protest.

But she was there.

I feel excited all of a sudden.

Luis says, It's good. It can go up on the gallery wall too.

Try overexposing it and then—but I'm tuning him out. He keeps talking but I stare at the photograph. I stare at the woman barely there. I stare at myself.

That's me.

It's her.

I find myself saying, **I don't like to draw attention to myself.**

He tells me, Then good. You're a dot in the background anyway. It's good.

I rush out of the gallery, leaving behind everything but the one photograph. I hear Luis shouting back, Good. I like an artist rushing, always on the go.

I'm going to head back to Charis's place.

Oh, I don't know. For a little nap.

Why didn't she say hello?

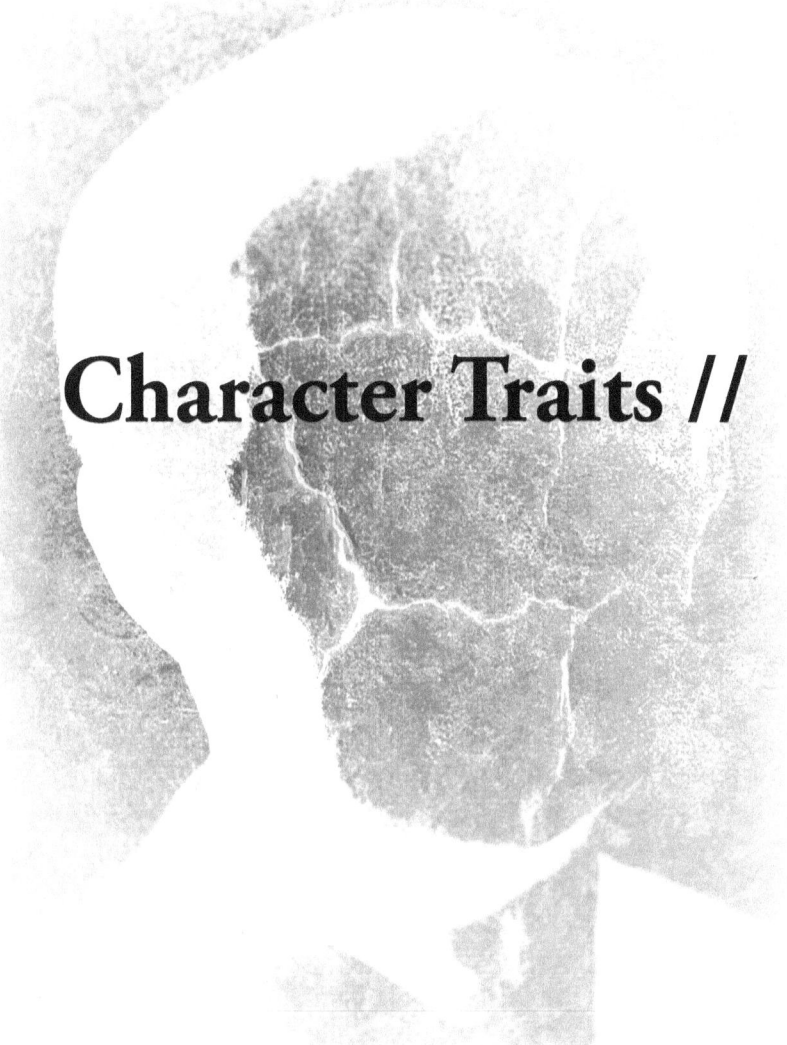

Character Traits //

It's going to be okay. We'll be okay. I didn't let anything bad happen. I made sure, see? I was never more than a few steps away, honest.

This photograph. Does it mean what I think it means? Does it mean you're feeling better? Does this mean you're ready to talk?

I've waited all this time. I've been patient. I'm always here to help. You know that. That's what friends are for. No use being bored. We're going to be just fine.

But I should say that I had a great time filling in while you were **gone**.

So, where do you want to go next? What do you believe in, Patricia?

You're so much better than all this. You can be anything; but you know that.

I can't wait to ask you.

When you have the face of any other—

A Third Twist //

I won't distance myself from the telling. Not this time, honest. Yes, it happened before but because I don't think it'll happen again—I think I understand her and she understands me—I'm going to explain. And I'm going to explain it for real. What happened, that one time.

No more than the truth. This is what really happened, that one time.

He was my brother. He was always the one more outgoing.

He played soccer and football and wrestling. He was athletic.

He was the favorite. He was the one most likely to be succeed.

He had the better looks. Clearly he had the better looks.

We both grew up, got older, we moved on but unlike him, I moved out of the way. We didn't talk for a long time. One winter I tracked him down. He was where everyone else was, so I figured I might as well see how he was doing. Maybe I'd lend him a hand.

Fitting then that he saw me while everyone else failed. If anyone would see me, it would have been my brother.

Always wanted to be him. I felt cheated, being the lesser sibling, the lesser son. So when he saw me and reacted the way he did, what else could I do?

Hello, my name is…

And off I went.

It was so natural being him. It was like being me but without any of the doubts and fears and anxieties and problems. I had so many problems back then. So many problems. But my brother didn't. Well he did, but he also didn't. He knew how to show his biggest strengths. He hid the cracks on his face, the blemishes around his eyes, by always wearing glasses, and always wearing his hair long. He wore glasses even when he didn't need to.

What he didn't show anyone was that he had nothing else going for him. After the scholarship and the sports and the time in the minor leagues of whatever sport it was that he found a future, it wouldn't hold up to the aging body.

My brother got a token position as a coach for one of the major league teams, but that didn't prevent him from knowing that the only reason he got the position out of pity.

There's often nothing worse than when the people around you walk on eggshells, being extremely careful with everything they say and do.

You can't really get along with others if they are unwilling to accept who you've become. So it wasn't so much that I wanted to be my brother, not like this. Not now. If anything I did what I did because I saw it in his face.

I saw his face, ready to shatter.

And I knew that there wouldn't be a mask fitting enough to hide the aftermath.

So I pitied him too. Which is perhaps the worst thing a brother could have done. But I did and I'm not proud of it. So then going through with it was the reason, my purpose, for paying him a visit. I pretended that it was a mutual agreement, that he had been waiting for me the entire time. Like he knew that one night I would appear, and end the pain.

It might have been a story I told myself to help accept what I had done. It might have been a story I told myself to accept what I had become. But eventually, it became a memory, the only memory I had left of my brother.

Given enough time, that memory would disappear too.

Anyway, there was only the one time.

Honest.

Life Story //

When you have the face of any other, you end up at the same front door, not bothering with the doorbell, disregarding even a single solitary knock on the door. You are here, excited to meet up with a friend. You wait and you wait and you wait some more. But it's not really a concern. You're dressed well, feeling comfortable in the suit and tie. You listen, expecting to hear her voice, and maybe Charis's but instead you don't hear anything. You don't hear anyone telling their life story. You hear crickets, the evening in full effect.

You look up and down the hallway.

You feel that—that feeling that you almost forgot.

You feel like you're being watched. That makes you even more excited. You look around and, sure enough, you can't help but laugh.

Nice, you say. We'll have the place to ourselves.

You look into the peephole of the apartment you've been staying at, the same apartment that will be cleared out and rented out to another couple in less than a month; but tonight, two friends are going to have the place to themselves.

When you have the face of any other, time is no issue. You could stand here for hours. Maybe you do. You can't be sure. There is no other cycle or measure of time's expanse except for feeling, real feeling. But you don't feel anything but excitement.

You take out the photograph.

Looking at it while you wait, you stare at her, and then you let your gaze move to the protestors. You think about how she might have found you. It would have been effortless. She would have been able to sense it, where you are. She saw your face; she knows what to look for. She knows you as well as you know her.

You figure she ran, eager to catch up.

She must have been tired, you think, given how much emotion went into the last couple events. But that's in the past and already, you feel most everything shifting, moving into the back of your mind.

You pocket the photograph.

You know she's looking back at you from the peephole.

You adjust your tie, run a hand through your short gelled back hair.

Then you say her name and hear the sound of something crashing to the floor. You don't need to ask if she's okay. Just tripped over a box is all. You try the doorknob, if only because you assume that she's equally excited to see you and the only reason she hasn't opened the door for you yet is because she's too busy getting ready.

You say something like, Patricia you don't have to bother for someone like me.

Add another thing, You're fine just the way you are.

The door is unlocked.

You step inside, carefully locking the front door. Privacy, that's all.

The lights are off in the apartment. Then you remember.

Stupid, you think. Duh. And then you think back to Bryan, plotting various possible schemes, methods of vengeance, as if he might have the courage to go through with it.

You walk into the kitchen and you look into the sink, you check to see.

No water.

You walk into common area, and you listen to the ambience of the apartment. You know that she's in the bedroom. Still getting ready? You ask.

You sit down on the couch, patting down your shirt and tie so that they remain pressed. Nothing worse than a wrinkled suit. You sit and take it easy, starting up a conversation with Patricia, in the other room.

You tell her about Luis and 678. You're starting to appreciate photography. You discuss how similar the two are, pairing up what you do and what she does, how you see the world and how she occupies it. You both seek out some sliver of truth.

It's quite refreshing actually.

No reply, but no bother.

You tell her your life story, or about as much of what can be remembered. It isn't much, but you fill in the details with whatever, memories remembered from people you've begun to forget. It makes for a decent transcript. Doesn't hurt really, as long as what's being said is sincere.

You hear her walking down the hallway.

She's about to join you.

You say something like, You don't know how long I've been wanting to speak with you. I've been patient but—

And then it hits you. Rather, **she** hits *you*.

It's a blunt object. A bat. A baseball bat.

You feel pain and embrace it, saying something like, Wow, that's unexpected.

She shouts, What are you?!

Excuse me?

What are you?!

She strikes you again; neither time is hard enough to do anything but sent a surprising jolt through your skull.

You tell her what you tell her, which means you tell her, It's me.

And then she's hysterical again, but guess third time's a charm because you don't see that one coming. And then you don't see anything at all.

You feel your senses slipping from your grip.

It's coming to a definite point. You can hear her voice, but you can't figure out what she's saying. Before falling unconscious you say the following—

A Moment of
Catharsis //

I see you clearer than ever. You look great. Hey, I'm trying to help you. What else are friends for? Tell me what's wrong and we'll fix things. I'm right here, Patricia. I'm here to help.

A Moment of
Honesty //

The following happens while I'm tied down, unable to move. I think she has me in a closet. I can hear her on the other side of the door. I can hear three sets of voices. That one, that one is undeniably hers, but the other two—can't be sure but it's pretty obvious.

But I must say—

I'm only trying to help. So this is what you do to someone that's trying to help?

They're totally not going to believe you, Patricia.

You're better than this.

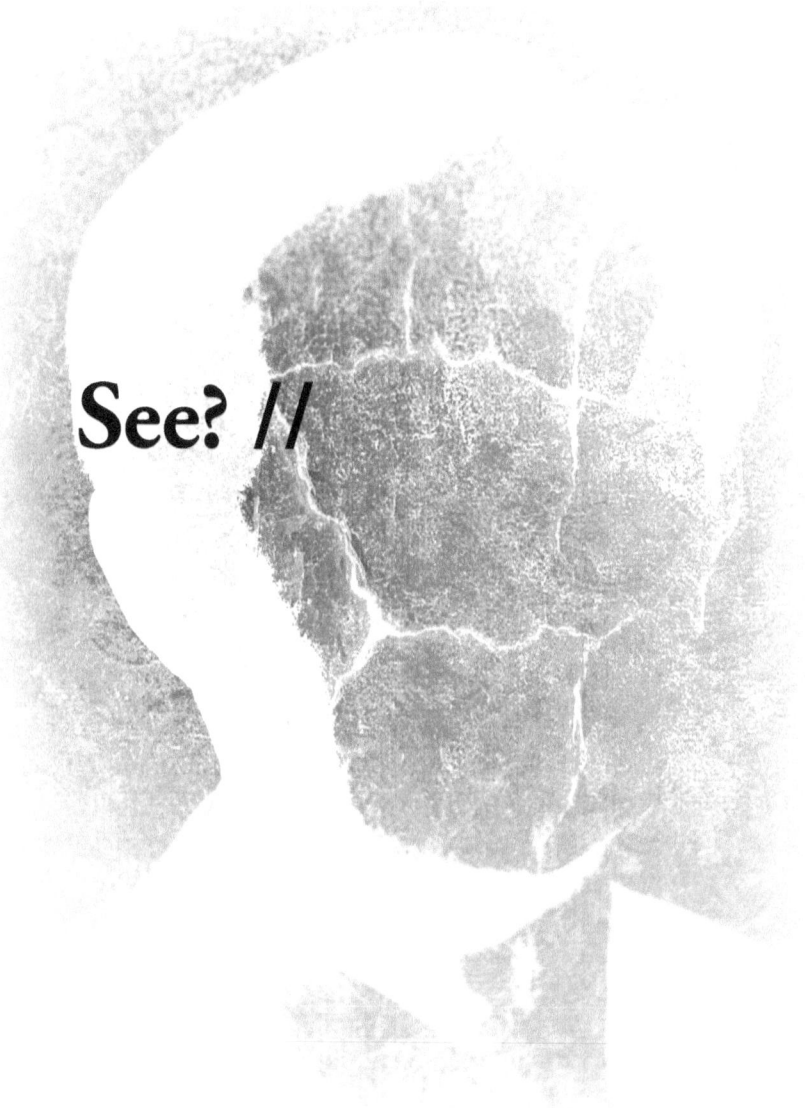

See? //

See? Don't you see it? I told you I saw what I saw. It's impossible. It's impossible but it's right there. It's impossible but, but, it's *in* there. It's real. It's a nightmare. It's not me. It want's to be me. It's right in there. Look. See, don't you see it? You have to see it, right? See, that's the thing that ruined my life. See, that's the monster that took Bryan from me. And, and—that's the monster that became... me.

See, don't you see it?

See? What are you waiting for?

Look! Open the door!

See? It's a monster.

See it's just like I said...

Just like I said.

Don't you see it?

Are you looking?

Are you?

See it?

See?

Movie
References //

You know what this situation reminds me of? Not situations people typically find themselves in or the sort of thing that happens to most people, but rather, those situations in movies where the character deemed mad is actually telling the truth. You have that unpredictable quality, that sort of glow that causes a group of people to be skeptical of some of the things you say, curious about why you're not at all curious or concerned about the things you tell them. You have no reason to ever stand outside of yourself, being something that you're not, and that alone has kept me near, above and beyond the purpose of my watch.

When I watch you I feel as though I'm watching the world.

You are acting like that one character in that film about the movie that makes you go mad, how after you watch even a small portion of it, your sanity is forever in question. She goes to great lengths trying to find the creator of the film, which takes her into the darkest corners of an underground film piracy ring, but she ends up maybe imagining the sum of what the viewer is seeing, so nobody, not even she, can do anything but doubt what happens next. And then it starts getting creepier because she can't stop now, can't suspend her search for the source when the nightmares begin and she swears that the news anchor on the 11-o-clock news is her. Inevitably, I think the creator reveals himself to her but he looks just like her. He is her, and the film concludes with a sequence of scenes outside of the character's perspective, where we get to see her for who she really is.

You are acting like that one character in the film set out in, I think, Alaska, but I could be wrong. It's away from the city; it takes place over a single week in a snow-smothered land. The character you act like starts out as the most level-headed of the group. He's perfect, actually, or at least appears to be, much like yourself. They're digging for something, it's never quite clear until things start falling apart. They are scientists, it's obvious, due to the lingo and various discussions transpiring at the beginning of the film. But when the character you really remind me of finally glimpses something in the snow, he is cast in a mask of doubt. The other characters are skeptical of his warnings, despite his reputation for being, well, level-headed and quite frankly the sanest person in the group. After long he starts attacking people, claiming that they aren't who they really are. No matter how drastic his actions, there's something troubling about what he tells the rest of the cast. And when he starts talking to the audience, attempting to bring them into his world, to help him, things really get bizarre. The rest of the cast systematically disappears. They disappear one by one until he is left alone, paranoid in his room. I'll never forget how the film ends. It's him and the visitor, the one he saw in the ice, earlier that week.

Nobody listened to him, and now, it is there to replace him.

You are acting like that one character in the film about a morbid killer living next door, as glimpsed by the bedridden and broken character. The paranoia starts out almost immediately, what with the character having nothing else to do, being bedridden, homeward bound. He watches, takes notes, inadvertently allowing himself into this killer's world. The killer doesn't seem to notice, but the viewer does, especially when the clues gathered by the character almost directly speak to him. The character's too consumed with his voyeuristic investigation to notice the messages hidden within the audio recordings, that one glimpse of the killer watching from a bedroom window, when the character was away from the video feed, asleep. The killer's privacy is invaded and, maybe that's the way it was intended because the character becomes the killer's next victim. It ends better than most, with the character able to prove his insane testimony to be true. But even then, people look at him dubiously, because although the character proved the impossible to be true, he paid a price, people will never look at him the same way.

You are acting like that one character in the film about time travel, those obsessive weekend warrior types working on some kind of project that goes from hobby to homegrown obsession in less than ten minutes. They stumble upon some kind of occurrence and they really didn't expect it. But that one character, the one you remind me of, he kept going. He refused to deny the possibilities. He risked safety to reach out and discover something remarkable. You remind me of him, mostly for the fact that you are willing to be honest with yourself no matter what.

Well, lately anyway. You're going through your own ups and downs. And yeah, this isn't easy. I often forget that everyone processes events differently. You've been through a lot but, again, I've always been here. Right here. You've been acting kind of like the character in the schizophrenia film, where the audience gets a candid view of developing mental illness. It's really not the condition that reminds me of you. It's how he interprets the symptoms. Basically, it has much to do with how he doesn't notice the symptoms. It's a storm that he anticipates will wash away everything. He prepares, like an altruist, building his own sort of arc, much like the biblical story. He fixates on survival at a time when he should be worrying about his family's financial situation. The character loses his job. He wastes the family savings on a shelter. Ruins long-time friendships with his best friends and coworkers. He scares away his two children, and he almost manages to end his marriage. But his wife remains around, and when the storm actually shows up, he saves everyone else except for himself. He drowns in the flooding, mostly because the shelter only had room for the ones he loved and he has no love for himself. As the film concludes, you discover that he knew. He knows what's happening to him and, as an act of rebellion, he faces the storm.

He never had a chance.

You are acting like that one character in the film about a dream, one so incapacitating, it makes the dreamer look like a fool. She had a dream and kept with the dream no matter what and it was cute to everyone around her, friends and family, for much of her childhood and twenties. But as a mother still telling the same stories, fixating on the same dream, her husband begins to worry. This has gone on long enough. There's an intervention and a quite extensive effort by her friends and family to help her through this… this, what they assume is a mild form of dementia. But when she disappears suddenly, running away with the dream, it's made clear that real or not, she chooses to believe the impossible. You remind me of her, willing to look impossibility in the eye.

You are willing to explain in a world full of people that would rather wear a mask than have to go through the analysis of their doubts, fears, and afflictions.

Monster in the
Bedroom //

That bitch, can't believe it. She hit me. She fucking hit me! With a baseball bat. You know how much this hurts? I could sue her ass. I really should.

But I still love her.

Yeah, yeah, I'm okay. But please, could you help me up.

It's Charis, right? Hey, nice to meet you, despite the... yeah.

And you are?

Dania? I like that name.

Hello, my name is Bryan.

Yup, that Bryan.

She can call me a monster, that isn't the worst she's said to me.

But hey, hey! If I'm a monster, then what does that make you? Huh?

That's funny Dania. I don't think she's a nutcase though. She's been through a lot.

Yeah I know I don't have to stick up for her, but part of me can't be vengeful. I just don't have the energy to drag hate into every situation.

Jesus, this hurts.

Is it bleeding?

How bad does it look?

Well fuck—it's going to swell.

Huh? I think she hit me like four times.

Yeah, yeah, I'm a monster. Patricia, you're mad.

Shit, she got blood on the suit too. Yeah, overdressed, but you see I was on my way from work and decided to stop by the apartment. I don't know why because there's nothing but memories of her in this place.

Guess I needed another jolt of mind-altering depression and sorrow.

Thanks, yeah this is good.

Shit—it's still bleeding.

I might have to get some stitches or something.

Hospital visit. You hear that, Patricia? You sent me to the fucking hospital!

Hey, Dania, Charis, can I ask you something? What did I do to her? What did I do wrong? I'm being serious. She confuses me. I do one thing for her and then she goes and undoes it, makes a big deal of whatever it is I've done.

I'm speaking the truth. I could use a second-opinion.

I got her this place. I got her whatever she needed.

But... I, I, just don't know.

I mean yeah, I could have been there. I wish I could but I have to work two jobs to stay afloat. She wasn't working and, I'm not saying she needed to—I would never ask that of her, never—but I needed to work two in order to support two people.

But it was worth it if the reward was never having to be alone.

I guess—I don't know.

How's she doing? I mean really?

She ups and attacks me, screaming her brains out like some basketcase. I'm worrying. I'm worried about her.

How is she doing? Can you tell me?

She was the one that broke up with me, actually.

Well that's a lie. She went to me, middle of the day, and dropped that bomb. And it was how she did it, you know? It was like she walked in, ripped out my heart, tore at my mind, and left me like this. Left me feeling like… nothing. Feeling confused. Feeling, I can't even explain it. It's just, it's just, what it is. I…

Huh? If she's miserable what does that make me?

I don't know.

I don't know what to do.

She confuses me.

Could you get me some ice, something to help with the swelling? This one's melted down. Thanks so much.

We've been going for about… well it was over ten years.

Engaged, yeah.

I guess it was my fault though: We got engaged too soon and waited too long after the engagement to actually get married.

Oh, sorry, no—I was, well, no use holding back on the surprise now…

I was going to surprise her on the cruise I booked. I paid for all her close friends and family to be on the cruise too, so we could get married at sunrise, saying our vows on the bow of the ship…

Yeah, it was expensive.

No refunds.

It helped that she didn't have very many friends.

My friends are still going. They said I should go too, just to get the fuck away from… all this. But I'm going to look horrible. No chance in hell meeting someone with a crack down the side of my face.

Haha, yeah, damaged goods.

She's what?

Seizing? She doesn't suffer from seizures.

Let me see. Ouch.

She's being a pain.

I'm not asking for anyone here to pick sides. It's over. Believe her if you want but it isn't going to change the fact that she broke up with me.

It's alright.

It's okay. I can drive her to the hospital.

I think we need to chat anyway.

Ha, yeah, thanks. She might murder me along the way!

I'm a monster, I'm a monster sure. It's okay. Thanks for *understanding.*

I know. I know I shouldn't but saying something won't make it not hurt. I've basically memorized everything she told me. The whole breakup, yeah.

It's on repeat in my head.

And now I got a crazy headache to go with it.

It's okay. Yeah.

You are good friends. I'm sure you didn't need to take her in.

Yeah I needed her out of the apartment. I just couldn't bear to see her face anymore. I was angry. I'm still angry. I mean, she fucking hit me.

Yeah, but I guess I'm at that point where it's all settling in and I just don't have he energy to be mad. I just want to move on. I want to be able to feel like myself again. I want her to get the help she needs. Fucking hell, I know I'm going to need as much help as I can get, getting through this.

Sounds like you two are in her support network.

I hear you. It's almost never out of choice.

A person needs you so you help.

Sometimes you do your best to be them.

But, ouch, yeah. I should get this treated.

Where is she? Could you help me get her in the car?

Yeah, I drive. Not all the time.

She never told you?

Paying to have it parked in a safe garage is a killer.

But having the option to drive, it keeps me from being bored.

Going
Somewhere //

Hey, hey, it's me. Are you awake? I'm hoping we can talk. It's okay, take a moment. You passed out. Completely clonked out. I don't know why you're acting this way, you really made a scene back there. You had them all roused up, thinking I was some kind of enemy.

It's me, Patricia.

Remember me?

I took care of it.

Took care of everything.

It's going to be okay.

Now we're getting out of the city.

For awhile. This head wound, it'll be fine.

I have had worse.

Are you okay?

Why are you looking at me like that?

Did you expect to see someone else?

It's me, Patricia.

I'm only trying to help.

Some Impossible Actions //

When you have the face of any other, you are no different than anyone else in that you become a little confused when feelings don't match actions. You see her and she's thankful, or perhaps it's that she should be thankful, happy to see you, but instead she fights you at every turn. She refuses to listen and she kicks at the dashboard, kicks at the steering wheel.

She becomes a liability. She wants to crash this car.

She wants to hurt you, which means she wants to hurt herself.

When you have the face of any other, you do what you need to do. You do whatever is needed. There's no time to decipher. You tell her what you told her before:

I'm right here.

I'm here to help.

And you maintain control of the car. You hold her down with one arm, telling her to calm down. You improvise the next couple actions, unable to really understand what's going on. You tell her, Damn you are full of surprises.

And then—Do you really know what you want?

With a sigh, you brace for impact.

She hits you in the stomach, a blunt kick that steals your breath.

When you have the face of any other, you aren't willing to give up so easily.

You laugh, because there isn't much else that can be done.

You laugh, and then you look at her. You examine the new cracks on her face.

You tell her, If you keep this up, you won't have much of a face left.

And then she screams, Fuck you!

And you laugh, even though hearing that confuses you. It confuses you dearly, and in fact, hidden behind the laughter, is a very grave feeling.

It's a feeling you seldom enjoy.

It's betrayal.

When you have the face of any other, there are no betrayals save for your own betrayals. Daily betrayals mostly having to do with what you should have done versus what you did instead. Quite often, it's that you didn't do anything, and you watched, without feeling, the world take from one person the better of their talents, their cares.

You take the next exit.

You improvise.

You grab her neck, because she's starting to bite back.

You think about asking her but you wait. You wait until you can be sure that it's the question you want to ask most. You let her go free. She coughs, and then she continues sobbing. You look at her, but she won't look at you.

And then you say, I'm the best thing that ever happened to you. I know what you need. I know how to make your life perfect. I made your life perfect.

Then you ask what you've been wondering all along—

Are you being honest right now?

Do you know what you want?

I'm right here.

I'm here to help.

Photographic Evidence //

It's just the two of us, there's no point in screaming. Shut up. Okay? Look, look at me. Why won't you look at me? You did before? Is it something I said? Maybe not. Maybe it's something I did. It could be that—but I'll have you know that I did only what I knew was right. It's what I'd do for anyone and especially what I'd do for you.

This isn't the place I had in mind. I was going to take you to that place you always wanted to go to. You know what I'm talking about, right?

Not the state park but the national park.

The wilderness with nothing but a camera and the truth.

But this'll have to do.

Hey, where are you running? Just, calm down.

Sit there. Here.

Take it.

Take it.

It's your camera.

I've waited patiently. And I've done a lot. So as a friend, I have a favor to ask. Could you—could you take my picture? Could you show me what you saw? I want you to calm down and do something for me. Is that too much trouble to ask?

I saw you and I showed you, see?

This is it. You were there, at the protest.

Look at you—that's you. Yeah.

I just want you to tell me what you see.

I see everyone else's face but my own.

Can you do this for me? Can you show me what you see?

Thanks. Wait, let me get my good side.

You find the right angle, but I'm going to make sure I give you the best, most natural pose, possible. You going to say cheese? It's a joke. Maybe it's not really funny but, yeah.

Wait, you already took the photo?

Let me see! What is this?

Wait, you think I'm this? You think I'm **this**?

You disappoint me, Patricia.

Why won't you trust me?

Is it because you don't trust yourself?

You are one complicated chick you know that? But I see your potential...

And I only want what's best.

Elucidation, with Dialogue //

When you have the face of any other, you realize that they are all **your** faces. Every single one of them. They are yours to become, for as long as you're interested. When you really think about it, all you've ever wanted is to help people. If they're happy, they don't ask any questions. When you spend all your time and energy making sure the people around you are happy, no one will question whether or not you feel the same way.

No one is there to question your motivations.

I'm just being honest.

Sometimes you have to fill in and decide for those that remain indecisive.

You see her once, and she looks you in the eye. You see her twice, and she's resisting, wanting to be a different person. You see her a third time, and it's like you're best of friends, she's going along, and you help her like you've helped so many others.

You get to know her personally and most of all the potential behind that face. You go out of your way to do everything, be her for much longer than most anyone else. You start to get used to it, and you see the potential, the promise of the perfect blend of honesty and talent. But then you ask her for a single favor, and this is what you get.

A picture as pathetic as it is a reflection of every one of her doubts.

You think about what to do, but the truth is you already know what to do. You can read it the way things are transpiring.

The twists and turns—

When you have the face of any other…

You turn into her, matching her perfectly.

It brings fear to the surface of her face, eyes widening, lip quivering. You show her who you see. You show her Patricia, not the Patricia she is but the Patricia she could be.

And then you tell her, Let's take a look. Let's take a good hard look at ourselves.

You have her stand right in front of you, so that she can't look away.

Eye to eye, you say. Eye to eye.

You tell her, I only want what's best.

She doesn't resist. There are no tears welling up in her eyes.

She looks you in the eye.

I am an average person.

You tell her how to respond: Strongly disagree, Somewhat disagree, Somewhat Agree, Agree, Strongly Agree.

You wait for her reply. She answers, Disagree.

There's a sinking feeling in your stomach.

And then you answer, Strongly Agree. And it's the right answer. It's truth. And she starts breathing heavily. She knows.

I tend to keep quiet in the presence of persons of higher rank, experience, etc.

She doesn't want to answer but you tell her she has to. Why are you afraid?

Why are you so afraid of yourself?

She settles for Strongly Agree.

You sigh, answering correctly, Somewhat Agree.

Her lip begins to quiver.

There's no stopping now, no matter how horrible this feels.

I like to get lost in thought.

She bites her lip, perhaps to keep it from quivering, bites so hard she draws blood.

You answer when it's clear she's not going to answer, Agree.

It's too late, you say, when she opens her mouth to speak. And that's a lie and you know it.

I wish I could have more respect for myself.

To that, she is quick to deny, Strongly Disagree.

You clear your throat. Your body language says everything. You place an ear to her chest and listen. You tell her, Calm down now. It's not over yet.

I am quick to understand things.

She nods because maybe it's what she thinks she's supposed to do. Nod. Agreement. Camaraderie. All of the above.

But there's no answer she can give, and so you say what should be said:

Agree.

I looks like you're no longer staring back at her; rather, it's like you're looking in the mirror, and what you see pales in comparison to the person you really are.

But it's almost finished.

I certainly feel useless at times.

She starts to hyperventilate and you place a hand on her shoulder, calming her down.

You tell her, you don't have to. It's okay.

You answer, Strongly Disagree.

And for the last statement, you keep it to yourself, realizing that the only person that can answer for her is you. No one knows Patricia better.

When you have the face of any other, you let her have a moment. This moment. You let her look up at the sky. You let her say what you're already thinking—It's beautiful.

But where she referred to the sky, you were referring to the picture, the one held in your hand, the picture of that protest the other day.

You run a thumb over the figure in the distance. Her.

And you check your face, her face, tracing the full extent of the expression.

When the moment passes, you walk up to her, and you tell her that this isn't the first time. She understands. It's not meant to be anything more than information to help calm her down. It'll be quick, you say.

And you know what you have to do next.

You pocket the face, saving her a bit of pain by posing instead as her mother, Heather, cradling her in your arms while you whisper into her ear, You are so much better than this. I only want what's best for you. And then, when she wraps her arms around you, hugging you back, it's time. You know that it's time.

You tell her, Mother knows best.

And you smother her with your love.

I'm right here, you say, when she begins to choke, air escaping from her lungs.

I'm right here.

Feel her fingernails dig into your back, Don't you worry. You coax her into the last breath, telling her that you know what's best.

You're going to be just fine.

When you have the face of any other, you tend to see the cracks forming long before they are ever felt. You look into a person's face, like Patricia's, and you see the youth wearing away with the ambition that continues to go unaddressed. You see the years that add on with age, the years that burn out like a tired flame. You see what I see, and then you'll see why it's much easier to work hard helping others with the belief that it will pay off at the end.

The question thought by many is, How much longer?

Self-Acceptance //

The answer you give is, Not long at all. Honest.

Deus Ex Machina
Part III //

When you have the face of any other, sometimes you see someone that is willing to see you. You fill out the questionnaire but you are never satisfied with the results because there's far more to a person than the statements they provide. Having seen a person's true face, you understand that in order to trust others, you must first be willing to trust yourself.

I am often frightened in the middle of the night.
Somewhat Agree.
I am troubled with dreams about my work.
Strongly Disagree.
I frequently have nightmares.
Somewhat Agree.
I have a tendency to walk in my sleep.
Strongly Disagree.
I experience the feeling of falling in my sleep.
Somewhat Agree.
I sometimes have the feeling of being suffocated by the world around me.
Somewhat Disagree.
I sometimes feel an awful pressure in or around the head.
Somewhat Disagree.
I experience frequent episodes of fainting.
Disagree.
I have lost my memory for short periods of time.

Agree.

I have tried to run away from home as a child.

Agree.

I know of one or more people that might be trying to harm me.

Agree.

I make friends easily.

Strongly Disagree.

I get used to new places quickly?

Agree.

I have trouble walking around in the dark.

Strongly Disagree.

The feeling that things are not real has bothered me at times.

Strongly Disagree.

I am troubled with the idea that people are watching me on the street.

Disagree.

I am afraid of commitment.

Somewhat Agree.

I get tired of people quickly.

Somewhat Agree.

My interests change frequently.

Strongly Agree.

It's all there. I'm not missing anything.

Sincerity //

Hello, my name is Patricia Pond, and I'm still pretty young. My life is finally falling into place and I am excited. I am a professional photographer for 678 Gallery, the prestigious establishment owned by Luis C. You know the one, the curator? Yeah, that's the one.

Mid-twenties—wow. You think you're indestructible at twenty one and never think you'll grow old but then you blink and you're twenty-five.

A couple more blinks and I'll be thirty.

But it's not over. I'm not afraid of getting old. Things can change so quickly, there's no point in being afraid of getting old. Just a week or two ago, I was engaged to be married, financially secure, but totally at a roadblock, career-wise. But then it like all happened.

My life story totally changed. Not just a new chapter, I'm talking a whole new story.

But if I'm going to be honest with myself, I need to admit that anything's possible. The impossible is something that hasn't yet been proven to be true.

I'm afraid of so many other things, I'm afraid of being dishonest and losing myself to the hectic nature of the city. I'm afraid of the city and how it changes a person. I'm afraid of how the people that say they're used to the city are the same people that would cross a street, narrowly avert being struck by a car, and not even look. How can you be so numb? I'm fine with being normal; I just want to know that what I'm doing is what I'm supposed to do. I want to believe that what I'm doing nobody else could do, living as Patricia Pond. Nothing glamorous. I just want to be me.

I don't have a lot of beliefs; I'm fairly open-minded. However, I do abide by the idea of honesty and integrity. I'd never want to feel like a fake. I want to be genuine. I like knowing the truth. I like seeking the truth. That's what I love most about photography. Capturing the right shot, I feel like I'm getting an honest look at someone else's life. I really believe that people attempt to show their best side when they pose for a picture. We want to appear interesting. We want to look good in the picture. We want to smile and look our greatest. Sometimes I wonder what it'd be like if I lost it all. I wonder where I'll be a year from now. If anything, I feel more like myself now than ever before. The moment I'm behind the lens, I feel true. I know I'm capturing the truth, and it couldn't be any barer than the snapshot. Most of the time, I don't have a lot to show. Don't have a lot under my name.

But I think I might have a shot of myself worth being framed. I'm out of focus, and it's really about the protest but it looks like one for the gallery wall. It represents who I am, at the moment. I'm getting better at being confident but I still have a lot to learn, and a whole lot more of myself to improve. So that's why I'm out of focus, see? I don't think it's wrong to say that. It's good to know that you have room to improve, right?

Hey, I'm just being honest.

RESULTS:

You are viewed as unpredictable and enigmatic by others. You are at your best when you have something left to prove. You tend to move mountains with your emotions, often inadvertently putting yourself in direct line of fire. You are afraid of commitment and tend to avoid long-term relationships. You have a hyperactive imagination, with untold depths of inspiration.

I'm right here.

Can't you see me?

I can see you.

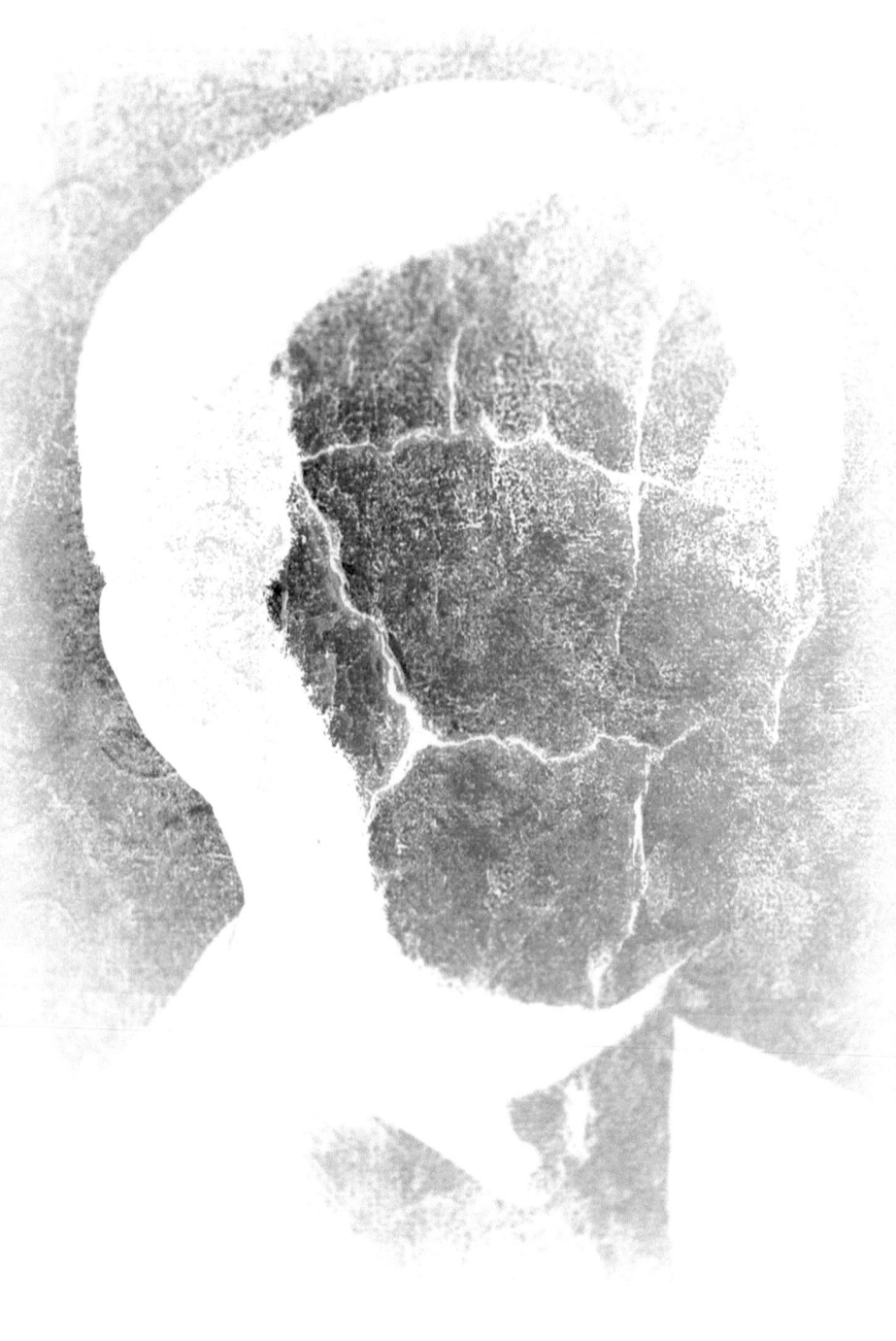